PLAYBOY
PILOT

Copyright © 2016 by Penelope Ward & Vi Keeland
ISBN: 978-1-959827-32-0

All rights reserved. No part of this publication may be reproduced, distributed, or transmitted in any form or by any means, including photocopying, recording, or other electronic or mechanical methods, without the prior written permission of the publisher, except in the case of brief quotations embodied in critical reviews and certain other noncommercial uses permitted by copyright law.

This book is a work of fiction. All names, characters, locations and incidents are products of the author's imagination. Any resemblance to actual persons, things, living or dead, locales or events is entirely coincidental.

PLAYBOY PILOT
Cover model: Sahib Faber
Photographer: Greg Vaughan
Cover designer: Letitia Hasser, r.b.a. designs
Interior Formatting & Proofreading by
Elaine York/Allusion Graphics, LLC/
Publishing & Book Formatting
www.allusiongraphics.com

Praise For *Stuck-Up Suit & Cocky Bastard* (co-written by authors):

"Graham and Soraya stole my heart! This book left me wonderfully content at its conclusion-->simply **beautiful** from cover to cover with twists and surprises I didn't see coming. These ladies can WRITE, and they can write ROMANCE, and they do it so well I'm impatiently waiting for their next collaboration. Five **Fabulous** stars for Stuck-Up Suit!" - Raine Miller, *New York Times* Bestselling Author

"Vi Keeland and Penelope Ward have created yet another **cocky bastard** to steal our hearts, and this one wears a suit - my favorite. I call dibs on Graham Morgan. Must read!" - Laurelin Paige, *New York Times* Bestselling Author

"Vi Keeland and Penelope Ward are two of the very **best authors** in contemporary romance right now. Both have already released books I loved this year that are sitting on my list of Best Books of 2016 (The Baller by Vi Keeland and RoomHate byPenelope Ward) so when I saw that this book was written by both of them together, I absolutely couldn›t resist diving right in and I **highly recommend** you do the same! This is definitely a new top favorite!" - Aestas Book Blog

"Witty & **HIGHLY addictive** standalone with a surprising plot twist we didn't see coming! Confidently one of our top reads this year!" - The Rock Stars of Romance

"I don't even know what else to say, but STUCK-UP SUIT by Vi Keeland &Penelope Ward was **SUPERB** in every single way! I wasn't expecting to **feel** so much, but HOLY HELL, I can't even right now..." - Shayna Renee's Spicy Reads

"This will be, without question, one of my **favorite reads for 2015**!" — 5 stars from Three Chicks and Their Books

Money can buy a lot of incredible things...
But
Can't Buy Me Love

-The Beatles

CHAPTER 1

CHRIS HEMSWORTH.

I flipped the page of the American Airlines Worldwide Destinations catalog through the section on Australia. The pages were filled with colorful pictures—kangaroos, turquoise water, that big white building that looked like a bunch of sails blowing in the wind. Pretty. But not what I was really interested in.

Liam Hemsworth. *Australian accents. Oh my God. Two of them.*

The next page had a worldwide map. I followed the dotted route line, my finger tracing Miami to Sydney. *Crap. That's a long ass plane ride.*

Sighing, I moved on. The next page—London.

Robert Pattinson.

Theo James.

More sexy accents, with less than a third of the flying time. I dog-eared the corner of the page and kept flipping.

Italy. *George Clooney.* Who cares if he's practically the same age as my father? The man was like a good bottle of Cabernet—better with age and meant to be savored in your mouth. Another dog-eared corner.

The bartender interrupted my destination shopping and pointed to my half empty martini glass. "Can I get you another Appletini?"

"Not yet. Thanks."

He nodded and headed to the other end of the packed bar. I was already on my second drink and had no idea how many hours I was going to be stuck in this airport lounge. It was probably a good idea that I pick where I'd be spending the next ten days before the alcohol kicked in too much.

Santorini. *Hmmm*. The pictures looked beautiful. Stark white buildings with bright royal blue doors and shutters. Yet...I really had no idea where I wanted to go. Nothing was jumping out at me; not even a tropical island was calling my name.

Blowing out a deep breath as I realized I was just about at the end of the thick vacation catalog, I lifted my drink to my mouth and mumbled to myself, "Where in the world should I go?"

I wasn't expecting an actual answer.

"My place isn't far." A deep, baritone voice said from next to me. Not realizing anyone had taken the bar stool on my right, I startled, tipping my martini glass and spilling what was left of my drink all over my brand new top.

"Shit!" I stood, quickly grabbing for a napkin from the bar and started to blot at my brand new blouse. "This is a Roland Mouret."

"Sorry about that. Didn't mean to scare you."

"Well then don't sneak up on people."

"Relax. I'll pay for it to be dry-cleaned. Alright?"

"It's going to stain."

"Then I'll buy you a new one, sweetheart. It's just a shirt."

My head snapped up. "Did you hear me say it was Roland Mouret? It was *eight hundred dollars.*"

"For *that?* It's a T-shirt."

"It's designer."

"It's still a damn T-shirt. Don't get me wrong. You fill it out pretty nicely. But you got ripped off. Ever hear of the Gap?"

"Are you joking?" I asked before finally giving up on my blotting and looking up at the man who had *some nerve.*

Shit.

He had some nerve alright.

Some *tall, dark and handsome* nerve. *Gorgeous,* actually.

I walked away for a moment to grab my bearings and went in search of more napkins. There wasn't another one in sight. When I returned to my spot, Mr. Beautiful called to the bartender, "Hey, Louie. Can I get a glass of club soda and some paper towels down here?"

"Sure thing, Trip."

Trip?

"Your name is Trip?"

"Sometimes."

"I'm in a freaking airport bar with a guy named *Trip?*" I couldn't help but chuckle.

"And you are?"

What the heck, I would never see this man again. I glanced down at the travel catalog I'd been sifting through when my eyes landed on the cover. "I'm..." I hesitated, then lied. "Sydney."

"Sydney..." he hissed out, skeptically.

"That's right."

Swallowing, I had to look away for a moment. Even with my gaze pointed away from him, I could feel the weight of his big hazel eyes on me. The heavy scent of his musky cologne was all-consuming. His tall, overbearing presence in my periphery made it difficult to focus my attention elsewhere.

The bartender returned and handed him a glass and a handful of napkins.

Trip lifted his brow at me. "You want to get the stain out?"

I nodded, my skin prickling as he leaned in. Within a few seconds, everything went from hot to cold as a shock of wetness hit me, seeping through the material of my shirt as he poured the soda water slowly and directly onto my chest.

"Ah! What the...what the hell are you doing?" I spewed, looking down at the wet spot on my designer shirt.

"You want to lift the stain out, don't you? The carbonated water will do it. It just needs to soak for a while."

"The stain isn't that big. You just poured water all over the front of my shirt!"

"There was no easy way to avoid that."

"You could have *not* done it!"

"That wouldn't have been any fun."

I looked down at myself. My nipples were peeking through the wet fabric. "You can see right through my shirt now!"

"I'm painfully aware of that." He sucked a breath in, his eyes glued to my chest. "Christ, are you not wearing a bra?"

"Actually, I'm not."

He finally looked up. "Might I ask, why you're at an airport with no bra on?"

Clearing my throat, I said, "I wanted to be comfortable on the flight. Plus...I'm...perky. I don't really need to wear one in general. Well, at least, I didn't until you poured seltzer all over me! I wasn't expecting a strange man to assault me with water."

His eyeballs descended upon my chest again. "Perky... huh?"

"Could you not stare at me like that?" I crossed my arms over my chest.

"I'm sorry. I wasn't expecting…"

"To see me practically naked? You don't say…"

He laughed guiltily. "What am I supposed to say? Look, I came here for a bite to eat and got way more than I bargained for. You have fantastic tits. You're right. They *are* perky…just like their feisty owner."

He suddenly took off his leather jacket and wrapped it around me. "Cover yourself with this." It was heavy and felt like a warm hug coated in his sandalwood scent. If this felt good, I could only imagine what his actual body would feel like wrapped around me. I shook my head at the thought.

Looking down while I zipped it up, I noticed a small pair of metal wings pinned onto the chest. "What's this pin? Were you a good little boy on your flight or something?"

He smirked. "Something like that."

When I cracked a smile, he reached his large hand out. "Let's start over. Hi, I'm Carter."

Carter.

Huh.

He sort of looked like a Carter.

I took his hand and felt shivers roll through me when he squeezed mine with a powerful grip. Narrowing my eyes, I said, "Carter…I thought your name was Trip."

"No. You assumed my name was Trip because that was what Louie called me. Trip's a nickname."

"Where does it come from?"

"Long story."

"How do they know you here anyway? Do you travel a lot on business?"

"You could say that."

"You're a little dodgy, you know that?"

"And you're fucking adorable. What's your name?"

"I told you my name."

"Oh, that's right. *Sydney*...and your last name's Opera-House. Sydney Opera-House." He laughed, lifting the magazine and pointing to the actual Sydney Opera House on the cover. "Why did you lie to me, Perky?"

I shrugged. "I don't know. I don't like giving my real name out to strangers."

"That's not it. You're not shy. You don't even wear a fucking bra in public, for God's sake. And it took you almost a full minute to cover your tits after you knew I could see them. You're not reserved, and you're certainly not being cautious."

"So, then why do you *think* I lied about my name?"

"I think it gave you a thrill to pretend you were someone else. You figured you're never gonna see me again, so why not? Am I right?"

"You think you have me pegged as a careless thrill-seeker? You've known me for what...ten minutes?"

"It takes one to know one."

"Oh really?"

"Yes. It's how I live my life...always looking for the next thrill, never in one place." After a moment of silence, he squinted his eyes with an examining look. "You don't know where you're going."

"How do you know that?"

"When I first walked up behind you, you were talking to yourself, wondering where you should go. Remember?"

"Oh. That's right. Yes. I'm taking myself on a trip...Trip."

"What are you leaning toward?"

"I still have no idea."

He startled me when he put his hand on my shoulder. "What are you running away from, Kendall?"

My heart beat faster. I moved backwards, away from him a bit.

"How did you know my name?"

He reached into his back pocket and waved a passport. "You really need to be more careful traveling alone. You walk away for one second, someone could slip something in your drink or take your belongings."

"That's mine? How did you get that?"

"When you walked away to look for a napkin, it fell out of your purse. I picked it up, took a peek at your name. Kendall Sparks. I like it. You're lucky you can trust me."

"I'm not so sure about that," I huffed, snatching the passport.

We stood there for a bit just staring at each other. His mouth curved into a smile, and for the first time I noticed the dimple on his chin.

"I saw her standing there," he said.

"What?"

"The Beatles song. *I Saw Her Standing There.*"

"What about it?" I asked.

"I have this theory. If you think about almost any given moment in life, there's a Beatles song that can describe it."

"So, that's the song of the hour?"

"Exactly. I saw you standing there. I walked over, and apparently I disrupted your decision-making. So, let me buy you another drink. We can figure out together where you're gonna go. We can work it out."

When he laughed, I repeated his last words in my head.

We can work it out.

God, he's a little nutty.

I shook my head in disbelief. "*We Can Work It Out.* Another Beatles song."

"Very good. You're too young to know The Beatles so well."

"My mother listened to them. What's your excuse?"

"I just appreciate good music, even if it was before my time." He looked down at his watch. "Speaking of time, I don't have all that much of it. How about that drink?"

When he smiled again, I couldn't help feeling like my resolve was melting. There wasn't any harm in one more drink, especially since I hadn't decided where I was going yet.

"Sure. Why not?"

Carter led me to one of the tables then left to put in an order at the bar.

"I hope you don't mind. I ordered a few appetizers for us."

"Thanks. That's fine."

"So, what's the nature of this voyage, Kendall?"

"I have some important things to think about. I need to get away from real life for a while to do that."

"Hopefully, it's all good stuff? You seem really on edge. That's why I assumed you were running away from something."

"Just an important decision that I have to make."

"Anything I can help with?"

Not unless you want to impregnate me.

If he only knew.

"No. It's a problem I have to figure out on my own."

"Seriously, though, how bad can it be? You're healthy, vibrant...beautiful, and you seem to have money. I'm sure it will all work out for you."

"You think you have me all figured out, huh?"

"You're young. Whatever it is...you have plenty of time to solve the issue."

Don't I wish that were the truth.

"How young do you think I am?"

He scratched his chin. "Twenty-two?"

"I'm about to turn twenty-five."

That's the exact problem. Twenty-fucking-five.

"Okay. Well, you look a little younger."

"And how old are you? Given your musical taste, I'd guess around fifty-three...but from your looks, I'd put you at twenty-eight."

"Close enough. Twenty-nine."

A waiter brought our appetizers over to the table. Carter had ordered a medley of fried mozzarella sticks, Buffalo wings, and egg rolls.

My stomach growled. "It's a good thing I'm not on a diet."

"Yeah. They don't really have much else that's any good here. Everything fried tastes good."

I noticed that he hadn't ordered a beverage. "You're not drinking?"

"I can't."

"Why not?"

"If you tell me what your dilemma is, I'll tell you why I can't drink."

Grabbing a fried cheese stick, I changed the subject. "There's no time to get into it. Right now, I really just need to make a decision about where I'm going. What about you? Where are you headed?"

"Hang on." He ignored my question, instead pulling out his phone and began to scroll.

"What are you doing?"

"This is a full list of international flights that are departing in the next three hours." He pointed the screen in my direction.

I took the phone. "Okay...Madrid. Iberia Airlines, 8:55."

"You don't want to go to Spain."

"Why?"

"It's July. Super hot there. You'll sweat your ass off. And you can't take off your shirt, because you're not wearing a bra."

Feeling flush, I looked back down at the list. "Okay...um...what about Mexico? American Airlines, 10:20."

"No."

"No?"

"The new norovirus that's going around."

"The what?"

"Jesus, woman. Don't you watch the news?"

"No. It's too depressing."

"Just trust me. You want to avoid the food there right now."

"Alright. What about Amsterdam? KLM, 9:45."

"I don't think that's a good choice for you. Prostitution is legal there. You walk around the city with no bra, you could get mistaken for something you're not."

My eyes widened. "You think I could be mistaken for a whore?"

"The whores are pretty classy there, actually."

"And how would you know?"

"Whoa...I don't pay for sex, if that's what you're getting at." He let out a throaty laugh. "I have the opposite problem, actually."

"Wait. Women pay *you* for sex?" I covered my mouth. "Oh my God. You're a male prostitute! Or an escort? Is that what you're doing hanging around in airport lounges?"

He bent his head back in laughter. "No."

"So, women just throw themselves at you. That's what you're saying."

"I'm saying that...sometimes it's fun to be the chaser. And I haven't had to do that for a very long time, nor have

I really found anyone *worth* chasing. So basically, the last thing I would need to do is pay for sex."

That didn't surprise me. I couldn't even conjure up a comeback. This man was gorgeous and charismatic. Cocky as hell. Women loved that.

When he grabbed the phone back from me, the quick touch of his hand felt really good. *Too good.*

"Ever been to Brazil, Kendall?"

"No."

"It's really nice there this time of year. It's winter. But it's still warm enough to enjoy." He slammed the phone in front of me "Rio. International Airlines. 10:05."

"What else is there to do there?"

"The beaches are beautiful. There are also a ton of clubs and bars in Copacabana and Ipanema. It's fun as hell."

"Is it safe for a single woman traveling alone?"

"You need to use the same common sense you would any place you go. Maybe buy a bra."

Carter suddenly flipped his phone back around to look at the time. "Shit. I have to go. I'm late for work," he said as he got up from his seat, throwing a wad of cash on the table.

He hadn't given me a chance to ask him what he did for a living, or where he was going. I really still knew nothing about this man, but a gnawing feeling of disappointment inside of me proved that I really wanted to know more.

"Um…okay. Well, thanks for the appetizers."

After a long pause, he said, "Let fate decide. But for the record, my vote is for Rio. Take care of yourself, Kendall."

As he started to walk away, I realized I was still wearing his leather jacket. I called after him, "Wait! Your jacket!"

"Keep it. It'll keep your tits warm."

That was oddly endearing. "Alright." I laughed slightly and lifted my hand. "Goodbye, I guess."

"Hello, Goodbye."

"What?"

"Beatles song." He winked.

"Oh." I rolled my eyes. "I should've known."

He smiled, and I realized it was probably the last time I would ever see that dimple on his chin for as long as I lived. As he walked away, I admired his ass, which I hadn't really gotten a good look at until that moment. He suddenly stopped and turned around. "Kendall..."

"Yeah?"

"If you don't choose Brazil, have a nice life."

Before I could respond, he turned back around and kept going at a faster pace.

An unwelcome feeling of loneliness washed over me. I watched him until he turned a corner and was out of sight.

That was an odd comment, though.

If I don't choose Brazil...have a nice life?

Was I stupid for listening to this stranger's advice? Time wasn't exactly on my side. I had to pick something. So...Rio de Janeiro? And if I ended up dead, I'd blame it on Rio.

Wasn't that a movie?

Blame it on Rio?

I started to sweat in his jacket. God, I was still so hot and bothered.

Blame it on Carter.

Chapter 2

I COULDN'T HELP BUT FEEL disappointment when the flight attendant pulled the plane door shut, even though I knew it was ridiculous to feel that way. Sitting in first class, instead of sipping my pre-flight champagne and enjoying warm roasted peanuts, I found myself looking up, hopeful as each passenger boarded.

I thought for sure Carter would be on this flight, although he hadn't exactly said he was heading to Brazil. A recording came over the cabin PA system, and a flight attendant followed along demonstrating the oxygen mask and seatbelt. After the demo was finished in English, she performed an encore, the second time moving along to a recording in... Brazilian? Wait. No. That wasn't right. Portuguese? I think. *Shit*. I was heading to a country I knew nothing about and definitely didn't speak the language.

Once we were in the air, another flight attendant came to take my dinner and drink order. Oddly, I noticed she resembled the seatbelt mime. Tall, thin, with a pretty face that was heavily made up, yet she could have done without it all. Both had their dark hair pulled back and done up in a tight twist in the back. A third flight attendant came up to the front of the plane, and for the first time, I realized they *all* looked the same. It was as if someone had built the ideal flight attendant, then cloned her.

After about ten minutes, the plane seemed to level out. Since the seat next to me was empty, I slipped off my Tory Burch ballerina flats and decided to close my eyes. Of course, that was almost exactly the same time that the Captain decided to make his welcome announcement.

"Good evening Ladies and Gentlemen, this is your Supreme Commander otherwise known as Captain Clynes. I'd like to take a moment to welcome you this evening to my home away from home here on this beautiful Boeing 757. Our flying time from Miami to Rio de Janeiro will be a little over eight and a half hours tonight. We anticipate a smooth..."

Holy shit. That voice. Is it...could it be?

Just then, the flight attendant arrived with my Appletini. "Excuse me. Do you happen to know the Captain's first name?"

"Of course." She lifted her hand up and wiggled her fingers, showing off a massive rock on her ring finger, then winked and leaned in. "I used to yell it every once in a while. Engaged now to someone else, so I don't anymore. That's Captain Carter Clynes, though. The man gives new meaning to flying the friendly skies."

Captain Carter Clynes. It all made sense now. The wings on his jacket, being on a first-name-basis with the airport lounge staff, even the quick way he pulled up the flight schedule on his iPhone. How could I have missed the clues? I knew how. I was distracted by his looks and cocky attitude.

It was definitely not easy to relax after that. Knowing that Carter was on board, that my life was in his hands for the next eight hours, made me anxious, to say the least. Although it wasn't the type of anxiousness I have waiting in the chair for the dentist to come in. It was more like that anxious feeling I get when I hear the clank of the lock bolt into place after I'm seated on a roller coaster. It would either be the ride of my life, or I'd wind up splattered on the ground.

A few hours later, another announcement came overhead. Carter's voice was low and raspy as he spoke. "This is Captain Clynes here. We're just about across the Caribbean Sea right now. I'm going to go ahead and dim the cabin lights and hopefully you'll be able to catch some shut eye." A minute later, the lights turned off and the cabin became dark, except for a few reading lights illuminated above some of the seats. Deciding to try to get some sleep, I reclined my seat all the way back, pulling the blanket up to my chin, and shut my eyes. Low music started to play after that. At first, I wasn't sure where it was even coming from. Until I recognized the song being played—*Lucy in the Sky with Diamonds*. And the singer—it wasn't John Lennon crooning about Lucy—it was Carter singing over the cabin PA system.

He really was nutty. But for some reason, I couldn't stop smiling for the entire song.

I WAS MOMENTARILY confused when my eyes opened the next morning. At least I thought it was morning. It took me a minute to figure out I was still on a plane. Was I really going to Brazil, or had last night all been a dream? The seat next to me was no longer empty, too. A flight attendant was drinking coffee and reading a paper. I pressed the button to upright my seat and smiled at the woman next to me. It wasn't the same attendant who had shown me her sparkly ring and dished about Carter.

"Morning. Hope you don't mind me sitting here. We take turns on our breaks and it's much more comfortable to sit in one of these big cushy seats than in that fold up jump seat."

"I would imagine." I hesitated before I asked the question I was thinking, figuring she might think I was a little crazy. "Can I ask you something?"

"Sure."

"Where are we heading to?"

Her manicured brows rose. "Rio de Janeiro. Is that not where you're supposed to be heading?"

"No. It is. I just made a last minute change in plans last night and for a second, I thought I had dreamt I was heading to Brazil."

"Nope. We should arrive in about an hour. It's good you got some sleep."

I nodded. As long as she already thought I was a little off, I might as well jump in with both feet. "Did...the pilot sing *Lucy in the Sky with Diamonds* last night to the cabin?"

She chuckled. "Sure did. Sings it on every night flight. Not sure why."

"That's a little strange."

"That's Captain Clynes for you. A little crazy, but a whole lot gorgeous and fun."

"The other flight attended alluded to him being *fun*."

"I'm sure there are a lot of flight attendants who would tell you how much *fun* he is."

"But not you?"

She shook her head slowly. "Men like that aren't usually my thing."

Feeling deflated, I had to agree. "Mine either, I suppose."

Something in her face changed, and she inched closer. "You know what is my thing?"

"What?"

"Petite little blondes with big blue eyes and pouty lips. We have a full two- day layover in Rio, if you want some company."

What in the lord's name? Was everyone crazy on this plane? Maybe the oxygen was too thin flying around at thirty-five thousand feet all the time. "Umm...thanks. But, I don't...ummm...just no thank you."

She smiled politely and folded up her paper. "Shame. But enjoy your trip anyway. I have to serve breakfast in steerage before we land."

When our plane finally touched down on the tarmac, I stalled while the rest of first class disembarked, waiting for the cockpit door to open. I'm not even sure why I did it, or what I would have done if it had opened, yet I felt compelled to see Carter at least one last time. Wasn't he at least curious if I was on the plane?

That answer became abundantly clear ten minutes later. Pretty much the entire plane was already off, and I was still sitting in my seat like an idiot stealing fleeting glances at a cockpit door that never opened. *"What the hell is wrong with me?"* I grumbled to myself. I'd met a random man in the airport lounge, whose first words to me were an invitation to go home with him, he then made my blouse see-through and talked about my boobs. So, of course, I did the only logical thing any woman in my place would have done—bought a three thousand dollar first-class ticket to follow him to Brazil. My actions pretty much went with the current fucked-up state of my life. This was supposed to be a trip about finding my own answers (and maybe finding some great shoes along the way), not about being a notch in the bedpost of Captain Freelove, no matter how fuckably handsome he was.

Standing, I picked up my Louis Vuitton Venus bag, smoothed down my crumpled top, and took a deep breath.

Later, Captain Clynes.

IT TOOK MORE THAN an hour to find my luggage and wait on the taxi line. The heat outside was oppressive even though it was supposed to be winter in Brazil, and I felt beads of sweat beginning to form on my back. I needed a cool shower, gigantic cup of iced coffee (vanilla or hazelnut might be nice), and possibly a ninety-minute massage at a hotel spa. When it was finally my turn at the front of the line, I couldn't wait to slip inside the air-conditioned taxi while the driver packed my bags into the trunk then joined me.

"Oi! Onde você gostaria de ir?"

Shit. "No habla Portugese." Wait...was *no habla* the same in Portugese as it was in Spanish?

The driver turned to face me. "You speak English, yes?"

"Yes."

"Ok. You tell me where you want to go, understand?"

"Oh. Sorry. Give me a second." I quickly typed *luxury hotels with spa in Rio* into Google. The Internet connection was slow, but eventually I began to scroll through hotels looking for a chain I was at least familiar with. My search was interrupted by the cab door opening.

The driver began to shout something in Portuguese. The way his finger was wagging, I assumed he was telling the person that the cab was full. But the passenger didn't listen. Next thing I knew, I was sitting next to someone in the back seat.

Someone wearing a uniform.

Captain Carter Clynes in the flesh.

He turned to face me with a wicked grin on his face. "My layover just got more interesting."

Damn. He seemed to have grown that stubble overnight.

"How was your flight, Perky? Did you enjoy the ride I gave you?"

"My shirt's dry. I think you can drop the Perky."

His eyes lowered to my breasts. Of course, my nipples were standing at full attention since the sheen of sweat on my skin had met the cool air-conditioning inside the cab.

Carter scrubbed his hands over his face. "Damn. You weren't kidding about those things. I haven't slept in eighteen hours, and they just woke me up. I think they're contagious, and *I'm* fucking perky now."

"That's not really an appropriate thing to say to a woman you just met, you know."

"We didn't just meet. This is our third date."

"Third date?"

"I bought you dinner in an elegant restaurant for our first one and took you up for a plane ride for our second one. Those were damn good dates. Some women would kill for that kind of lavishness. Seems fitting date three we should be heading to a hotel." He winked.

I wasn't sure if it was the time change, my being tired from restless sleep on the plane, or if it was possible this man could say *anything* and I wouldn't be offended. *Why am I not offended?*

When I didn't respond, he continued. "I'm glad I saw you. Didn't think I would ever see you again."

"That might be because you didn't look for me."

"I never thought you'd actually take my suggestion and fly to Brazil."

I mumbled. "Neither did I."

The cab driver interrupted, looking between us to ask, "You share cab, yes?"

Surprising me, Carter answered. *In Portuguese*. The language that sounded choppy and frustrating just two minutes ago, suddenly sounded sexy and romantic.

He turned back to me in English. "What hotel are you staying at?"

"I was just trying to figure that out with a little help from Google. Do you have one to recommend?"

"You trust me to pick out where you'll stay tonight?"

I considered his question for a minute. It was illogical, that much I knew, but I *did* trust him to pick my hotel. Lord knows why. "I think I do."

That response earned me another sexy grin that had me more excited than I'd been in the last year.

Almost a half-hour later, we were finally off the highway and traveling into what looked like a residential neighborhood. "Barra da Tijuca." I read the street sign aloud.

"Very good. I should probably warn you. It's probably not the type of hotel you're used to."

"What does that mean?"

"You look like you're more of the luxury chain with a spa type of woman, that's all."

Even though that was exactly what I'd typed into Google, when he said it that way, it sounded like a bad thing. It made me defensive. "And what's wrong with a luxury hotel? Sometimes a girl needs a massage and a soak in a nice bathtub while traveling."

"Well, you certainly won't be getting either of those where we're heading." Carter caught my eye. "Unless I'm the one doing the massaging, that is."

I blushed, which caused Carter to chuckle. "You really are fucking adorable. I'm not sure what's sexier, the fact that you're up for letting me take you on this little adventure, or that you secretly like the thought of me giving you a massage."

"I do not!" My quick, defensive response only confirmed he was right.

He leaned to me. "Do, too."

"You're off base."

"That's a shame. I've been told I'm really good with my hands." He held out his hands in front of him, examining them. *Big hands.* Hands that looked like he used them to do some actual work when he wasn't flying a plane.

Damn.

I needed to be back in control of my body and this conversation. "Actually, I've heard you were good...*with your hands*."

Carter furrowed his brow.

"Your crew. They might have mentioned something."

"What did they mention?"

"It's not important."

Carter was about to push for more information, until the taxi came to a stop. I looked around. "Where are we?" We were still in the middle of a residential neighborhood.

"Maria Rosa Rio Guesthouse."

"You mean like a bed and breakfast?"

"It's more like a bed and dinner. Maria Rosa doesn't usually get up before noon. But she makes the best damn feijoada south of the equator."

He exited the car and surprised me by offering me his hand. "Fei-what?" I asked as he helped me out of the taxi.

"Trust me. It's fucking delicious. I get hard just thinking about it."

"You're a pig, aren't you?"

"Perky, you have no idea. I've been holding back, trying to be a gentleman since you seem a little more refined than I'm used to."

Carter handed a wad of cash to the driver and toted my carry-on bag on top of his wheeled suitcase as we walked up the driveway. After he rang the bell and we were standing on the doorstep waiting, the taxi drove away. It was at that moment that he decided to let me in on a little information.

"Don't let Maria Rosa scare you. She's not really as crazy as she seems."

CARTER WAS A LIAR.

"Meu filho Americano!" Maria was wearing a bright-colored house dress as she took Carter's face in both of her hands, planting kisses on each of his cheeks. An aroma of saffron and other herbs and spices filled the air.

Carter introduced me. "Maria, está é a minha amiga, Kendall."

God, he sounded sexy. Even if the only thing I understood was my own name. He'd even used an accent to say, *Kendall*, lingering on the L a little at the end.

Maria looked me up and down, a thin black moustache expanding across her upper lip as she smiled. "Aha! Você nunca trouxe um amigo antes..."

I turned to him. "What did she say?"

"She's pointing out that I've never brought a friend here before."

"Exactly how often do you stay here?"

"About every other time I come to Rio. This place feels sort of like a home away from home to me."

The chattering sound of an animal suddenly registered. Before I knew it, a weight landed onto my back, nearly causing me to topple over from the impact. Then, I felt a spray of warm liquid on my neck.

I stiffened and waved my hands erratically. "What is on me? Get it off of me!" I screamed. "Get it off!"

The creature let out a series of high-pitched screeches as its nails started digging into me. Carter was laughing hysterically as he lifted the thing off of my back.

When I looked over at him, I discovered the animal was a tiny...monkey. Maria Rosa was shaking her head almost dismissively and saying something in Portugese.

Carter couldn't contain his amusement. "Maria apologizes. Capuchin monkeys sometimes piss on people to mark their territory." The monkey let out a loud squeal as if to agree with Carter.

"I have monkey piss dripping down my Roland Mouret. This is just fantastic."

"That shirt needed to be washed anyway. Don't worry. I'll clean you off nice later."

His words sent chills through me. As much as this situation was freaking me out, I couldn't help my attraction to Carter as he stood there towering over me, still dressed in his pilot's uniform. The monkey was now comfortably perched on Carter's shoulder.

When Carter smiled at me, I again took notice of the dimple on his chin, and my demeanor softened. "How come he's not pissing on you, Captain?"

"Because we're old friends. Aren't we, Pedro?" The animal flashed his teeth. I could have sworn it laughed before hopping away to the other side of the room.

Maria seemed upset about something as she spoke to Carter.

"What is she saying?"

"She didn't realize I was bringing a guest, wanted to make sure I knew that the only other spare bedroom is being rented out. She says we'll have to share a room."

"I'm not okay with that."

He whispered, "We'll figure it out."

"There's nothing to figure out, Carter."

"Let's just go to the room and relax for a bit. I need to get out of this uniform and take a nap. Then, I want to show you the beach before dinner."

"This isn't going to work…sharing a room. I need to find a hotel."

"Perky…you didn't follow me all the way to Brazil only to leave me now. You can say you're going to get a hotel, but the fact of the matter is, you don't want to be alone. You wouldn't be here if you did. Now calm your tits and come with me to our room. Believe me, even if I *wanted* to take advantage of you right now, I haven't slept in eighteen fucking hours. I need to crash."

As I quietly followed him down the hallway into the corner room, I cursed at my inability to argue this. He'd safely flown that gigantic plane all the way to Brazil. My life had been in his hands the entire time. He had a point; he needed to sleep. Honestly, I was tired from the flight, too, and I hadn't even piloted the plane.

The room was small but charming. A bright red bedspread with embroidered purple flowers made of yarn was draped over the queen-sized bed. A single window letting in a cool breeze displayed a nice view of the water in the distance.

There was a bathroom off of the room with an antique white ceramic tub. I noticed fresh flowers on the edge of the sink along with a variety of soaps.

"This is cute. How did you ever find this place anyway? It's really off the beaten path."

"I was driving around one day, exploring Rio. I got out of my car to take a walk and smelled Maria's cooking through the window. I basically followed my nose. When I discovered she rented rooms, I cancelled my reservation at the other place and stayed here. I'd choose this any day over a hotel."

"You said you only stay here half of the time. The other times, you opt for the big hotel?"

He hesitated. "I come here when I'm alone. I go to the hotel when I—"

"Never mind." I held out my palm. "I get it."

The hotel was his fucking ground, probably with the stewardess of the week. I didn't want to hear anymore.

"Why did you bring *me* here then?"

"I wanted to show you the authentic side of Rio. I feel responsible for you being here. The least I could do is be a good tour guide."

"How long are you here before you have to fly again?"

"Two days."

My stomach sank. That wasn't very long at all.

"Then where are you off to?"

"I don't know. I haven't checked the itinerary."

"Two days here..." I repeated.

"Yeah. So, let's make the most of it."

Carter began to unbutton his crisp white captain's shirt. He hung it up in the small closet. His bare chest was just as perfectly contoured as I'd imagined it. I got the sudden urge to lick a line straight down from his chest to his navel and down the thin happy trail of hair leading into his black dress pants. He was bigger than most of the guys I'd dated. I could only imagine how the weight of his body might feel pressed down over my petite frame. I wanted to feel the weight of him on me, and that was not where my head should have been.

I'd almost forgotten that the purpose of this trip was to try to straighten out my life, not complicate it further by falling for someone I couldn't be with. It wasn't going to be possible to be with *any* man in the near future if I went ahead with my plans.

Carter lifted a brow, a silent acknowledgement that he took notice of my ogling him. I suddenly looked away, although he'd already caught me in the act.

"Let's get you out of those clothes," he said.

"Excuse me?"

"I'll be right back."

What?

He retreated to the bathroom and closed the door. I could hear him peeing. Then, the bathwater ran for the longest time. Sitting on the bed with my back still soaked in monkey piss, I wondered what was taking him so long.

The door creaked open. Carter exited, still shirtless and now barefoot, wearing nothing but his black trousers. He'd left them unbuttoned at the top.

So incredibly hot.

I cleared my throat. "Did you take a bath?"

"No, I was preparing yours. Whatever's bothering you is written all over your face. You're very tense. That's been the case from the moment I met you. You need that bath more than I do right now." He slowly approached and put his hand on my shoulder. "Let's just forget about our troubles for a couple of days. Stop overthinking this room situation. You have my word that I'll keep my hands to myself. I won't try anything if that's what you're worried about—unless you ask for it. Until then, no monkey business. Well, not figuratively at least. There *will* be an actual monkey from time to time."

I broke out into laughter. It felt good. How did this situation become my life?

"What do you say? Will you just chill with me, Kendall?"

God, I really did want to just relax and enjoy these two days.

For the first time, I glanced over at the bathtub and really took notice of what he'd done. The foamy bubbles had risen to the top. Carter had lit two small candles and placed them at the windowsill above the tub. He might have been a womanizer— stewardess fucker—but he was damn smooth... and sweet.

Without saying anything further, he collapsed stomach first onto the bed. My eyes were glued to his ass as he grinded into the mattress, practically making love to it. "Fuck, this bed feels good," he muttered. Carter let out a groan that sounded almost orgasmic. Spreading his arms out wide in the shape of a T, his back was rising and falling as he relaxed into the pillow.

I took a moment to admire that sculpted back, realizing how much I wanted to lie on top of it like a carnival ride as it moved up and down.

When I'd assumed he was safely dozing off, I faced toward the wall and lifted my dirty shirt over my head, tossing it onto the ground. I tiptoed into the bathroom and undressed.

Immersing myself into the warm water, I closed my eyes and breathed in the steam. I felt like I'd been transported into another world. I suppose that *had* happened—a strange place with a strange man. And a monkey. Even though I couldn't explain it, somehow being here at this point in time felt exactly right.

I'd left the door open somewhat because I assumed Carter was asleep. So when I heard his sleepy voice, it sent a shiver down my spine.

"I'm glad you chose Rio, Perky."

CHAPTER 3

carter

I'M PRETTY SURE MY DICK woke me up as if to say, "Dude, look what you're missing."

The shades were down, the room was dark, and I was hard as fuck.

What time was it?

The clock showed four-thirty in the afternoon. I'd been napping for two hours. As I looked to my left, the reason for my painful arousal became abundantly clear. My brain may have been sleeping, but my body was fully aware of the fact that Kendall's tight ass was planted against my side as she curled into the bed.

Fuck me.

She'd been lying down next to me all this time. Maybe she did trust me after all. That was probably her first mistake. Two days with this girl, and I'd promised to be good? Smart.

I knew nothing about her, yet from the moment she entered my consciousness, she'd been all I could think about. This might seem hard to believe, but I'd never actually picked up a woman in an airport before. Yes, I'd fucked my share of co-workers, but that was sort of par for the course with being a pilot. The single members of the crew fucked around with each other, plain and simple. Hooking up with flight attendants during *LAYovers* had seemed exciting in the early days of my career. Over time, though, it had become stale and monotonous. It was all too easy. I liked a challenge, and Kendall was the first woman in a long time who played hard to get. That made *me* hard.

I was shocked to see her at the airport. I'd been thinking about her the whole flight, secretly hoping she was on it, but never really believing she was. I certainly never thought I'd end up lying in bed with her.

Kendall Sparks.

Who the hell are you?

Why do I need to know so badly?

She was complex; that was for sure. Just when I thought I had her pegged as an uptight rich girl, she announced she rarely wore a bra. The more she spoke, the less I knew what to make of her. All I really knew was that I was incredibly attracted to her and really freaking happy she gave me the chance to see her again.

My eyes trailed down the length of her lithe body. God, how I wanted to nestle my face in the back of her neck and bury my nose in her hair. I needed to get rid of this stiffy before she woke up, though.

Quietly lifting myself off of the bed, I headed to the bathroom to rub one out. The first thing that caught my eyes was her white panties lying on the floor.

Fuck me.

I picked them up and held them in my hand for a few minutes. They were small and delicate just like her. I couldn't help the urge to smell them. Taking in a long whiff of her scent, I wasn't prepared for my reaction. Her smell was addicting and only made the need building within me uncontrollably stronger.

I turned on the water and let it fill up. Lying back in the tub, I placed her panties over my face, imagining her pussy there. *Don't judge.* I took my cock out and began to stroke myself. If this was wrong, I didn't want to be right.

I took in another deep breath of her sweet feminine smell as I jerked myself harder.

Was I a sick fuck?

I didn't care.

Telling myself no one was being harmed in this process, I kept at it, needing to get rid of the sexual frustration that had been building from the moment I first spotted her perky little nipples at the airport.

It only took me a matter of seconds. I came hard all over myself, panting as I collapsed farther back into the tub.

After a few minutes, I still couldn't move. That was when I heard her voice.

"Carter?"

I shot up and threw her panties across the room. "Coming! I mean...be right there. Just need to take a quick bath."

After that, I washed up as fast as I could.

Kendall was sitting up on the bed when I reentered the bedroom. I felt a little guilty for what I'd done but still would've done it all over again.

I held my towel around my waist to prevent it from falling. "You ready to explore the beach? We'd better get going before the sun goes down." I couldn't help noticing the way she was checking me out.

Fuck yeah. There may be hope after all.

"Yeah. I'd love to head down there."

Kendall slipped into the bathroom to change into her bathing suit. When she came out, she was wearing a casual cotton sundress over her bikini.

I'd changed into my swim trunks and put on a plain white T-shirt.

When we emerged from the room, we had to pass through Maria Rosa's main living area to get to the front door.

When Pedro leapt toward me, Kendall instinctively ducked. The monkey hopped up onto my shoulder and began to nip at my hair before practically flying away again.

Kendall was caught off guard when Maria suddenly led her by the hand to a table in the corner of the room.

Oh shit.

We're never getting out of here now.

"What's going on? What is she saying?" Kendall asked.

Not wanting her to get even more freaked out when we'd first arrived here, I'd chosen not to immediately tell Kendall that Maria was actually a psychic and clairvoyant. The majority of her business came from people who walked in off of the street for readings. I translated what Maria was trying to convey to her.

"Maria's a psychic. She said she's sensing some negative energy surrounding you."

Kendall swallowed. The fear in her eyes was palpable. We both watched as Maria took both of Kendall's hands in hers. The old woman's eyes were closed as she concentrated. I continued to decipher what she was saying as best I could.

"Maria says she's seeing a baby...and it has two heads."

Kendall's head whipped toward me. "What?"

I struggled to understand Maria's ramblings, which were a bit fragmented.

"There's a curse that's been put on you, one that you may not be able to rid yourself of without her help. She says there is something going on involving a baby and that the baby or you could be in dire danger if the curse isn't removed. I don't understand what she's talking about with the two heads."

I had to say, as much as I loved Maria, this shit she pulled always creeped me the fuck out. One night as I was getting ready to leave for the airport, she cornered me and told me that there was a dead girl on the other side who was coming through and wanted to speak with me. I freaked out so badly thinking it was Lucy that I almost never came back here again. Thankfully, Maria never brought it up after that day.

I decided to play around a bit to deter Kendall from getting too weirded out. "She said in order to remove the curse, you have to kiss me."

"Are you serious?"

My expression gave me away, and she rolled her eyes.

I listened more closely to Maria. "Okay...I think I've been translating wrong. She doesn't see a baby with two heads. She sees a baby, but the head of the baby is actually a coin with two sides, heads and tails. Does that make sense to you?"

Kendall turned pale. Either Maria was freaking her out, or something about this crazy shit was actually resonating with her.

I continued translating. "This represents a decision having to do with money that may also involve a child in the future."

Kendall placed her head in her hands. This was upsetting her. I needed to get her the fuck out of here.

I turned to Maria. "Vamos à praia. Podemos terminar mais tarde?"

"Come on. It's getting dark. I just told her we're heading to the beach."

She'd been quiet most of the short walk down the steep hill that led to the water. I needed to get her to open up to me a little or at least get her to relax.

Playfully pulling on her ponytail, I asked, "Are you alright?"

She forced a smile. "Yeah. I'm fine."

"That shit Maria was saying…did it make any sense to you?"

To my surprise, she nodded yes. "Somewhat."

"You want to talk about it?"

"No. I really don't. I just want to try to have some fun while we're here."

"Fair enough."

The sun was starting to set. It was getting too late to really enjoy the beach. When we'd arrived close to the shore, the people around us started clapping.

"What's going on?"

"They're not clapping for us." I chuckled. "There's a tradition here, that when the sun slips below the horizon, everyone stops, stands and claps.

"That's pretty cool."

"It would be nice if people appreciated life and nature more often like this, wouldn't it?"

"Yes." She grinned. "Definitely." She looked around in amazement, and I truly loved watching her face as she took everything in for the first time.

A familiar site at the opposite corner of the beach caught my eye. "Come on. I know exactly what we're gonna do."

A small sign on a stick buried in the sand read, *Samba na Agua*.

"What is this?"

"They do samba lessons on the beach at sunset here. They take tips, but it's free. I happened to be walking by one night and got roped into a dance by some old lady once. You wanna try it?"

Kendall's smile lit up her face. "Sure." What little sun was left seemed to shine into her aquamarine eyes. Seeing her smile like that made me realize just how naturally beautiful she really was and how damn good it felt bringing her joy. I couldn't quite figure out why making her happy was so important to me, considering I barely knew her. But there was a gnawing voice inside of me that seemed to whisper, *"Pay attention. This girl is important."* I couldn't explain it and sure as hell wasn't going to ask Maria to investigate.

The samba lessons didn't turn out exactly as I'd hoped. I was thinking I'd get to use it as an excuse to make physical contact with Kendall, but they'd assigned her to dance with an old man instructor. That gave me no choice but to dance with his female counterpart. Probably made sense, since neither Kendall nor I knew what we were doing. Still, I enjoyed watching her trip over her feet as she laughed and looked over at me doing the same

Quick. Quick. Slow.
Quick. Quick. Slow.

Even across the sand from each other, we were connecting somehow in that experience. A thrill shot through me as I realized I was going to get to sleep next to her again tonight. Then, I quickly mentally slapped myself in the head for getting excited over a girl I might never see again after this trip…and whom I'd vowed not to touch.

Quick. Quick. Slow the fuck down, Carter.

We'd have one more full day tomorrow before I had to leave for the airport the following night. I realized I didn't even know where she lived. It was time to break out the truth serum. In Brazil, that was otherwise known as Caipirinha.

"WHAT'S IN THIS? It's strong...but good."

"It's lime, sugar, and Cachaça."

Kendall giggled. "Say that again."

"Cachaça." I smiled.

"I love when you speak Portugese, Captain."

"I'll have to keep that in mind."

We'd stopped at the small bar on the beach. After a couple of drinks there, we took the last round to go in SOLO cups and continued our party sitting on the sand.

"So, Kendall Sparks. You love when I speak Portugese. What else do you love? I need to know more about my travel companion."

"What do you want to know?"

"For starters, you never told me where you're from. What do you do for a living?"

"I live in Texas. I come from a family of oil magnates. I work on and off for the family business but don't really have a clear career path."

"Was that so hard?"

"I don't always like telling people about my family. There are a lot of preconceived notions about people from wealthy backgrounds."

"Your economic status doesn't define who you are any more than my job defines me."

"Why didn't you tell me you were an airline pilot when we first met?"

I dug my feet into the sand and thought about my answer. "I wasn't trying to hide it, really. It just never came up. I would've told you eventually if we'd had more time together.

I was secretly hoping you would choose Rio, though, so I could surprise you. Why did you do it by the way?"

"Choose Rio?"

"Yeah."

"I had to make a decision."

"There was no part of you that took that flight because you thought I might be on it? I was obviously trying to give you hints."

Even though it was dark, I could still see her cheeks blush. "What do you want me to say? That I'm attracted to you and flew across the world because you gave me your jacket?"

Yes.

"If that's the honest answer, then yeah. What's wrong with just being honest? People spend half their lives bullshitting. Why can't we be upfront with each other?"

I laughed inwardly. *Yeah, right. Then why don't you tell her you were whacking off with her panties on your face?*

Some things *are* better kept a secret.

"Go ahead and ask me anything you want. I'm not going to lie to you, Kendall."

She finished off the last of her drink. "Anything?"

Looking deeply into her eyes, I repeated, "Anything."

She gazed up at the sky. "How many of the stewardesses on that flight have you slept with?"

"All but one." I swallowed.

"All but the lesbian."

"Yes."

"That's disgusting."

"Why is it disgusting? Because I'm a single guy who fornicates? It's just sex among adults who live a similar lifestyle. I'm responsible. I use protection. I don't promise them anything I can't deliver. The majority of the time, I'm the one who's being approached."

I realized all of that made me sound cold, but it was the truth.

"You don't want anything more than that? A deeper connection with someone?"

"I didn't say that. But it's just the way things have been up until now." Taking her empty plastic cup and stacking it inside mine, I asked, "What about you? No boyfriend?"

"No. Not at the moment."

"Why? I'm pretty sure you could have any guy you want."

Looking conflicted, she paused before saying, "I'm in a time of transition."

"The reason you're running away. Does it have to do with a man?"

"No. It doesn't."

"You can talk to me about anything. I won't judge."

"You can't promise that if you don't know what it is."

"How bad could it be? Does it involve murder?"

"No."

"Then, you're good."

She chuckled, looking so beautiful with the ocean breeze blowing around her blonde waves. "I barely know you. I can't open up about everything going on with me after knowing you for less than a day."

"I bet it would only take a minute for me to know everything I needed to about you, Kendall."

"What do you mean?"

"The important points in anyone's life can be summed up in under a minute. Most of the mundane stuff that happens in between is insignificant." I took out my phone and handed it to her. "Wanna test it? Go to the stopwatch feature and time me. I'll tell you all about me in thirty seconds."

She opened the timer. "Okay. Go," she said, pressing start.

PLAYBOY PILOT

"Carter Clynes. Also known as Triple C, which stands for Captain Carter Clynes, sometimes shortened to Trip. Almost thirty years old. Grew up in Michigan. Class clown. Catholic family. Parents still together. Two sisters. One girlfriend. Broke her heart before I went away to college. University of Michigan. Played the field. Dropped out. Went to flight school. Fly all the time now. Get lonely sometimes. Own a condo in Boca. One niece, one nephew. Upfront person. Love pizza and every kind of music. Horny as hell. Sitting on the beach in Rio."

That *was* pretty much it. It's funny how a life could be dumbed down to just a handful of details. Of course, there was one thing I chose to leave out. Not that I wouldn't tell her, but it was neither the right time nor place to elaborate on Lucy, so I chose to omit the one not-so-minor detail that had basically shaped who I am.

"Wow. That was exactly thirty seconds."

"Now you know almost everything you need to know."

She squinted. "Almost?"

Ignoring her question, I grabbed the phone for the timer. "Your turn."

"Hang on. I have to think."

"No. That defeats the purpose. You're not supposed to think about it. Just say the first things that come to mind. Those are the most significant details."

She took in a deep breath, and I started the timer.

"Okay. Kendall Sparks. Dallas, Texas. Twenty-four. Only child of rich parents who blew through most of their money. Grew up on a ranch. High school cheerleader. Father is dead now. Mother is an alcoholic. I skipped college. Worked on and off for the family business. Charmed life on the outside but not so much on the inside. Unsure of where I fit in this world. Scared for the future. Sitting on the beach in Rio."

When she looked down away from me, I placed my hand on her chin, bringing her eyes toward mine. "That last part is nice, though, isn't it? Our one commonality."

Closing her eyes briefly, she said, "I have to say...it is."

"Thank you for sharing this time with me, Perky."

I stood up, and she followed me as we walked back in the direction of Maria Rosa's.

"What are we going to do tomorrow?" she asked.

"That's the beauty of a vacation, right? We don't have to decide."

"I suppose."

Just before heading back up the hill, we stopped at a shopping plaza. I noticed a lingerie shop. An idea popped into my head. I was hesitant to leave her alone, but I didn't want her to see what I was up to, either.

"Stay right here. I'll be right back."

When I returned with a small plastic bag, she was smiling from ear to ear.

"What did you do?"

"I bought you a present." Handing it to her, I said, "It's for tomorrow."

"Can I open it now?"

"I insist."

She shook her head when she peeked inside and got a look at the white full-coverage bra I bought her. The material was completely opaque. It was the unsexiest bra I'd ever seen.

"This reminds me of the Cross Your Heart bra my grandmother would have worn."

"Did I get your size right?"

"Actually, you're close. I'm 34B, and this is 36B. It'll fit." She draped it over her chest. "Well, there is definitely no way anything is showing through this material."

"Exactly. If I have to be good, they can't be saluting me every second of the day. It's too tempting."

"I do own a bra, you know." She laughed. "I just don't wear it. But I'll wear this if I've been distracting you."

"It's more of a joke than anything. But you should consider wearing one if you're traveling alone."

A bad feeling at the pit of my stomach developed at the thought of her continuing this trip by herself. I definitely wasn't ready to leave her after tomorrow.

"Thank you for looking out for me, Captain."

"Anytime."

We were halfway back to Maria's when I said, "Kendall..."

"Yeah?"

"I want to hold your hand." My mouth curved into a smile. She immediately got it.

"*I Want To Hold Your Hand.* The Beatles song. I thought you were serious for a split second."

Laughing, I said, "Actually, I am serious. Very serious. Can I?" I reached out my hand.

She handed me hers. "Yes." Her fingers looked so tiny intertwined with my large ones.

I didn't let go the entire way back. The truth was, I wanted to do a hell of a lot more than hold her hand...I wanted to wrap my entire body around her.

Too bad there wasn't a Beatles song titled, *I Want to Ravage You.* Would have been way more appropriate for how I was feeling at the moment.

CHAPTER 4

carter

IF I WAS GOING TO BE a fucking panty sniffer, I might as well go all in and shoot for the title of biggest piece of shit of the year. I'd just taken a long morning piss and had to practically bend over the bowl to get my wood down enough to be able to aim for the water. Kendall was still sleeping in the bed, and my self-control was slipping. Not that I'd spent very much of my life actually practicing controlling myself. But this girl made me want to.

Last night, when it was time for bed, I could see she was uncomfortable. I was pretty damn uncomfortable too, but mostly because I had a stiff cock that I'd been trying to talk down for at least an hour after she'd changed into that paper-thin nightshirt and short shorts. So being the chivalrous man that I'm not usually, I insisted on taking the floor to sleep. Now my back was killing me, and I figured there was no harm, no foul if I climbed into bed and got a few hours of good shut-eye on the mattress. It was 4AM, and she wouldn't find out until morning. By then it'd be too late anyway. So I lifted the sheet and gently slipped into the bed, careful not to shake the mattress too much.

Kendall had been facing the other way, and when the old wooden bed frame creaked, she turned over in her sleep. I froze and waited to see if her eyes would open. After a minute, she was still in dreamland, so I took some time to openly ogle her. That's when I noticed the top button of her nightshirt, which had been only buttoned to a low V-neck already, was open. And her entire left tit was on full display. *Damn straight those things are perky.* And not just the breast itself. The nipple, which was a nice size for a breast that wasn't more than a good handful, was fully erect. It was pointing at me. *Daring me.* Inviting me.

Fuuuuck.

My mouth was salivating. I wanted to suck on that nipple more than I'd ever wanted to touch any woman.

Just one little lick.

She might not even wake up.

My eyes flicked up to hers. She was sound asleep. I doubted she would even feel it in her current state. I could be gentle. Just flutter my tongue over the swollen little bud, enough to take the smallest of tastes.

Just one little taste.

One tiny lick.

Fuuuuuucck. My head moved a few inches closer to her breast. I was such a piece of shit. I'm pretty sure I went through a real momentary lapse in sanity, because I could have sworn there was a tiny little devil sitting on top of her right shoulder. I could actually hear the thing, see it clear as day. Of course, my devil wasn't your run of the mill bald, menacing looking man painted red with a tail. No, *my devil* was a tall brunette with her hair pulled back in a twist, a skimpy flight attendant uniform, and cute little horns on her head. She winked at me and whispered in my ear. *Do it. Do it, you pussy. She wants it anyway.*

My conscience responded. *She trusts you. Don't be a dick all your life. Suck it up, dude. Find another pair of panties, you disgusting pig.*

Kendall shifted in her sleep again, this time raising one arm up and over her head. The entire breast was then fully on display. Her skin was creamy, and her nipple was such a deep shade of pink, it was truly a magnificent sight.

What the fuck is wrong with you, pussy. Suck it. Suck it now. The damn she-devil had grown to twice her size.

I scrubbed my hands over my eyes to wipe my imagination clean. It didn't help. Not one bit. My she-devil was unbuttoning her own shirt over Kendall's shoulder.

Fuck. *I've definitely lost it.*

Out of the blue, blocking out the sinful thoughts I was having, a Beatles song popped into my brain. *You're Going to Lose That Girl.* The lyrics started playing in my head, and she-devil was smiling and gyrating her hips to the beat.

Goddamn you, John Fucking Lennon.

He was right. He's *always* damn right.

Whipping the sheet off me before I could change my mind, I grabbed my running shoes and a baseball cap and took off.

KENDALL WASN'T IN BED when I returned to the room two hours later. I'd gone for an hour-long run and then sat on the beach to watch the sun rise. The fucked up thing was, I longed for a girl I barely knew to be sitting next to me as it rose over the ocean, almost as bad as I wanted that succulent nipple this morning.

I was growing soft.

Although I was generally fucking hard around her.

I sat down on the bed and began to take off my shoes when Kendall came out of the bathroom. "Hey. Where'd you disappear to so early?"

"I went for a run."

"You should have woken me. I would've gone with you."

I wanted to wake you, trust me.

"You looked so cute sleeping, smiling with one hand down your pants. I couldn't ruin that for you," I lied and winked.

Her eyes widened to saucers. "You're lying."

I shrugged. "Maybe."

She punched me in the abs and laughed.

"Careful there, little girl. Don't want you to break that fragile little hand on my rock hard six-pack."

"You're so full of yourself." She smiled and shook her head as she walked to the bed. Climbing on, she sat Indian-style and pulled a book from the end table. *Eyewitness Travel: Top 10 Rio de Janeiro.*

"Where did you get that?"

"It was in the end table."

"It's in English?"

"No. But I was looking at the pictures."

She is so fucking cute. "Anything spark your interest, Sparks?"

Her face lit up when she spoke again. "Everything! To be honest, my idea of traveling is usually finding those few blocks of high-end stores and shopping all day. Then going to a fancy restaurant to show off what I bought. My mom trained me well. The only difference between us is, I don't generally have eight whisky sours and plant my face in the spaghetti bolognese. I'm not sure what it is about this place. Maybe it's being here at Maria Rosa's, but I want to see everything." She paused and started to flip through pages she had dog-eared. "The train up to Sugar Loaf Mountain, the Christ the Redeemer statue, Tijuca Forest—the giant waterfalls, the favelas...I want to see it all!"

"That's an awfully tall order for one day."

Her bright smile fell. "I wish we had more than one day."

There was no way in the world I would ever be able to deny this woman anything that made her face light up like that. I scratched my chin. "You know what? I have an idea."

"What's that?"

"I think it should be a surprise."

"I love surprises!"

Maybe I shouldn't have left this morning then.

"Alright. You trust your life in my hands for today?"

"It was in your hands for an entire plane ride. So I don't see why not."

It wasn't the time to mention that I was a fuck of a lot more reckless when I wasn't in the sky. "Okay. Get dressed. And you'll need to wear something tight. No loose clothing. If you have any of those bicycle shorts and a tight tank top, that would work best."

"Okay."

"I'll head to the kitchen and whip us up some *ovos picantes e salsicha*."

"Mmm...sounds delicious."

"It is. You're going to love my sausage." I winked and left her to it.

MARIA ROSA HAD AN OLD, beat up, open-air Jeep that boarders could use for seventy-five Brazilian Real a day, roughly about twenty bucks. I loved the thing, and Kendall seemed to, as well. She hadn't stopped smiling since she laid eyes on the hunk of junk. Once, I had rented a Mustang convertible while I was on layover in Barcelona and had planned to spend the day with one of the flight attendants who had been in my bed the night before. She made me put the top up so it wouldn't mess her hair up. That was the last time I bothered attempting to do anything outside of fucking when I stayed at a hotel. But Kendall, the woman with a T-shirt that costs more than my entire wardrobe, just pulled an elastic band from her bag and tied her hair back without even thinking about the mess the wind may cause. It made her that much more sexy to me.

"How much longer? Are we seeing Christ the Redeemer first?"

We had been slowly driving up a winding mountain road for the last ten minutes, so her guess was a good one. Although she didn't know it yet, it was more likely she would be praying to Christ to save her ass in a few minutes, rather than snapping pictures of him for Instagram. "We're almost there. I haven't decided what we're going to see first. But we will see the statue at some point."

She scrunched up her face. "How could you not have decided on our first stop if we're almost there?"

"Ahh...a riddle. That's for me to know and you to figure out, my perky friend."

She rolled her eyes, but I was certain she was having a great time, even though we hadn't gotten to the fun part yet.

When we were a minute or two away from where we would be leaving from, she caught on that I wasn't wearing tight clothes, yet I had told her she needed to.

"Where are your bicycle shorts?"

"Don't have any."

"Don't you need tight clothes?"

"Nope."

"How come? You told me I needed them for what we were doing today."

"I actually didn't. I told you *I* needed you to wear tight clothes. But I never mentioned that it was for what we were going to do today."

"I don't understand."

"I just wanted to see you in tight clothes."

Her eyes flared. But instead of getting mad, she threw her head back in a fit of laughter. "You are such a perv."

"Do you like pervs?" I asked, sounding like a total perv.

She sighed. "I guess they're starting to grow on me."

I parked in a dirt clearing in the middle of a field on the top of a mountain. There were a few cars parked, but she couldn't see the main attraction because we needed to climb down about 100 stairs to get to the bluff where we would take off from. "We're here."

She looked around. "Where's here? What are we seeing?"

I grabbed a backpack out of the back of the Jeep and jogged around to open her door. Extending my hand, I said. "We're not seeing anything here. We're doing."

Cautiously, she stepped out. "What are we doing, exactly?"

I couldn't have staged it any better than it happened. Just as she finished her question, a glider soared above the edge of the mountain. It was a tandem glider, just like we'd be doing. I pointed, even though she had already seen it. "That."

Chapter 5

kendall

CARTER WAS INSANE. I'd suspected he had a few screws loose, but thinking I was going to fly off the side of a cliff with a few scraps of metal and a flimsy piece of polyester, confirmed he was certifiable.

"I'll watch you do it."

We'd been standing alongside the Jeep for the last ten minutes arguing. "You're one of those, huh?"

"What's that supposed to mean?"

"You're a sideliner."

"Elaborate."

"You sit on the sidelines and watch your life happen. If you don't play in the game, you can't get hurt. Spectators are safe."

"In this case, I prefer safety to hurtling to my untimely death at twenty-four."

Carter rubbed the back of his neck and stared at me for a moment. "Every spectator who watches an event is watching it because they want to *be* the player. But they either don't have the talent or the balls."

"Well I certainly don't know how to fly a hang glider. So in this case, you're right. I don't have the talent."

"You don't *need* any talent for this. You fly in tandem, with a trained and experienced glider. No talent necessary. You know what that means?"

"What?"

"That you're a spectator because you don't have the balls."

"I have plenty of balls." I stood taller.

"Yeah. When was the last time you took a risk?"

"I'd say two days ago when I got on a plane to Brazil at the recommendation of a crazy person I met in a bar."

"Alright. I'll give you that one. That did take some balls. But when was the last time you had a real adrenaline rush? The kind that pumps through your veins so powerfully that it makes you think you haven't really been alive before then?"

I knew the answer to that. When *you* got in that cab yesterday. Only I didn't have the *balls* to say that either. "I don't remember."

"It's an experience you'll never forget. I promise."

"You do this often?"

"Hang glide? Not so much anymore. I used to do it all the time though."

"I didn't mean hang glide. I meant do things that give you an adrenaline rush?"

"I still get one every time I take off. When I'm barreling that plane down the runway at a hundred and eighty miles an hour and I pull back on the yoke to lift the nose and we break from the ground...it's like the first time, every time."

"So you're a thrill seeker."

Carter shrugged. "At times. Life without a little thrill is boring, beautiful."

I really like when he calls me beautiful. I couldn't believe I was even considering doing this. But he was right. The last few years of my life *had* been pretty boring. And this trip was supposed to be about finding me. Getting answers. He could tell I was reconsidering.

"Come fly with me." He held out his hand.

"That's Frank Sinatra, not the Beatles."

"I know, but I figured it would be more convincing right now than *In Spite of All the Danger*." He smiled, and I actually felt goosebumps break out on my arms when I put my hand in his.

THE REQUIRED PRE-GLIDE training class lasted an hour and a half. My instructor really seemed to know what he was talking about, and it put my mind at ease. Well, as much at ease that was possible when you were about to jump off the side of a mountain. And I do mean *jump*. It was probably best I had no idea that we literally *ran* off the side of a mountain to take off when I agreed to this craziness. That crazy run was what I was about to watch when Carter came and sat next to me. He hadn't needed to do the training class since he'd been here plenty of times.

"Nervous?"

"I'm afraid my legs won't move when it's time to run off the platform."

He smiled and put his hand on my thigh. "They'll work. You got this."

I *really* liked his hand there, so I smiled back. Together, we sat on a patch of grass about ten yards away from two people who were about to take off. When they raced the seven steps and literally ran off the side of a mountain, they disappeared from view immediately. I shot up to look at what had gone wrong. Carter chuckled. "They'll pop up in a minute. Relax. That's how it happens."

Thirty seconds later, the two were flying high above our heads in the distance. My instructor called over, waving for us to come. "Vêm aqui mulher bonita. Come."

"You ready?" Carter asked with an unexpectedly serious tone.

I took a deep breath in and out. "Now or never."

He smiled. "That's my girl." And took my hand to walk over to the prep area. In that moment, I realized, with Carter holding my hand and calling me his girl, there wasn't much I wouldn't try. The thought was comforting, yet scared the shit out of me at the same time.

Instead of my instructor helping me suit up, Carter did. He helped me step into my harness and checked the connections on my suit by pulling at them a few times. He then suited himself up. "Which one of us is going first?"

Carter's brow furrowed. "Going first? We go at the same time?"

"You're my glide pilot." I had assumed the instructor that did my training was taking me up in tandem. Couples would be in the air at the same time, but were always with an instructor.

He saluted with two fingers to his forehead. "Captain Carter Clynes, at your service."

"But...but...are you experienced enough?"

"I'm very experienced." He wiggled his eyebrows.

"Seriously. This is my life we're talking about."

"And you're about to put it in my hands. You're a lucky lady."

I was near panic. "Carter. Be serious for a minute. You're trained to fly that thing? You've flown it by yourself before?"

He put both his hands on my shoulders and spoke into my eyes. "I would never let anything happen to you." Then he surprised me by pulling me against his chest for a long hug. After my breathing calmed from being in his arms, he spoke. "You good?"

"I think so."

He kissed my forehead. "Let's fly, baby."

MY LEGS WERE STILL RUNNING, even though there was no longer ground beneath my feet. When we immediately dipped and started to lose altitude, I dug my nails into Carter so deeply, I might have punctured his skin. "Carter!"

"I got you. Hold tight. Here we go." And just like that, just like the instructor had explained, we picked up a gust of wind and began climbing back up. My heart was beating out of control, and I was holding my breath. My harness was fastened slightly higher than Carter's, so I was leaning partly on his back and clinging to him while he held the long metal steering bar.

After a few seconds, I took a sharp, very needed breath, and Carter began to circle us around, flying higher and higher above the mountain we had just launched from. My grip around him loosened slightly as we began to soar. Catching small gusts of wind, we glided smoothly through the air.

"Oh my God, Carter. We're flying! I feel like a bird."

His entire face smiled at me. "Feels incredible, right?"

"Yes!" It was an indescribable feeling. Looking down at the sparkling turquoise Atlantic, miles of sandy beach shoreline, and the lush green mountains around us was completely breathtaking. I was glad Carter had talked me into it. And I was even more ecstatic that I was experiencing it *with* Carter.

As we flew around, Carter was whistling. Even though we were right next to each other, it was sometimes difficult to hear because the wind was filling our ears. But after a while, I caught on to the song he was whistling. *Lucy in the Sky with Diamonds.*

"You sang that song on the flight, over the PA system after you turned down the lights. I almost forgot. Is it your flying song or something?"

"Something like that."

For more than two hours, we glided around the sky of Rio de Janeiro. I don't think the huge smile left my face once. We saw everything I wanted to see—Sugar Loaf Mountain, the Christ the Redeemer statue, Tijuca Forest, giant waterfalls, the favelas, beaches, extraordinary landscapes. We didn't *see* Rio, we experienced it. I felt like if there was a canvas in front of me, I would be able to bleed the beauty from my veins. It was the most incredible, invigorating experience of my life.

When we had seen everything I wanted to view and more, the wind began to die down, and Carter said it was time to land. We touched down on a beach with only the slightest of bumps. My legs were wobbly when I attempted to move on the sand.

"Careful. You have air legs. Takes a minute or two to get your vertical balance back." A team of guys from the glide company unhooked us and then made us drinks on the beach.

I was still smiling as I sipped my Caipirinha from a hollowed pineapple. "I'll admit, I definitely can see how you can get addicted to that feeling. Is that what it feels like every time you're sitting in the pilot's seat?"

"It's different, but still a rush. Today had that adrenaline that it always has. But—" He hesitated and seemed to rethink what he was going to say. "I'm glad you liked it."

"What were you going to say?"

"Nothing."

"Liar."

Carter did that squinting and staring at me thing he seemed to like so much. Then he chugged back the entire contents of his pineapple in one gulp. When he was done, he leaned in. "I was going to say today felt better than it ever has for me. That I fucking loved your arms wrapped around my body the entire time, and the way it felt when your nails dug into my skin and your tits pressed into my back. That seeing your smile, knowing I had something to do with putting it on that beautiful face, was a fuck of a lot better than just raising the tip of a plane or flying a solo glider."

I swallowed. Our eyes locked, and Carter was searching for something in mine. Then he turned away. "You ready to blow, Amelia Earhart?"

"Excuse me?"

Carter laughed. "Bad choice of words, I suppose. I meant, you ready to hit the road?"

"Oh. Yeah. I'm ready."

The ride back to Maria Rosa's was quiet. Carter seemed to be lost in thought, and I was coming down from the high brought on by spending the day flying like a bird. I couldn't remember the last time I had felt so free. It had to have been back when I was a teenager, riding horses with Emilio. I quickly shook the thought of that from my mind, focusing instead on the realization that Carter and I only had half a day left in Rio. Tomorrow morning, Carter would be flying off to some other exotic destination, and I couldn't stop thinking about whether he would be staying at hotel or a place like we were staying tonight. Knowing what staying at a hotel meant, it hurt to even think about it.

And me. I had to go back to reality. My reality. The one I had been dreading for the last two years, and now there were only eight days left before I had to decide which way my life would go. I was on the cusp of a proverbial fork in the road and still wasn't ready to chose my path. Honestly, I wasn't sure I would ever be. But that's the thing. If I didn't choose by next week...my path would be chosen for me by default. I couldn't do that anymore. My whole life had been a series of following down paths that someone had set me on. It was time I picked my own path, no matter which it was.

As we drove through the residential neighborhood, Carter must have realized how quiet I'd been. "What are you thinking about over there? You're somewhere else entirely."

"Just life. In general, I suppose."

"Anything you want to share?"

"Not really."

He nodded. "Have you thought about what you're going to do after I leave tomorrow? Will you stay at Maria Rosa's?"

My heart sank. *He was really going to be gone tomorrow morning.* "No. But I guess I should leave Maria's. I don't speak Portuguese or know my way around. Without you there, I'd feel uncomfortable I think."

Carter's eyes slanted to mine and then back to the road. "There's a Westin not too far from the airport. It's nice, clean, and I'm pretty sure it has a spa. We can share a cab in the morning if you want."

I nodded.

When we pulled up to Maria Rosa's, Carter cut the engine then turned to me. "Is there anything you want to see tonight? Anything you want me to show you before I take off tomorrow?"

"No. I think I'd just like to have some dinner and hang out tonight, if that's okay?"

"It's perfect. It's exactly what I'd like to do, too."

THE MOOD HAD DEFINITELY shifted from this afternoon. Dinner was good, and although Carter and I talked the entire time, it felt like there was a giant elephant in the room neither of us were mentioning. When we were done, Carter asked if I was up for a walk on the beach.

We both took off our shoes and left them near the boardwalk that led to the sand from the parking lot. I really loved that Carter took my hand as we started to walk.

"Do you know where you're flying to tomorrow?"

"Dubai. I checked my schedule while you were in the shower before."

"They don't tell you until a few days before?"

"No. They plan months ahead of time. I just don't like to know."

"You don't like to know where you're going?"

He shrugged. "Eventually, I know. I mean, I have to know before I get into the cockpit. I guess there's just no reason to check in advance."

"Don't you ever want to make plans ahead of time when you know you're going to be in a certain city?"

"Not really."

"That's odd, Carter. You know that, right?"

"Never said I was normal."

We walked for another fifteen minutes, eventually coming across two random chairs set up at the water's edge. There was no one around. Carter pulled my hand over to them and repositioned the chairs so that they were facing each other.

"They were set up to watch the water."

"I know. But why would I look at the water when I have you to look at?"

We both sat. At first our feet were right next to each other in the sand. But as we started to talk, Carter rubbed his feet up against mine. The pad of his foot massaged my ankle. It felt good, so I returned the favor. Our feet stayed intertwined as we chatted.

"So tell me, Kendall Sparks. Why are you on this trip? What is it that you are trying to find?"

I was embarrassed to admit the truth. I didn't want Carter to know how shallow and desperate I was. How much control money had over my life. "If I told you, you would think I was horrible. That I needed therapy for what I was likely going to do."

"I'm sure I wouldn't."

"You would."

"Would not."

"We're all fucked up in some way. All have secrets to keep and crosses to bear in life."

I scoffed. "Maybe. But I'm more fucked up than most."

"I doubt that."

"Well I'm more fucked up than you. You have a great job, own a place in Florida, and know how to enjoy life."

"Is that what you think? That your story is more fucked up than mine and you'll look bad?"

I nodded. "Maybe."

Carter looked up at the sky for a while and then started to speak quietly. "I was sixteen when I met Lucy Langella. She had long black hair, big blue eyes, and wrote poetry. We were together for more than two years. She was my first, and for a long time, I really thought she would be my last. Thought I was in love. Told her I loved her even.

During our senior year in high school, she started to change. She never wanted to go out, and she slept a lot. It was senior year—parties, friends, sports, road trips—I wanted to do it all. For a while I could get her to do things with me, but it became harder and harder as the months went on. She started to have some crazy mood swings, too. It got to the point where I had no idea what Lucy I was going to get when I went to her house. So I slowed up on going to her house. Basically, I was eighteen and thought she was becoming boring. She had been a better student than me, and when we first started dating we had talked about both applying to the University of Michigan. When the time came to send out college applications, she didn't even send any. By the time we graduated, she rarely went out, and being around her was a total downer.

The summer before college started, I knew I had to break it off before I moved three hours away for school. When I did it, she cried for a week. I felt like shit because all she kept saying was, '*You told me you loved me. You told me you loved me.*'"

Carter stopped talking for a minute. Then he cleared his throat and continued. "My first day of college, I'd just finished classes and brought a girl I'd met at orientation back to my dorm room. We ended up in my bed, and my cell phone kept ringing while I was screwing a girl I'd just met. Thought college was the greatest thing in the world that day." He scoffed and shook his head. "The next morning, I looked at my phone and saw that all the calls had been from Lucy. I didn't call her back. Another day passed, and I was in bed with my new girl when it started happening again. My phone was ringing over and over. But when the name flashed on my screen, I noticed it was my mother. I knew if she called that many times, something had to be wrong. So I picked it up. She was hysterically crying." Carter stopped again, staring down at our entwined ankles in the sand. "Lucy had committed suicide. What I thought was boring was clinically depressed."

I gasped. "Oh my God, Carter. You couldn't have known."

"Anyway. Today you asked me what the significance of the song I sing every time I take off is. *Lucy in the Sky with Diamonds*. I'm singing the Beatles to my dead ex-girlfriend every time I start to fly into the sky. And you think *you're* the one who's fucked up?"

"I'm sorry. That's horrible that you went through that."

"Thank you. But I didn't tell you this story so you would have sympathy for me. It's your turn, Perky. I bet it will make you feel better to share whatever it is that's been bothering you. Plus, I want to hear how my beautiful girl got so screwed up that she's traveling to foreign countries with the likes of me."

"You won't look at me differently after I tell you?" Even though we had less than twelve hours left, the thought upset me.

"Not a chance."

"Okay." I took a deep breath and started at the beginning. "My grandfather, Rutherford Sparks, was a very rich man. He was also domineering, eccentric, racist, homophobic, and controlling. And very much a chauvinist. Lucky for him, he had two sons and no daughters. But the first son died at age four of pneumonia. The second was my father who is Rutherford Sparks the Third. I should note that Rutherford

Sparks, Jr., was my father's older brother who died before he was born.

"My dad died five years ago of a heart attack. So my grandfather basically buried his two children, both his namesakes. Even though I was only nineteen when my father passed, my grandfather began pushing me to have a child. He literally started harping on me at my dad's funeral, demanding that I have a child as soon as possible—a boy, of course—so that he could be sure that his precious name lived on. I had no interest in having a child, so I kept ignoring him, even though he basically funded my lavish lifestyle since the day I was born.

"Anyway, without boring you with all the details, my grandfather died two years ago. I have a trust fund that pays for all of my living expenses, but that cuts off when I reach the ripe old age of twenty-five. There's a second trust fund, one that is worth millions of dollars, that was also left to me. However, my grandfather put a little condition on that one. In order for me to receive the funds, I am required to have a male child by the time I turn twenty-six. Oh...and the child must be named Rutherford Sparks."

"Is that shit even legal?"

"Apparently so. I had my lawyers look into it. Restrictions on trusts are common. The only time a court will strike the restriction is if it's illegal or against public policy."

"Isn't forcing someone to have a baby against public policy?"

"Apparently not."

"So, you're thinking about having a baby and that's why you took this trip?"

"Actually...this is the part that wins me the contest for being the most fucked-up. I figured out a small loophole in my grandfather's will. I have to give birth to a male heir, but I don't have to *keep* the child. Most normal people would assume that it's implied that when you intentionally have a child, you keep it. I'm not ready to have a child. But there are plenty of gay couples who *are* ready to have children and can't. So I have an appointment in nine days with a married gay couple in Germany. I would be inseminated with the sperm from both men that is genetically modified to ensure that I had a boy. After I gave birth, little Rutherford Sparks would be theirs. Foreign countries are less restrictive with genetic modification of pre-implanted embryos. That's why I'm doing it outside of the United States."

Carter shook his head up and down a few times and grinned. "Shit. I didn't think I'd ever say this, but it's a close one. I'm not sure who wins the contest."

Oddly, as much as I was disgusted with myself and ashamed of what I was considering doing, I felt a weight lifted off of my shoulders by telling Carter. He didn't seem to judge me at all either. He was just staring out at the water.

"What are you thinking about right now?"

He laughed. "If I tell you, I might slant the contest in my favor."

"Tell me."

"I was picturing you pregnant and thinking you're going to look fucking hot with a big belly and swollen tits."

"You would."

The two of us cracked up for a while after that. Even Carter seemed a little lighter after our conversation.

"Alright. Anything else I should know about you, Sparks?"

"I divulged one thing. You divulged one thing. We're even, Captain."

"I want to know more."

"What do you want to know?"

"You sure you don't have a boyfriend back home?"

"I'm sure."

"Have there been a lot of boyfriends?"

"No, not serious ones."

"You've never been in love?"

Looking over at the waves, an old familiar ache developed in my chest. It was the second time today I'd thought about Emilio. I finally answered, "Once."

"What happened?"

It had been years since I'd opened up this old wound. This night was getting way too deep for me to handle. Still, I wanted to tell Carter everything there was to know about me; I didn't understand where that need was coming from.

"Emilio was a ranch hand who worked on our property back when I was a teenager. We started spending a lot of time together, particularly when my parents weren't home. We would ride the horses, talk about normal teenage things—our hopes and dreams. It was so refreshing being with him because none of our conversations had to do with money or the aristocratic lifestyle that had been shoved down my face from the time I was born. With Emilio, I was just Kendall—not some girl with money and a thousand expectations weighing her down. Talking to him and riding horses together in the wind...those were some of the best memories of my life. Whenever I was with him, I felt like my true self. I felt free."

"From the look on your face right now, I'm getting a sense things didn't end well."

Shaking my head, I continued, "Emilio wasn't exactly legal. He and his family had fled Mexico. At one point, I found out that he'd been helping take care of a sick family friend, who was also an illegal alien. He never once asked me for help, Carter. I had to beg him to let me help him."

"What did you do?"

"She was a middle-aged woman. Her name was Wanda, and she suffered from polycystic kidney disease, needing constant dialysis to live. She was getting weaker by the day. We had this old guesthouse on the property. I snuck her in there, basically gave her food and shelter, tried to take care of her as best as possible. But what she really needed was a new kidney. She had a family member who was willing to donate one, but they couldn't afford the surgery."

"That was really nice of you to take care of her like that."

"Well, it made me feel like I had a purpose for the first time in my life. Not to mention, I was falling in love with Emilio and would have done anything for him at that point."

When I started to tear up, Carter placed his hand on my cheek. "What happened, Kendall?"

"My parents came home early from a trip one weekend and caught me in the guesthouse with Wanda and Emilio. I was begging and pleading with my father. At one point, my emotions got the best of me, and I stupidly blurted out that I was in love with Emilio. My father threatened to have them both arrested and deported."

Carter cringed. "Did he do that?"

"When he found out about Wanda's ailment, he calmed down a bit. But he absolutely would not accept my being with Emilio. He bargained with me. He said he would pay for Wanda's kidney transplant, provided Emilio and Wanda never set foot on the property again and with the understanding that I never saw Emilio again."

He blew out a long breath. "I think I know where this is going."

"Yeah. So...I couldn't, in good conscience, deny Wanda her life for my own selfish need to be with this boy. Emilio and I both agreed that was the way it had to be. My father made all of the arrangements, Wanda had her surgery, and I never saw Emilio again."

"You did the right thing, Kendall."

"I tried to find him after that, but because of his illegal status, there was no real record of him or his family. I had one address where I knew they'd stayed, but when I went there some months after the surgery, it was abandoned." I looked up at the sky. "That's really where the story ends."

"I'm sorry, Perky. Thank you for sharing that with me."

"Well, that whole experience definitely had a huge impact on my life, made me afraid to open up to anyone ever again, for fear of hurting them or getting hurt. In the years since, I've just learned to suppress my feelings and go with the motions."

"Well, I'd say you did a pretty damn good job of opening up tonight, but I think we need a break." Eventually, he stood and offered his hand. "What do you say we go get shit-faced?"

"I think that would be a perfect conclusion to our evening of confessions."

WE WERE BOTH PRETTY DRUNK when we stumbled into our room at Maria Rosa's that night. Carter was lying in the bed with his hands folded behind his head when I came out of the bathroom after getting changed.

"I'll sleep on the floor tonight," I said.

"I was thinking we could share the bed tonight. I'll be on my best behavior. I promise. But I want to hold you in my arms while we sleep. I don't even care that I sound like a pussy saying that. Because it's the truth."

I didn't even have to think about it. "I'd love that."

Carter held open his arms for me, and I climbed into bed and rested my head on his chest. He wrapped his arms around me so tight, and I clung to him. It felt so good to be held by him. But my feelings were conflicted. The thought of leaving tomorrow morning caused a physical ache in my chest. I had to choke back tears while I reveled in how good his touch felt. Neither of us said another word after that, and it felt right to lie in silence on our final night together. His heartbeat eventually lulled me to sleep.

The next morning, we both overslept. Racing around and bumping into each other, we took quick showers and packed our bags. Carter had to be at the airport by nine, and it was already eight, and we had an hour drive ahead of us. Rather than risk waiting for a taxi, Maria Rosa drove us to the airport.

When we arrived at the outbound terminal, I was barely able to keep my tears at bay. *This was really it.* The thought of never seeing Carter again was sickening. I'd only spent two days with him, yet I felt like he knew me better than most people. I got out when he did so I could say goodbye. He rattled off something in Portuguese to Maria and then handed her cash.

After he unloaded his luggage, the two of us stood facing each other at the back of the Jeep. "Maria is going to take you to the Westin. She knows where it is. While you were in the shower, I took your phone and programmed in her number. If you need anything, call her. She's a little loco, but she's good people."

"Okay."

He cupped both my cheeks into his hands. "Don't go braless and talk to strange Brazilian men in bars. Got it?"

I nodded.

"Now give me a damn kiss already. I've been good for two days. No way in hell I'm letting you walk out of my life without a little taste."

Before I could say a word, which obviously would have been *yes, please,* Carter's mouth crashed down on mine. My knees went totally limp. My pulse was racing as he pulled me tightly against his body. He groaned when I wrapped my arms around him just as hard as he was holding me. Our tongues frantically collided, neither of us willing to waste another second before it was too late. We *needed* to taste each other, *feel* each other, *say it all* with that one kiss. When he started to release my mouth, I moaned and the kiss ramped up again. Even hungrier this time. I had no idea how long it lasted, I just knew when it ended, I was going to be devastated.

Carter leaned his forehead against mine. "Thank you for everything, Perky."

"You took care of me for two days. I should be the one thanking you."

"Nothing to thank me for. It was my pleasure. I'd stay right here with you if I could. Fucking hate leaving you. Especially after that kiss."

A tear fell down my face, and Carter caught it with his thumb. "Whatever decision you make, it's the right one. Don't let anyone tell you any different. Promise me that."

"I promise."

We kissed a few more times. "Gotta fly, beautiful. You take care of yourself."

"You too."

I watched as he walked to the door. He turned and waved one last time before disappearing inside. Then I cried like a baby.

CHAPTER 6

carter

ALMOST IMMEDIATELY AFTER walking through those automatic doors, it just felt wrong—unnatural—to have said goodbye to her.

You fucking idiot.

I spotted a few members of my crew approaching; their rolling suitcases sounded like fingernails against a chalkboard. Two of the flight attendants were chatting in another corner. One of them winked at me, and I offered her a slight nod.

I looked around at the lines of people. A feeling of emptiness consumed me. For the first time in years, I didn't want to be here. I didn't want to fly. I didn't want to escape to the next destination. All I wanted was to return to that car, head back to Maria Rosa's and hold Kendall again. Even after that whacked out inheritance shit she'd confessed to, she was all I wanted right now.

I missed her already, and it hadn't even been a full five minutes. I'd programmed her number into my phone earlier, so I impulsively dialed it. There was no answer.

So, with my heart pounding, I sent her a text.

Remind me why we just said goodbye?

I sent another.

Because for the life of me, I can't think of one damn good reason.

Another.

What would you say if I told you I wasn't ready to let you go just yet?

After several minutes, there was still no response. Sweating through my polyester uniform, I decided to do something rash.

I went to the ticket counter and purchased her a seat on my flight. I didn't even have her email, so I had the e-ticket sent to the email address on Maria Rosa's psychic website. It was a long shot. There was almost no chance of her getting back here from the hotel in time to board. But I wouldn't have forgiven myself if didn't at least try.

I have no idea if you'll get this in time, but I just sent you a ticket to get on my flight. Ask Maria to check her email account. It's in there. We leave in just over an hour. You'd need to grab your stuff and jet back here. No pressure, but I would love nothing more than to continue our little adventure. If the answer is no, I'll understand.

I chuckled at my attempt to seem casual. *"No pressure."* What I really wanted to say was, *"Kendall, get your ass back here because I can't imagine how I'm gonna breathe through this fucking flight without you."*

Again, no answer after I tried to dial her one last time.

I headed to the pilot's lounge to check in, get the forecast and go over the flight details. Still no word from Kendall. There was no choice but to stick to the itinerary because this plane wasn't going to fly itself.

Checking my phone constantly as I met with the crew, it was beginning to feel like Kendall getting on this flight just wasn't going to happen. In a last ditch effort to stall, I did something I'd never even considered doing once in my entire career: I intentionally caused a delay.

As the first officer, it was my responsibility to inspect the plane when it arrived. I created a fake concern that one of the instruments in the cockpit wasn't calibrating properly and needed to be looked into. That resulted in an engineer having to run some tests on it. Although the inspection ended up delaying the plane for over an hour, it was all in vain. No Kendall.

I finally closed the cockpit doors, and when my pre-flight paperwork was completed, I got the go ahead for push back.

Ten minutes later, I lifted the plane to a smooth take off while images of blonde hair, honest blue eyes and the most beautiful smile I'd ever seen flashed through my brain. I wondered if we would ever cross paths again.

Once we were at cruising altitude, I decided to use up my last glimmer of hope. The ticket I'd bought for Kendall was for seat 12C. Sometimes a few stragglers boarded at the last minute. Could I have missed her?

When a flight attendant entered with water, I asked, "Is there anyone sitting in 12C by any chance?"

"Let me check," she said.

The lives of nearly two hundred people were in my hands, and it didn't make me nervous in the least. Waiting for that flight attendant to come back with the answer? It was torture.

The door opened.

"Actually, Captain, no. That seat is empty."

"Thank you, Cammie."

With confirmation that Kendall was definitely not on my plane, I released the breath I'd been holding and took to the intercom to do what I always did when I was feeling down.

But this one was for her.

CHAPTER 7

kendall

I TRIED TO RELAX into my seat, even though I was a nervous wreck.

The flight attendant made the announcement to shut down all wireless devices, but that wasn't necessary in my case, since my phone had died. In my haste to get ready this morning, I'd left my phone charger plugged into the wall back in the bedroom at Maria's.

Shortly after dropping Carter off at the airport, I had what felt like a panic attack in Maria Rosa's car. The thought of continuing this trip alone seemed unbearable.

We were almost to the hotel when it all suddenly became clear.

I didn't even know how to speak Portuguese, so I took a wild guess as to how to relay my thoughts to Maria.

Pointing in the direction behind us, I said, "Aeropuerto!"

She nodded and kept driving toward the Westin.

"Maria, I need to go back to the airport."

She must have understood me because she suddenly made a sharp left u-turn, up and over the median. Then, we were finally heading the way to the airport. My heart was beating a mile a minute during the drive back.

When she pulled up to the drop off area, I gave her a quick hug. "Muchas gracias!" Immediately realizing that was Spanish, I simply didn't have enough time to figure out the correct way to thank her. Later, I'd send her a translated thank you note along with some cash to remove the apparent curse on me.

Rushing through the door to the International Airlines ticket counter, I nearly tripped over my own suitcase.

"Has the flight to Dubai left yet?"

The attendant clicked a few buttons. "Actually, that's been delayed due to technical issues."

Thank you, Jesus.

"Is there still time to get on that flight?"

She made a phone call before answering, "You'll have to hurry, but I've alerted them to expect you at the gate. Give me your credit card, and we'll get you set up as fast as possible."

She printed my boarding pass, and I ran as fast as I could to security. Thankfully, there were no issues getting through, and I was able to make it onto the plane.

He hadn't asked me to come with him. This was a huge risk.

Despite my growing insecurity, I held onto the memory of the look in his eyes when he turned around to wave to me that last time. His expression had seemed filled with regret and doubt. He'd looked how I had felt.

It would be fourteen hours before I would figure out whether this was a big mistake. The cockpit had already been closed when I made my way to the back of the plane.

Now, I would try to just relax. Well, as best as I could with the knowledge that most, if not all, of the leggy brunettes walking these aisles had likely slept with Carter.

As the plane taxied down the runway, I closed my eyes and let myself feel his presence in every movement of the vessel as it ascended toward the sky. Memories of our tandem gliding ran through my mind. The thought that Carter was the one controlling this aircraft was just as comforting as it was a huge turn on. There was nothing more powerful than holding dozens of lives in your hands. He was a hero, if you asked me.

Once the plane had leveled off, my heart nearly skipped a beat at the sound of his deep, soothing voice over the intercom.

"Good afternoon Ladies and Gentlemen, this is your Supreme Commander otherwise known as Captain Clynes. I'd like to take a moment to welcome you this afternoon to my home away from home here on this beautiful Boeing 757. Our flying time from Rio de Janeiro to Dubai is a whopping fourteen hours. We anticipate some pockets of turbulence in the first forty minutes or so, but after that, it should be smooth sailing. Again, welcome aboard International Airlines Flight 237 to the United Arab Emirates."

Then, without warning, Carter began to sing. While all of the passengers seemed amused, the flight attendants, who were clearly used to his singing, were completely unphased.

The Beatles song he'd chosen this time was *Ticket to Ride*. Two things weren't lost on me: the fact that the song was about a careless girl who was going away and the fact that he'd sung it instead of *Lucy in the Sky with Diamonds*. He'd replaced his signature song with one that I was pretty sure was about me.

If you wanted me to stay, why didn't you ask me?

I couldn't begin to imagine what his reaction was going to be when he saw me in Dubai.

The day had taken its toll on me. I normally couldn't sleep well on an aircraft, but Carter being at the helm made me feel safe. I ended up nodding off for a couple of hours.

When I woke up, I was greeted by a rude awakening. A few of the flight attendants were gossiping in the galley. My seat in the last row was located right in front of the area where they prepared the food.

I tried to block out the surrounding sounds to focus in on what they were saying.

"Did you and Trip hook up in Rio?"

"No. We're not seeing each other anymore. And don't you dare tell me 'I told you so.'"

"Honestly...you lasted longer with him than anyone else I've ever seen him messing around with."

"Two whole months." She laughed. I turned around so I could get a look at which one was speaking. It was the one named Jolene. Tall brunette. *Shocker*.

"Two months is a lifetime in *Trip* time. I was hoping it would work out for you. But I knew better...because of personal experience, unfortunately."

"I should've listened to you."

"Sometimes we need to find things out for ourselves."

"I'm sorry that I almost risked our friendship to be with him."

"By the time you told me you were sleeping with him, I was happy with Brian. Someday, you'll meet a good guy, too. Fuck Carter."

"That's the problem. I already did. Now, I just need to get over it."

I couldn't stand to listen anymore. Putting my earbuds in, I blasted the music.

Was I sick in the head?

There were just so many reasons why I could potentially be delusional. This guy had a proven track record of being an asshole to women. *Attractive* women. Suddenly, I was going to be the one to change him? A girl who was potentially about to get pregnant by another man?

Not knowing whether to laugh or cry, I felt trapped. Both literally on this long-haul flight, and figuratively by my own idiotic heart. Because as much as I knew I should get out of this situation—my heart wouldn't let me.

What if.

What if.

What if.

What if what we have is different?

When Jolene came by to take my dinner order, I couldn't help myself. "Can I ask you something?"

"Sure." She smiled, flashing her perfect white teeth. God, could she have been more opposite from me physically? She was like an Amazon woman. They all were. What did he want with me, if he liked them?

"I noticed that the pilot likes to sing Beatles songs. I was on another flight with him, and he sang *Lucy in the Sky with Diamonds*."

"Uh-huh. Usually, he just sings that one. For some reason, he did a different one today."

"My dad used to sing the Lucy song to me," I lied. "Is there a story behind why he sings that one in particular?"

Without hesitation, she shook her head. "I don't think so. He told me once he just likes the song."

I examined her face for any sign of dishonesty. "Okay. Thanks."

I knew she was telling the truth because she had no reason to protect him at this point. If anything, it probably would have given her pleasure to spill his secret. He hadn't told her the meaning behind the song.

As Jolene took my order, my heart was doing a bit of a happy dance. The fact that he'd dated her for two months and never opened up to her like he did with me gave me a bit of hope. The cynical side of me, however, quickly concluded that maybe he opened up to me because he figured he'd never see me again.

The rest of the entire flight was spent ruminating. I asked God to give me a clue that my being here wasn't all a huge mistake. At one point, I was able to fall asleep again.

By the time I woke up this time, the sun was shining through the plane windows, and we were almost in Dubai. I had no clue what time it even was there.

I noticed that the man sitting across the aisle from me had a charger plugged in. Thankfully, he let me borrow it to power up my dead phone.

When Carter's voice came on the intercom, it sent chills through me, not only because I hadn't heard it in a while, but because he sounded down and tired.

"Ladies and Gentleman, we are now on our final approach into Dubai International Airport. The time here is a little after one-thirty in the afternoon. This is the hottest time of the year in the UAE. Current temperature is a scorching ninety-three degrees. Stay cool and thank you again for flying International Airlines. We hope to see you again soon."

Closing my eyes, I said a little prayer for a smooth landing. My ears popped as the plane lost altitude. My heart began to beat out of control in anticipation of revealing myself to Carter.

The landing was smooth as could be. When the engines were shut down, I powered on my phone, shocked to find that there were several missed messages—all from Carter.

Oh my God.
He'd bought me a ticket.
He wanted me here.
He must have thought I'd been ignoring him.

Sweat started to permeate me. My heart felt like it was going to burst.

Unable to see past the line of people waiting to exit the aircraft, I stretched my neck to search for him.

There he was, standing tall at the front of the plane with one hand crossed over the other as people thanked him for landing the plane safely.

He didn't look like the Carter I knew. His eyes were dark and empty as he nodded to them, going through the motions.

It seemed to take forever to get to the front. With every step forward, my pulse raced faster. Only a few more steps to him.

Someone had asked him a question and in the middle of answering, he stopped mid-sentence when he finally turned and saw me standing there. For a few seconds, he froze in apparent shock. His chest was rising and falling as his breathing quickened. Then, the previously sullen look on his face slowly gave way to a massive smile.

This was one of those times in life where words were not necessary. Carter slowly shook his head in disbelief, looking deliriously happy. Did I still have my doubts about his intentions? Yes. But he sure as hell couldn't have faked the look of genuine happiness on his face in that moment.

We just stood there staring at each other for several seconds. All of the passengers had exited the plane, but the crew was still scattered about.

Carter leaned in and whispered, "I see you got my texts."

"No."

"No?"

"No. My phone died shortly after dropping you off. I only saw those texts just now. I ended up rushing back and buying my own ticket."

His eyeballs were moving back and forth as he processed that. "Perky..." He paused.

"What?" I smiled.

"I don't know what this is."

"Neither do I. I—"

"Let me finish," he interrupted. "I don't know what the fuck is happening here, but when I thought you were gone, it felt way worse than it should've after only knowing someone for two days. So, I don't know what this is. I just know I want more of it."

He looked around then placed his hand around my waist, leading me into the cockpit and shutting the door behind us.

"I can't believe you really came." In an instant, I was against the wall as he pressed his lips hard against mine and groaned into my mouth. I opened wide for him and relished the flavor that I'd only experienced once before—the one I thought I'd never get to taste again. Our tongues desperately explored as I ran my fingers through his hair and tugged at it.

He pulled back first. "I needed this so badly."

Panting, I said, "That was a long fourteen hours."

He tucked some of my hair behind my ear. "Listen, part of the reason I just attacked you like you're my last meal...is because of where we are, okay?"

"I don't understand."

"Once we are off this plane and in public, we're not allowed to touch."

"What do you mean?"

"Things are very different in Dubai. We're not allowed to show affection in public. We could literally get arrested. Even married people can only hold hands. Kissing or even hugging for them is considered indecent."

"Are you fucking kidding me?"

"You can't swear in public, either. It's a criminal offense."

"Jesus, I need a drink."

"That's another thing. We're only allowed to drink in hotels and clubs here." He looked me up and down. "We need to cover you up before we go out there, too. I hope you brought that bra I bought you."

"It's in my suitcase."

He took off his jacket. "Take this for now. We have to get out of here."

Carter placed his hand on the small of my back and led me out of the cockpit.

"Where are we headed?"

He winked and flashed a mischievous grin. "I might know of a little hideaway."

CHAPTER 8

carter

MY USUAL HIDEAWAY was booked solid. Amari had offered me the couch free of charge until one of his three bedrooms freed up the next morning. If I were alone, I'd have taken him up on it, knowing I was going to crash and be dead to the world when I got there anyway. But Kendall deserved better than sharing a couch while random strangers came and went. Plus, even the thought of anyone checking her out while she slept in her little thin nightshirt riled me up. Rather than take a chance on trying somewhere new in a place like Dubai, I took a room at the hotel the airline put the crew up in. It sure as shit wasn't ideal, but it was safe, and I needed to get some sleep.

Outside of the airport, I steered Kendall away from the airline employee van that would have taken us to the Hilton Dubai Jumeirah Resort with the rest of the crew. I didn't want her exposed to any more of my past indiscretions than she already had been. At the cab line, we managed to find a shared van without too much of a wait. Kendall and I sat in the rear bench seat, and the other rows were filled with people speaking something I thought might be Farsi.

The back of the seat in front of us held a plastic pouch filled with laminated *Local Laws of Dubai* pamphlets in different languages. I'd perused them before and figured Kendall would get a kick out it. Slipping the English version out of the seatback, I held it and pointed to the first rule: *No public displays of affection. This includes kissing, cuddling, and hand holding.* Her palm was flat on the seat. I checked that no one was paying attention and then slipped my hand over hers, weaving our fingers together. She gave me a sidelong look with a gleam in her eye.

Keeping her left hand entwined with mine, she reached over with her right and took the law card out of my hand. She set it on the seat and silently pointed to the second rule: *Clothing should be conservative. Females must avoid wearing transparent, low cut, or short clothing. Stomach, shoulders, and back must be covered. Men must cover their chest and shall not display their underwear.* She looked straight ahead, making sure that no one in the rows above us were watching, and then slowly began to hike up the skirt on the sundress she was wearing. Knowing it was illegal, and following the slow, sensual movement of her hand as she inched it up little by little, it took everything I had to stifle a groan. By the time she reached the very top of her thigh, I had to shift in my seat. I'd seen her in a fucking bikini, but this... sneaking while people were right there, was purely erotic.

With entwined hands, her skirt pushed up barely covering her underwear, she handed the card to me. Not wanting to draw attention to us by acting strange, and needing a minute to slow the swell of my cock, I spent a minute looking outside the window, pretending to be interested in anything other than the sight of her thighs and the feel of our skin on skin. Then I pointed to rule six on the card: *No foul language or indecent gestures whatsoever will be tolerated.* I waited until the driver was busy merging onto the highway and the family in front of us was deep in a loud conversation. Then I leaned in and whispered in her ear. "My cock is rock hard wondering if I pushed that skirt up a little higher, if you would stop me."

She gasped; luckily no one seemed to notice. A few minutes later, we were already getting off the highway, and I knew we weren't far from our hotel. Kendall turned the rule card in her direction and looked up at me with a devilish grin that said, *what other rules could we break?* She browsed the list once again and then caught my eye as she sucked her bottom lip between her teeth before pointing to rule number nine: *Sex outside of marriage is not permitted in Dubai, and it is a fact that this law applies to visitors no matter where you are from.*

There wasn't a law in this damn country I wasn't going to try my hardest to break while I was here.

UNFORTUNATELY, THE EXCITEMENT and sexual build up from the van ride didn't last long. The Hilton hotel lobby was fairly empty when we arrived. Except...for a few flight attendants I'd rather have not run into. When two of them approached, I wanted so much to pull Kendall close to me, wrap my arm around her possessively to offer some sort of physical reassurance, but I also didn't want to get her in trouble with the law. These people in Arab countries didn't screw around. A few months back, two British flight attendants from a different airline were jailed for ninety days because they were caught sexting each other. *Three fucking months.*

"Trip," Jolene purred. "I wasn't sure you would be here for this layover." Standing next to Kendall, being with Jolene felt like a lifetime ago. But the reality was, it wasn't. It was less than a month ago that we were fucking in this very hotel.

Kendall stiffened when Jolene moved closer to me. She spoke quietly but loud enough that both Kendall and I could hear as she slipped a keycard into my lapel pocket. "If you want company later, I'm in room 4030. Lana is next door to me this time, so at least we won't get complaints about all the banging and loud noises again." I took a step back away from her, and Jolene noticed Kendall for the first time. "Who are you? Oh...from the plane, right?"

Kendall stared at Jolene. At first, I thought Kendall was going to be upset. But then I caught the fire in her eyes. *She was pissed.* Although she plastered on a fake smile and extended her hand with a heavy Texan accent I'd never heard before, "Kendall Sparks, nice to meet you."

Jolene reluctantly gave her hand. Once Kendall had Jolene's hand in hers, she held it and leaned in. "I'm Carter's personal therapist. I'm afraid he's on hiatus from *banging* and *loud noises* for a while. Stress-induced erectile dysfunction." Kendall took the keycard from my pocket and held it out to Jolene. "He won't be visiting room 4030." Jolene's mouth was hanging open as we walked away.

"You know my manhood needs to prove that everything you said back there was bullshit."

"Maybe if you kept it in your pants once in a while, your manhood would get that opportunity someday."

"I'm going to hold you to that, Perky. I'm going to hold you to that."

My layover was three nights in Dubai this time, but I told Kendall to only take a room for tonight when we checked in. I hated that we weren't sharing a room like at Maria Rosa's. But at least this shit was only for one night. Once we were at Amari's tomorrow, there would be no eyes watching anymore.

Our rooms were on the eighth floor, three doors down from each other. Arriving at Kendall's first, I tried to charm my way inside. "Thank you for continuing this journey with me, Perky. There is no way I was ready to let you go. I don't know what this is, but it's the best thing I have in my life right now, and I don't want to lose it."

"I'm glad I came, too."

When she opened her door, I attempted to step inside her room, but she stopped me with her palm to my chest. "The hallway has cameras."

"I'd go to jail for a kiss right now. Might even do hard time to cop a feel at those tits of yours."

She shook her head but smiled. "You have a wicked tongue."

I arched an eyebrow.

"Go. Get some sleep. You must be exhausted. Tonight I want you to take me out on the town. Take me dancing."

She was right. I definitely needed a few hours of sleep. But there was no way in hell I was going to do that without another little taste. I'd had it twice, and now I was addicted. I pushed inside her room before the door closed. When she saw the determination on my face, she let the door close behind me.

"Carter...we could get in trouble."

"All the more reason to make it worthwhile."

Ten minutes later, I left her room with a raging hard on. I hadn't even noticed what I was humming until I showered and climbed into bed. The Beatles, *I Want to Be Your Man*.

I was fucking done for.

Chapter 9

kendall

I WAS SOAKING IN THE TUB after a long nap when the hotel room phone rang. Conveniently, there was a corded phone in the bathroom, and all I had to do was reach over and pick it up.

"I had this dream you were next to me in the bed when I woke up." Carter's voice was still raspy from sleep. The sound traveled from the receiver, through my ears and straight down between my legs. "Disappointed when I reached over, and all I got was an empty bed."

I sunk back down in the tub, leaving only my nipples above the warm water. Between the cool air and Carter's voice, they were standing firmly erect. I splashed some water to warm them, but it didn't help. "Are you saying you were dreaming about me?"

"Been dreaming about you since the minute I laid eyes on you at the airport lounge. Although not sure some of the things I've been thinking would be called dreams. Fantasies might be more like it."

"Is that so?"

"It is."

I cupped a handful of water and let it drip down onto my nipples as I spoke. "Did you have a good sleep, or did those dreams make it hard to rest?"

"Oh, it definitely made it hard. But I got a few hours shut eye at least. How about you?"

"I slept a little. I was achy from the long flight, so I thought taking a bath might help relax my muscles."

"You're in the bath right now?"

"Mmmm-hmmm."

Carter made a noise that sounded like a groan. "You're fucking killing me, Perky. I finally got my sail down, and now you tell me you're lying naked in the bathtub talking to me?"

"It feels so good. You should try it."

"You don't have to ask twice. I'll be right there."

I laughed. "You have stress induced erectile dysfunction, remember?"

"I'll show you how dysfunctional my erection is."

"Be nice. I could have told them you had an STD, you know. Then you'd have trouble getting back in with the sky sluts, even after I'm gone."

"Sky sluts, huh?"

I sighed. "Let's talk about something else. I don't like to think about you like that. You seem...so *different* when you're with me."

"I *am* different when I'm with you."

I was quiet for a minute. *Can one person be two different people?* I didn't think it was really possible. More than likely, one of the two personalities was an act. I couldn't even let myself think about that...maybe *I* wasn't the one seeing the real Carter.

"You went quiet on me. What are you thinking about?"

"To be honest, I'm wondering which Carter is the real you. The guy who slept on the floor in Rio without being asked because he knew I was uncomfortable. Or the guy who shacks up with a different flight attendant each week."

"I'm sort of confused about that myself, too. But I know which one I like better. I *like* myself better when I'm with you. I think you bring out the best in me, Kendall—a side I haven't seen for a really long time. Kinda forgot that part of me even existed anymore until you got on my plane."

"I think that's the sweetest, realest thing anyone's ever said to me. I like you too, Carter Clynes."

For the next few minutes, we just listened to each other breathe. Oddly, those minutes relaxed my muscles more than my nap and the warm tub had done combined.

"Are you still up for dancing tonight? I understand if you're not. You flew a plane for fourteen hours and only took a nap, really."

"I don't require much sleep. I'll be good to go in an hour."

"I went through my suitcases before. I honestly don't have much to go out in that covers all the parts that are required to be covered."

"You have a light jacket?"

"I do."

"Dress your sexiest. Throw the jacket over you to cover up. Rules don't apply in licensed clubs, and I'm looking forward to seeing some skin."

"Okay. Well then skin you shall see, Captain."

FORGET DUBAI, there was a chance I could get a ticket in Texas with this outfit. I turned to my left, then to my right, modeling my dress in the mirror one last time to make sure all of my important parts were adequately covered. They were...barely. From the front, it looked like a simple little black dress, although it was really, really short. It wasn't until I turned to the side that you could see that the entire sides were see-through. A strip of sheer fabric about eight inches wide held together the black material and showed off that it was impossible to wear anything at all underneath. Braless wasn't unusual for me, but going without panties to a dance club was a first. It was why I hadn't worn the dress even though I'd picked it up at a trunk sale four months ago.

To go with my high-class call girl look, I'd teased my blonde locks to give them extra body and made up my eyes in a smoky purplish gray. There was a fine line between sexy and whore, and I hoped I was teetering on the right side. When Carter knocked, I was suddenly nervous with butterflies.

"One minute!"

I gave myself a last onceover in the mirror and took a deep breath before strutting to the door in my stilettos.

Apparently, *slutty* was a look Carter really liked. His eyes bulged from their sockets and he cursed under his breath. "Jesus, Mary, and Joseph. You're trying to fucking kill me."

I spun a slow circle to give him the full view. "You like it?"

"You have no bra or underwear on under that thing, do you?"

"There are no sides; you can't wear any. Is it too much?"

He stayed in the doorway, holding on to both sides so tight that his knuckles turned white. The way he looked at me with such raw intensity made my skin prickle. "You look gorgeous, Kendall. It's not too much. I just hate the thought of sharing you with anyone else in that outfit."

"You said you wanted to see skin. So I wore it for you."

"Thank you. It made my day. Fuck that, it made my year. Now grab your jacket and cover yourself up before I do something that you might not be okay with."

My coat was on the bed. Slipping it on, I cinched it tight at the waist, and I was glad it fell all the way to my knees. No one could have imagined what little I had on underneath. Carter held the door as I passed, but I stopped to whisper. "I can't think of anything you'd do that I wouldn't be okay with."

CLUB BOUDOIR WAS MORE glamorous than any club I'd ever been in. And that includes the annual girls' trip I'd taken the last few years to New York City. There was a long roped off line to get in, but Carter surprised me by walking to the front. When he gave his name, we were escorted right inside. He'd reserved a table that came with an expensive bottle of champagne.

"This is beautiful."

He pulled out my chair. "I'm glad you like it. Because I might not be able to afford dinner for the next few days after this." He'd said it jokingly, but I knew it had to cost him a small fortune for a bottle of American Dom and no-wait entry. We shared a table full of appetizers and drank the full bottle of champagne while people-watching together. It was so effortless to spend time with Carter, whether I was sitting in our room at Maria Rosa's or swaying to music in my chair at a swanky club in the middle of ritzy Dubai. The more I thought about it, the more I realized how weird the entire situation was.

"I can't believe a few days ago a monkey peed on my

shoulder at a boarding house and now I'm sitting in a club full of beautiful people drinking champagne with you."

"Which do you like better?"

"I don't know. You haven't shown me your moves yet. Can you dance, Captain Clynes?"

He gulped back the last of the champagne in his glass. "Maybe."

I stood and offered him my hand. "Show me what you got, hot stuff."

One brow arched. "Hot stuff?"

The champagne had me feeling no pain. I wrapped my arms around Carter's neck. "You're gorgeous, confident, funny, and an airline pilot. The only thing that can make that package any better is if you have rhythm."

Carter leaned in slowly, brushing his cheek against mine and whispered in my ear while his fingers slowly trailed down the side of my body. "Oh, I have rhythm. But that you're going to see later in private. I promise."

When he pulled his head back, my lips were parted and my breathing was labored. I wanted him so damn much, it physically hurt. "We could skip dancing?"

"No way. I'm grinding myself against you out on that dance floor. It's going to be your foreplay. Because I'm not sure how much you'll get when I rip this dress off of you later."

CARTER MOANED INTO MY mouth when I slipped my hand into the back waistband of his pants. We were in a hallway by the bathroom, both of us soaked with sweat from hours of dancing. We'd laughed and danced, swayed to slow songs and grinded to American R&B. *Lord, Carter Clynes could dance.* The way he moved his hips, pushed his unrelenting erection into me, I could almost come from that alone.

The last ten minutes, though, things had changed. The kissing became more urgent, the need ratcheting up to a level that felt like if we didn't both have our clothes off in the next few heartbeats, I'd pass out from sex deprivation.

A slow song had just come on again. I didn't know the words, but Carter sang along at parts, our bodies swaying as we stayed pressed against each other in the privacy of the dark hallway.

"You're driving me crazy. We need to go," I said. There was an emergency exit at the end of the corridor. It didn't matter that we had no idea where it led. All that mattered was that *outside* was one step closer to us getting back to our hotel. I tugged Carter's hand. He followed as I pushed the side door open. The fresh air felt so good on my sweaty body, sending tingles everywhere that the air met dampness. I couldn't remember ever feeling so alive before. Even my skin felt the excitement. Just before the club door was about to close, Carter caught it. "Fuck. I left my credit card with the waiter. I need to close out the tab and grab it. We have to go back inside."

It was the most incredible summer night. I could smell the salt water in the air, and the light breeze felt so good. The street was quiet and no one was around. "I'll wait here."

"No way. I'm not leaving you out here by yourself."

I slipped my shoes off my feet. "I can't go back in. You go. Hurry up." He attempted to protest again, so I wrapped my arms around his waist and leaned up on my tiptoes. "If you don't hurry...I'm going to start without you."

Carter groaned. "Don't move. I'll be back in two minutes."

I could still hear the music from inside even after the door closed. Shutting my eyes, I smiled feeling freer and happier than I could ever imagine. Beyonce's *Dangerously in Love* came on, and I swayed my body to the music thinking how in tune she and I were. I felt free, even though the man I was falling for was dangerous. Lifting my arms in the air as the chorus came on, I twirled around a few times singing along *Dangerously, Dangerously in Love*. I was so lost, so happy, so falling for this man, I wasn't even paying attention to my surroundings. Which is probably why I didn't notice the police car coming down the road until the sirens were blaring.

THE TRANSLATOR WASN'T making any sense.

"But it wasn't on the rule card. How can dancing in public be illegal? No one told me? I wasn't even really dancing. It was more like swaying."

"It's considered an act of indecency. Don't worry, you'll go in front of the judge, and you'll plead not guilty. It's unlikely you'll receive a sentence of more than ninety days since it's your first offense."

"Ninety days! I can't do ninety days in jail. I didn't do anything wrong. Where's Carter? I need Carter. Or my lawyer. Can I call my lawyer in America? He'll know what to do."

"After you speak to the judge, you'll be taken over to the holding facility. They'll get you settled in and then, in a few days, you can make some calls."

"No. I can't. You don't understand. I didn't do anything wrong." My heart was beating out of my chest, and I had a horrible itch on my arm. I kept scratching and scratching, but it just wouldn't go away. Hives had broken out all over my body just like they did when I was a kid.

This cannot be happening. How can this be happening? It's insane!

"Miss. You need to calm down. The judge will be very upset if you act like this in his courtroom. The expectation is that you will remain silent unless you are spoken to." *Speak when spoken to. I was not in America anymore.*

A little while later, my translator disappeared leaving me alone in a room that reminded me of a bad interrogation scene from *CSI*. It had no windows, only two chairs and a dirty old table. I wanted to cry, but I was afraid once I started, I'd never be able to stop. The reality of where I was set in. A woman alone in an Arab nation where I'd broken their indecency law. Scared didn't begin to describe how I felt.

They'd taken my phone, and there was no clock on the wall, so I had no idea how much time had gone by. My head was resting on the table, but it was impossible to fall asleep. Hours after my interpreter left, a uniformed officer wearing a beret and not one, but *two* holstered guns, came in. He was carrying a plate with a sandwich and threw it in my direction. The dish clanked loudly on the table, and I startled, jumping out of my seat. I wasn't sure if he didn't speak English or just pretended not to, but he ignored every question I asked and walked right back out the room.

At some point, I must have dozed off. A different officer slammed the door to wake me. Wiping the drool from my face, I jumped to my feet. "I need to make a phone call."

"You'll see the judge now."

"But I haven't spoken to my lawyer yet or made a phone call. Don't I get to do that first?"

Again, I was ignored. Instead, I was handcuffed to a dozen other people and we were led in a straight line down a series of long hallways. Eventually, we came to a door, and we were ushered in. Once inside, I realized the bars on the other side of the room looked out to an empty courtroom. I felt like an animal in a cage about to go on trial for a crime I barely even committed.

A few minutes later, two uniformed officers unlocked the back doors of the courtroom, and people started to fill the galley. I held onto the bars, frantically searching through the people entering. *Carter! Thank God.*

"Carter!" I raised my hand to wave, yanking up the arm of the person next to me I was still cuffed to, without warning.

He tried to come to me, but one of the guards stopped him from getting that close. "Don't say anything. I got you a lawyer. She'll take care of everything."

I nodded, feeling the first sense of relief since this nightmare had started. Tears started to stream down my face, but I couldn't even wipe them away without bothering the person next to me. So I just let them fall.

A little while later, court was called into session. A judge wearing an ankle-length, traditional, white Kandura robe with a red and white-checkered headdress draped over his head, took the bench. He spoke fast and furious in Arabic and rarely looked up.

So much was going on at once. The judge would be speaking to one person while two or three others were having side conversations in different languages—some of which I wasn't even sure what language they were speaking. I just kept looking back and forth between the front of the courtroom and Carter sitting in the back. It was the first time I saw Carter look anything other than his calm, laid back, confident self. That alone scared the shit out of me.

Eventually, an officer called my name. He uncuffed me from the chain of prisoners and led me into the hallway where a woman wearing a suit was waiting for me. She spoke perfect English, but with a thick Arabic accent. She was also stunningly beautiful.

"When the judge calls your name, I will speak for you. We're going to plead not guilty. The arresting officer will not show up to give his testimony, and this will upset the judge."

"What? How do you know the arresting officer will not show up and why do we want to upset the judge?"

She sighed as if I was annoying her. "Because the officer was told not to appear today. And this judge is a stickler for hearing testimony at the initial arraignment. There's a fifty-fifty chance that it will annoy him so much that he'll release you to prove a point."

"What happens if things go in the other direction? What happens if the other fifty percent chance wins out?"

"Then you go to jail for a maximum of thirty days until such time the officer can be located and appear."

"But..." Before I could object, an officer called my name.

"It's our turn. Let's go."

"Wait..."

"No. We go in now."

Everything that came next played out before me as if I was watching it from a distance. I was physically present in the courtroom, but my mind was floating somewhere above watching it all play out. I glanced back at Carter before standing next to my lawyer in the front of the court. He was sitting on the edge of his seat and looked as nervous as I felt.

The judge said a few things I didn't understand, and then my lawyer responded in Arabic. I held my breath watching the judge as he grew angrier and angrier with each stream of words he barked. After a heated debate, the judge picked up his gavel and slammed it down angrily. I jumped from the sound.

"Come with me." An officer took my elbow and began to lead me out of the courtroom.

"Wait. Wait...What happened?" I asked my lawyer. "What did the judge say?"

She rolled her eyes. "You're free to go. The officer will take you to collect your belongings now."

CARTER WAS WAITING ON the front steps of the courthouse with my lawyer. My initial reaction was to run and throw my arms around him. But then I remembered that was how I got in trouble in the first place—being indecent in public.

"You okay?" His face was so full of concern.

"I think so."

He turned to my lawyer. "I don't know how to thank you, Serine."

A sly grin crossed her face, and she nodded. "I'm sure you'll think of something the next time our paths cross on a flight to America, Captain." She turned to me. "Good luck with your sister. Try to keep her decent from now on."

I stood with my mouth hanging open as she walked away. "Your sister?"

Carter attempted to explain. "We met a few times on flights. I thought the chances she would help me were better if..."

I put my hand up and stopped him. "I don't even want to know."

"I'm so sorry, Kendall. I should never have left you out there by yourself. I should have made you come with me, and this would never have happened."

"It's not your fault."

He tipped his chin toward the parking lot across the street. "I rented a car. Can we get out of here please?"

"God, yes. I need to take a shower so badly and get out of these clothes."

"Good. I already have your bags. I got housekeeping to open your room. Pretended I lost my key."

"My bags? Where are we going?"

"Where I should have taken you the first night."

CHAPTER 10

carter

I'D REALLY FUCKED everything up.

Under no circumstances should I have left Kendall alone. Even though she kept trying to convince me the arrest wasn't my fault, I couldn't help but feel responsible for the whole ordeal.

She was unusually quiet the entire ride to Amari's. My friend secured us one of the bedrooms in his rooming house for the next couple of days. Amari's place was located in the heart of the desert, away from the commotion of the city. Thankfully, Amari wasn't conservative. As long as we were discreet, pretending to be married so the other guests weren't tipped off, he was completely fine with Kendall and me sharing a room. He could be trusted not to rat us out.

We'd just arrived to our room when I noticed Kendall staring pensively out of the window at the sandy desert.

"Are you okay?"

"I just need a shower," she answered without turning to me.

Her tone alarmed me. I needed to fix this. All I wanted was to undo the damage done by the arrest.

"Let me run you a bath."

Despite the fact that she didn't answer me, I proceeded to the bathroom to set up the tub until it was filled with water and soap. Still feeling anxious about her mindset, I returned to the bedroom and offered her my hand to lift her off the bed.

Leading her into the bathroom, I wanted nothing more than to hold her under the warm water.

"Take off your clothes," I demanded. "But leave your bra and underwear on because we're bathing together."

Relieved that she didn't protest, I took off my pants, keeping my boxer briefs on before immersing myself in the water. After she removed her dress, my cock swelled at the sight of her fit body in nothing but panties and a bra. I reached my hand out to her.

"Get in. I promise I won't bite."

She hesitantly dipped her legs in one by one then lowered her body in front of mine, situating herself between my knees. With her back pressed against my chest and her ass so close to my crotch, my hard-on couldn't be helped. Hopefully, she understood.

Kendall had her hair tied back into a ponytail. Pulling at the hairband, I watched as her beautiful blonde mane came loose. Cupping some of the warm water in my hands, I repeatedly wet her hair then poured a dollop of shampoo into my palm.

I began to slowly massage her scalp as she bent her head back. "Relax, baby," I whispered. "Just relax." I wanted nothing more than to take care of this girl right now, make her feel safe again.

It was quiet aside from the faint sound of men speaking Arabic in the adjacent room. After several minutes of near-silence, Kendall spoke for the first time.

"Am I a fool, Carter?"

I instinctively stopped the movement of my fingers through her hair to process her question. "What do you mean?"

"What am I doing here?"

My heart sank. Hearing that question was like a punch to the gut. "You regret following me?"

She sat up a bit and paused before speaking. "You're a beautiful man...so charismatic...such a free spirit. And you make me feel things I've never felt before. But I think I got carried away. I just don't understand how I'm going to get out of whatever this is unscathed."

"Why are you worrying about things that haven't happened? Why can't it just be about the present?"

"I can think of many reasons why it can't be."

"Okay...what are they? Talk to me. Aside from the arrest, tell me why everything that happened before that point led you to suddenly believe that all of this is a colossal mistake." The angry tone of my own voice surprised me. My body went rigid as I waited for her response.

"It's not just about you. I've been selfish. You wanna know why all of this is fucked up? Because there are two men, who I've led on, waiting to meet me in five days, two men who are leaving it up to me to determine if they're going to have a family or not. Because I'm supposed to be taking prenatal vitamins, not drinking. Because I haven't decided at all whether I'm going through with any of it. Because I overheard Jolene on the plane telling the other flight attendant—who you also screwed over—what an asshole you are. Because my lawyer who got me off the hook is yet another one of your cheap lays. Because I feel like maybe I'm a fool for thinking I'm somehow different than all of them. Because maybe my getting arrested was a sign that sleeping with you would have been a colossal mistake. Because I still don't know if I can trust you. I can really go on and on."

That was hard to hear, and I honestly didn't know what to say. I could understand her doubts about me, and no matter how strongly I felt about her, there wasn't going to be an easy way to prove it to her.

After a long silence, I finally said, "I understand the situation you're in, and you're right to have those concerns about me."

"There's just so much at stake, and I could be sacrificing everything for a man who's going to burn me. How am I different from them, Carter? Tell me. All the other women... how am I any different?"

I knew this was it. This was my only chance to answer that question in as honest a way as possible, or I was going to lose her.

I ran my wet hands through my hair and let out a deep breath. "I'm not proud of myself for the way I've lived my life thus far. Everything you've heard...it's all true, Kendall, all of it. I'm not trying to hide anything from you. But nothing has been the same since the day we met. I don't know how to exactly explain *why* this feels different. It's still too new. The only thing I continue to be sure of is that I want more time to figure it out, more than I want anything."

Her breathing became heavier, and I knew I needed to look her in the eyes.

"I need you to turn around and face me."

When she finally did, I repositioned my legs around her, locking her in. "This is me, the real me. Not the pilot, not the playboy or any of the labels branded on me because of dumb decisions. I need you to know that the last thing I want is to hurt you. I will do everything in my power to avoid that. But you have to understand that I can't change my fucked-up past."

Her eyes started to well up. "It's not just you. I'm so fucked up, too, Carter.

I wiped a tear that fell down her cheek with my thumb. "We're both fucked up. Maybe that's what it is. Maybe we see a little of ourselves in each other. We're two wrongs that somehow make a right. Inseparable we're miserable, but together…we somehow work. I know this isn't a simple situation. I know you have decisions to make."

"I'm scared."

"Wanna know the truth? I'm scared for you, too. When you told me what was going on with you back in Rio, I really hadn't let it sink in. I thought a lot about it on the flight over here, actually. That's some scary shit. But I understand your dilemma. It's a lot of freaking money—your family's legacy. You feel a responsibility to uphold that, and you're trying to do it in a way that would actually help people—these guys in Germany. But you're not ready to make a decision, Kendall. I don't want you to make a mistake you can never take back. It doesn't take a genius to figure out that you're just not ready to commit to having a child. That's not gonna change in five days, either. You need more time. You need to put off that trip to Germany at least until you're sure."

I need more time, too.

Just give me more time with you.

"If we continue this adventure, I can't sleep with you, Carter. As much as I want to, I decided that wouldn't be a good idea after all."

"I get it. I'm not gonna lie and say that makes me happy or that it will be easy for me. But I understand it and respect it. And I promise not to pressure you, either."

We stared into each other's eyes until I leaned in and kissed her forehead and kept my lips pressed against it. I momentarily lost my senses and my composure when I spoke against her skin, "Don't leave me yet, Perky."

She pulled back to look at me, and when she suddenly smiled, it felt like she'd released my heart from a chokehold. "What's on tap today then?" she asked.

Relief.

"Well..." I smiled. "We nap. Then when we wake up, we'll have an early dinner of some of Amari's shawarma, then some hookah."

"Did you just call me a hooker?" She laughed.

My laughter roared throughout the bathroom. It felt so fucking good to let it out after the tension of a few minutes ago.

"No. *Hookah.* Also known as shisha. It's a water pipe used to smoke flavored tobacco. They smoke it out back after supper. It's a tradition here. You don't have to do it if you don't want to. But I promise, it's the only pipe I'll ask you to wrap your mouth around tonight."

Kendall playfully pinched my cheeks. "There he is. I was starting to think you were going to make this no-sex thing easy for me by shutting your dirty mouth, too."

"Oh, I said I'd respect your decision, but there's no way that extends to my dirty mouth."

"I love your dirty mouth, actually."

"Someday, Perky. Someday...when you're ready, you'll realize just how dirty my mouth can be all over you. And you'll love it."

PLAYBOY PILOT

THE BATHTUB TALK WE'D HAD seemed to bring us closer together. That night, we sat outside in back of Amari's property, which was basically the vast, dry desert, sharing not only a hookah pipe but also stories of our childhoods.

Kendall told me all about growing up on the ranch in Texas, and I let her in on some funny secrets, like how my sisters used to put makeup on me while I slept when we were kids.

Kendall was a joy to watch as she sat with her legs crossed, blowing smoke rings from the hookah pipe with that pretty little mouth as she laughed and opened up to me.

I had never wanted her more, but as much as I was aching for a taste of her, I vowed to keep my promise not to push physical boundaries while she was in this state of limbo.

Later that night, she'd fallen asleep with her ass pressed against my side. Between the quiet of the desert and my raging hard-on, I couldn't sleep for shit.

Desperately needing relief, I quietly got up from the bed and retreated to the bathroom. With my back leaning against the door, I closed my eyes and thought back to our time at the club, but instead of us dancing, somehow my mind had envisioned Kendall fully naked, wrapped around me as she rode my cock on the dance floor.

We were so close to Nirvana that night before I fucked up and left her alone on the street. Shaking the upsetting thought from my head, I tried to focus once again on my club fantasy.

Panting, I fisted my cock, pumping it hard as I imagined fucking her hot, wet pussy, remembering the way she smelled when our bodies were close, how much she wanted me that night, the way her tongue tasted when we kissed.

I jerked myself harder before suddenly stopping at the sound of her voice from behind the door.

"Carter? What are you doing?"

Shit.

I laughed under my breath and banged the back of my head against the wood. "Praying?"

"Do you always breathe like that when you're praying?"

"It's an intense prayer."

"What are you really doing?"

"I think you might know what I'm really doing, Kendall."

"Can I come in?"

Still fully erect, I tucked my cock back into my pants as best I could before opening the door.

Her eyes trailed down to my massive erection. "I'm sorry....to make you resort to that."

"It's okay. My hand and I haven't spent time like this since I was a teenager. I think he missed me."

"What were you thinking about?"

"You."

"Yeah...but what specifically?"

"It was this fantasy of fucking you on the dance floor back at the club."

She looked down at me again. Her expression was serious when she asked, "You need some help?"

"I thought you said we weren't going to go there."

"I can't have sex with you. But I want to touch you. I could take my clothes off, let you finish what you started. You know...help you."

Looking up at the ceiling, I shook my head. "You have no fucking clue, do you?"

"What do you mean?"

"How crazy you make me. There's no halfway with you.

Jerking off with your naked body right in front of me...not being able to do what I really want to you...would be torture. I don't have that kind of willpower, not with you, not anymore. Even when I kiss you, all I can think about is burying myself inside of you. But you naked in front of me? Too much, Kendall. When you strip down for me, I want it to be when you're ready to let me have you. Otherwise, it's better if I don't know what I'm missing out on."

Looking filled with remorse, she waved her hands. "Okay. I get it. I'm sorry...for interrupting."

"Go back to bed. I'll be right there."

After Kendall left, I closed my eyes in regret. Was I crazy for turning her away like that?

Now that she knew what I was up to in here, I couldn't relax. Still needing release like a motherfucker, I turned on the shower and got in. Ironically, I jerked myself to thoughts of her naked body against the bathroom door and imagined she was watching me.

Fuck my life.

CHAPTER 11

kendall

WHEN I OPENED MY EYES the next morning, Carter was gone from the room. He was probably getting breakfast. I had no clue what time it even was.

God, I felt so stupid.

What the hell was I thinking interrupting him like that last night, offering him nothing but another giant cock tease? Hearing him panting like that, knowing what he was doing behind that door, was making me crazy.

Shit or get off the pot, Kendall.

Carter had no clue how badly I wanted to give everything to him. I just couldn't allow myself to go there until my head was on straight, because there was no way I could compartmentalize sex with him, no way I could keep my emotions out of it. I had to be sure not only of his intentions, but my own before taking a step like that.

I heard a thump against the window.

What the hell?

Then came another thump.

After sliding the curtain to the side, I literally jumped at the sight of what met me. It was the face of an animal that I quickly realized was a camel. On top of said animal was Carter, who was smiling and waving like a lunatic.

"Open the window," he mouthed.

I lifted the windowsill. "What the hell is going on?"

"Get dressed and get your beautiful ass out here. We're riding this guy. Long pants would be best."

"I'm not hopping on that thing."

"Sadly, it's not the first time you've said that to me," he joked. "But this time, you're not getting out of it. Come on! We only have him for an hour."

Carter flashed his beautiful smile and one look at that chin dimple was the push I needed to get out of bed.

The desert heat was already scorching for so early in the day. Carter was off of the camel and standing next to Amari.

Our host smiled at me. "Good morning." He petted the camel. "You guys have fun on Fouad here. After you're done, I have a nice traditional Arabic breakfast waiting."

"Thank you, Amari. That sounds great."

"Amari's gonna help us get on," Carter said.

Amari got the animal to sit, then said, "Getting on is the hardest part. After that, it's smooth sailing." After he helped both of us onto the animal, he said, "Carter's a pro at this. You're in good hands."

I whispered behind Carter's back. "You seem to be a pro at everything."

He turned around. "Except getting the one thing I really want." He winked. "Just kidding, beautiful."

"No, you're not."

"You're right. I'm not." Carter placed a tender kiss on my lips that was interrupted when the camel started moving forward.

"Off we go, I guess! How exactly does one direct a camel?" I asked.

"Actually, I have no idea. Camels don't really respond if you try to steer them. But I've always had luck just going with the flow. The main thing is just not doing anything erratic to spook them out."

Blinking to rid my eyes of sand that was blowing in the desert breeze, I leaned into Carter, relaxing my cheek onto his back. As always, I felt safe whenever he was in control.

We rode in silence for a while before I was the first to speak.

"I'm sorry about last night. It was stupid of me to do something like that if I had no intention of taking it all the way with you."

"Don't worry about it. I hope you understand where I was coming from, though."

"I do."

"When I finally take you, there's not going to be any holding back. That's why you need to be completely ready for it."

"I know you're not used to women thinking twice before opening their legs to you."

"Do you not remember me telling you that I liked a challenge?"

"I remember."

"I'm up for it, Perky. Don't worry. I'll wait as long you need me to."

"Can I ask you something?"

"Go ahead. Anything. You know that."

"All of the women…never letting anyone in…even your career which assures you're never in one place for too long… is it all because of Lucy?"

Silence.

God, I was such an idiot. *Again.*

After a few minutes, I finally spoke. "I'm sorry, Carter. I shouldn't have asked that. It seems I just keep sticking my nose in places it doesn't belong the last twelve hours. First the bathroom, now this. I was out of line. I hope you're not upset."

His voice was low. "I am upset, but it has nothing to do with you."

Carter steered the camel down a small hill. It was nothing but sand for miles. And us. The few buildings that sporadically dotted the desert were no longer in sight. "We don't have to talk about it."

"That's the thing. I've never talked about Lucy. Not with anyone. My parents tried for a while, but they quickly realized they weren't going to get anywhere and gave up. As horrible as it sounds, I just moved on. It's been years since I let myself stop and think about everything that happened. Pretty sure I've thought about my life more in the last forty-eight hours than I have in the last fifteen years. Didn't realize how much I was still holding onto."

"Sometimes the things we hold onto the tightest are the things we most need to set free."

Carter sighed. "Yeah."

"It sort of makes sense. The lifestyle you lead. Always moving around and blowing through women. You can't get hurt if you never get attached."

"And I can't hurt them if they never get too close."

"It's a protective mechanism. We all do it to some extent. I've been doing it the last year myself. In the back of my mind, I knew what I was going to eventually have to do, and I started pushing people away. My friends, the little family

I have left...I didn't want them to judge me when the time came."

Somehow, Carter reigned in Fouad, and we came to a stop. He managed to swing one leg over the camel and turned so we were facing each other completely. Pushing a lock of hair behind my ear, he said, "I won't judge you, Perky. Not ever. I give you my word."

His eyes were filled with sincerity. I truly believed he meant it.

"And I'm here for you if you want to talk about Lucy. Anytime, anywhere. Even when this trip is over." My heart squeezed thinking it wasn't long now, the end of the road was coming near.

Carter kissed my forehead and then wrapped me in a tight embrace. "Thank you. That means a lot to me."

Apparently, Fouad decided we were done with our little heart to heart. He started walking again, forcing Carter to swing back around and face forward. For the rest of the ride, I kept my arms wrapped around him from behind and did what I'd done since the first time I followed this man—held on tight.

"YEAH, WELL, THERE'S A FIRST time for everything." Carter was talking on the phone when I walked out of the bathroom wrapped in a towel after my shower. We'd spent the entire day alternating between sitting outside in the desert, eating traditional Arabic meals, and listening to Carter's friend Amari tell stories of the changes in Dubai over the last twenty years. In between, we snuck in snuggle time in our room. Now the sun had set, and I'd just scrubbed an inch of sand from my scalp. "Give me fifteen, and let me talk to my woman." Carter hung up and tossed his phone on the bed.

"Your woman?" I looked over my shoulder to the right and then to the left and teased, "You have a woman you own around here somewhere?"

Even though he was standing on the other side of the room, the way Carter was looking at me made my body warm. The towels weren't very long, and my smallish breasts were pushed up and popping out the top. "I'd like to own you. You keep standing there much longer in that little rinky-dink towel, and you're going to feel how much you own me in about two seconds."

I hid my blush by burying my head in my suitcase searching for some clean clothes to change into. "Who was that on the phone you were talking to?"

He walked up behind me and kissed my bare shoulder. "A pilot friend. He asked me to cover a flight for him tomorrow morning. He's here in Dubai and has a rapid turn trip."

"Is he sick or something?"

Carter ran his nose along my neck, his warm breath sending goosebumps down my skin, most of which was already exposed.

"Cold?" The smile in his voice was unmistakable. He knew the affect he had on me.

I ignored him. "Are you going to take his flight?"

"That depends."

"On what?"

"If you're up for another adventure."

I turned, and he didn't back up. "You want me to go with you?"

"I'm *only* taking it if you go with me. If you want to stay here for another two days, I'm fine with that, too."

"Where do you go in two days?"

Carter's eyes looked back and forth between mine. "Home. I have five down days after this. I fly from here back to the states and then pick up a connection as a passenger to get back home to Florida."

Wow. Our little trip *really is* coming to an end. The thought made me sick to my stomach. Carter must have sensed what I was thinking. He tipped my chin up so our eyes met. "Let's not go there yet. Stay with me. Whether it's here or on another adventure, we still have time. I don't want this to end yet either. Stay in the moment with me, Kendall."

"Where would we go?"

He smiled, and it was all I could do not to drop my towel in response. "That's a surprise."

"Give me a hint."

Carter scratched his chin for a minute. "Okay. If you want to continue our little adventure, you'll give me the green light, but you might wind up getting stopped at the *red light* along the way."

"What the heck is *that* supposed to mean? I said a hint, not a riddle."

He laughed. "What do you say, Perky? You up for one more adventure with me?"

"Can I get arrested for dancing, cursing, showing skin, or touching you, wherever it is we would go?"

"Definitely not." He kissed the top of my nose. "In fact, those things are strongly encouraged at the next stop on our tour." Carter smiled and that damn chin dimple joined in. *God, I'm a sucker for that thing. Who knew?*

I rolled my eyes. "Alright. I'm in. But if I wind up in jail again, I'm holding your dimpled self responsible."

PLAYBOY PILOT

OUR FLIGHT THE NEXT MORNING was at an ungodly hour. We had to leave Amari by three-thirty in order for Carter to check in. It was going to be what he called a rapid turn, meaning we would get to wherever we were going by late this afternoon and be back in Dubai within twenty-four hours. Then, we'd meet up with his regular crew and fly back to the states. It was after that I didn't want to think about. I'd probably go back home for a few days before heading to Germany. On the way to the airport, I stared out the window watching Dubai pass by, but not really seeing anything. Melancholy had swept my mood thinking how soon things were coming to an end.

"You okay?" The taxi had pulled off the highway following the signs to the airport.

"Just tired."

"I got you a seat in first class, so hopefully you can get some sleep on the flight."

"How long is the flight?"

"About seven hours."

"What do you do up there in the cockpit the whole time? I mean, I know you fly the plane...but seven hours is a long time staring out at the sky."

He shrugged. "I like it. It's the only place I've ever really felt relaxed."

"You must do a lot of thinking."

"Sometimes. It depends on who I'm flying with. Some co-pilots are like me and keep it quiet. Others talk non-stop. When I get one of those, I usually take a nap."

My eyes bulged. "You nap while flying the plane?"

Carter chuckled. "I do. But don't worry. We take turns. The airline frowns upon both pilots sleeping at the same time."

"Can I see the cockpit?"

"There's nothing more that I would rather do than show you my *cock*pit. I thought you'd never ask."

Carter had my boarding pass on his iPhone along with his orders, so we didn't need to stop for check-in. We breezed through the employee security line and stopped at the food court for some coffee and breakfast. I gave Carter my order and went to the ladies room.

When I came back, I found Carter sitting at a table with a tray. Only he wasn't alone. A gorgeous brunette was sitting across from him. *Figures*. She was wearing the same navy colors as he was, another flight attendant groupie I assumed.

She looked me up and down when I arrived at the table, blatantly sizing me up. Carter stood and pulled out my chair. "Kendall, this is Alexa Purdy. We work at International Airlines together."

The woman showed me her perfect teeth. Considering my parents had also spent a fortune in endodontic care; I smiled bigger. "Nice to meet you, Alexa. Are you on Carter's flight today?"

"I am. But it's actually *my* flight Carter's on, not the other way around."

Carter explained. "I'll be the co-pilot today. Alexa is captain, the pilot in charge. It's her route I'm filling in on today."

"Oh." I wasn't crazy about the woman when I thought she was a gorgeous flight attendant. Knowing that she was smart *and* going to be locked in a small room with Carter today, I immediately disliked her.

Carter was watching me. "I didn't know Alexa had relocated and moved out of the states. We haven't flown together in years."

He might have been trying to reassure me, but Captain Purdy clearly had other ideas. She batted her eyelashes at Carter. "It's been *too* long. We have a lot to catch up on. Remember *how much fun* we used to have on long flights together when we were reserve pilots?"

Carter coughed. "Alexa and I started out as reserve pilots, taking whatever flights we could get. So did *her husband*, Trent. How is Trent? Been a long time since I ran into him."

"He's great. Last I heard he was doing the Milan route and sleeping with a ninety-pound model he met on a flight."

"You're separated?"

"Divorced."

"Sorry to hear that," Carter said.

Alexa touched his arm and cooed, "Don't be. The divorce was my idea. I like my freedom. Being tied down made flying the friendly skies drastically unfriendly."

Luckily, we didn't have too much time to waste over breakfast, because if I had to witness one more flirtation, or hear one more story of their *good old times*, I might have lost it. I wasn't generally a jealous person by nature. I always felt like it was a waste of time and energy to worry about what others had and I didn't. But for the first time, I was thinking maybe the reason for my lack of jealousy before was there was nothing I really wanted enough to be jealous of.

We didn't shake off Alexa until we were almost at the gate. Luckily, she got a call and told Carter she'd meet him on board before excusing herself. Still being careful to discreetly touch me in public, Carter steered me down a hallway near the bathroom for some privacy.

He raked his fingers through his hair. "I'm sorry about that. I had no idea she was my co-pilot. I haven't seen her in years."

It was masochistic for me to ask the question, but I couldn't stop myself. "Did you two, used to..."

Carter blew out a loud breath. "Yes. But it was a long time ago."

"Did you two ever...fool around in the cockpit?"

"Kendall..." Carter warned. No answer was necessary because my brain had already conjured up a vivid picture of Miss Perfect Teeth with her head underneath the jet steering wheel. *Ugh.*

I put up my hand. "It's fine. We're both adults. And it's not like *we're* fucking or anything."

"That's not by my choice, and you know it."

"Whatever."

"You're not being fair here, Kendall. I've been honest with you from the day I met you. Would you prefer I lied to you and told you that nothing had happened between us ever?"

"I'd prefer to not *be here* anymore." I was trying to hurt him, to make him feel the hurt I was feeling. His face told me I'd succeeded.

He leaned in, lowering his face to mine. "Is that what you really want? You want to leave? Then go ahead. I can't change who I was. I like you Kendall. A lot. Probably a fuck of a lot more than I'm supposed to at this point. But know this. I have no interest in Alexa or any other woman. You want to know why? Because the only woman I have any damn interest in *is you*. So if you can't even trust me to fly a plane, then there's no point anyway."

We stared at each other, neither one of us giving an inch. "I gotta go. I hope you join me. But even if you don't, nothing is going to change. The life I led wasn't worthy of a woman like you, and all I can do is try to change going forward. The past is exactly what it is, the past." And just like that, Carter walked away.

Twenty minutes later, the gate attendant announced final boarding. I was still sitting in the waiting area chairs, unsure what the hell I was going to do next. There was no way I wanted to leave Carter, but staying was only going to make our inevitable goodbye even harder. And if by some miracle we didn't say goodbye in a few days, could I build something with him knowing he was always on the road? Could I sleep at night wondering who he was keeping company with on those lonely nights of traveling?

The gate attendants flicked off the illuminated destination sign and began to pack up their paperwork. This was it. Now or never. I was scared as shit to keep going, but the thought of never seeing Carter again was even more terrifying. Just as they began to close the jetway door, I yelled, "Wait!" The two women turned back at the same exact second Carter frantically ran through the door.

Screw Dubai and their stupid rules. I ran to him, and he wrapped me in his arms, holding me tight. "Don't leave me, Perky." Then he took my face in both his hands and kissed me passionately.

"I'm sorry. I was stupid. You promised me you wouldn't judge me and here I was judging you."

"I'm sorry, too, Perky. Sorry there's so much in my past *to* judge. Let's just go forward, alright?"

"Yes. That's what I want, too."

"Good. Now lets get the hell out of here before I get you arrested again." He extended his hand. "Come fly with me, beautiful."

Chapter 12

carter

WHEN WE LANDED IN the Netherlands, I couldn't get off of that plane fast enough.

Captain Alexa had been annoying the shit out of me the entire flight, alternating between bringing up stories from the past and talking about her divorce, neither of which I gave a flying fuck about. From the second we boarded, all I'd wanted was to be back with Kendall. Seven hours later, I got my wish.

After a bumpy landing, my little perky, blonde angel was waiting for me in the cabin when I emerged from the cockpit. Ignoring Alexa and other members of the crew, I pulled Kendall into me and planted a kiss on her that was just as intense as the one before we boarded—as if we'd taken up right where we left off.

I couldn't wait to show her Amsterdam and to be able to touch her freely in public wherever and whenever my heart desired. We didn't have very long here, so I wanted to make the best of it before we had to fly right back to Dubai. I knew that some big decisions were on the horizon after this jaunt. We could save the heavy stuff for then. This leg of our journey was going to be all about having fun in a place with no boundaries.

As we waited in baggage claim, I stood behind her, wrapping my arms around her waist and spoke into her ear, "All of the worries in that pretty little head, put them on hold. Forget about them for today, okay? We're gonna have the time of our lives. Are you in, gorgeous?"

"I'm so in," she said, turning around and playfully sticking her finger into my cleft chin.

I'd chosen a hotel near the Red Light District. Kendall and I took a quick catnap before taking to the streets.

Since biking is huge in Amsterdam, we rented a tandem, which we rode all around the city.

We parked in the Jordaan neighborhood. Walking hand in hand through the narrow streets, we visited some art galleries and antique shops along the way.

Later, we took a guided tour through one of the canals, where we watched what the locals called dancing houses—a bunch of tall, tilted historical homes.

By nightfall, exhaustion had caught up with us. After dinner at a quaint restaurant, we decided to check out the Red Light District before turning in for the night.

The street was lined with red-lit windows, each housing a cabin where revelers could partake in either a peep show or a prostitute—whatever their hearts desired. There was nothing like it in the world. I'd perused this street plenty of times, but never partook. Even *I* had limits. It amused me to see Kendall's reaction, taking it all in for the very first time.

"So, this is all legal?"

"Yup. And it only makes sense that there's a gigantic church in the middle of it all, right?" I said, referring to the

Old Church. "Probably the only location in the world where you'll find religion and prostitution all in one place."

"Kind of magical and perverse." She laughed. "Swans swimming through a dam, surrounded by a church, some whores and lots of pot for sale."

"It's like a trippy dream. You know what would make it better, though?"

"What?" She laughed.

"This," I said, suddenly pulling her into me and planting a firm kiss on her warm lips. Pressing my body into her, I knew she could feel the erection practically puncturing my jeans. An indeterminate amount of time passed as we continued to suck face in front of one of the brothels.

A knock on the glass interrupted our moment. The scantily clad, tall blonde inside of the window we were blocking waved for us to get out of the way. We must have been obstructing her view of the street.

"Sorry," I said, wrapping my entire body around Kendall from behind as we continued our lazy stroll.

"So, do any of these women appeal to you?" she asked.

"No."

"Liar."

"I'm being serious. They're attractive, but I don't want them. Now if it were *you* in one of these window brothels... that would be a different story. I'd definitely come inside, and I'd go broke. I'd just keep giving you more and more money to let me try everything with you." I stopped walking and pulled her into me again, speaking over her lips, "Just take my fucking money."

She laughed through our kiss and said, "I'd give you a pretty good discount."

While our joking was all in good fun, being in this sexually open environment with Kendall and all of the kissing was making me horny as hell. I was now sporting a full-on boner as we made our way back to the hotel. Feeling weaker by the second, I knew that if she so much as looked at me back in our room, I wasn't going to be able to fight anything happening this time.

The hotel we were staying at was a funky little place that played up on the Red Light District theme. The rooms even had optional red lighting, which was cool as hell.

"You know what I could really go for?" Kendall asked when we got to our room.

"I know *my* answer to that question."

She playfully smacked me in the chest. "A glass of wine."

"I could go get us a bottle or two if you want."

"I feel bad making you go back out, but really, that would be great."

"Why don't you relax and take a shower while I'm out."

"That sounds good."

Looking up the nearest liquor store on my phone, I rushed out of the hotel to avoid wasting too much time away from her. After all, this could technically be our last night together. I'd already decided to ask her to come back home to Florida with me. Although if she didn't agree, our adventure would end soon.

Fuck.

A feeling of panic started to build.

No.

I wasn't going to let fear in tonight. This night was about enjoying each moment in Amsterdam. Period.

Trying to block all depressing thoughts from my mind, I made my way inside the store and asked the attendant for the best bottles of red and white that they had.

On my walk back to the hotel, my phone chimed with a text from Kendall.

Kendall: Just play along.

What the heck did that mean?

Carter: Play along with what?

Kendall: Where are you?

Carter: A block from the hotel.

Kendall: Text me when you're almost here but before you come inside the hotel.

A few minutes later, I did as she asked.

Carter: I'm here.

Kendall: Stay outside and look up to the second floor on the Bloedstraat Street side of the building.

That was where I was. I looked up.
Oh.
My.
God.
Fuck.
Me.

My heart started to pump faster. Kendall had the red lights on in our room. The front of her body was pressed against the window as she wore nothing but a lacy bra and panties. She'd done her hair into two braids and swayed her body slowly and seductively, looking just as comfortable as any of the window ladies we'd witnessed tonight. Except this wasn't just any window lady. This was the girl of my dreams bringing a fantasy to life that was better than anything my wildest imagination could have conjured up.

With a come-hither stare, she lifted her index finger and gestured for me to come upstairs. Staying frozen on the sidewalk, I tried to burn this into memory—the sight of her in that window illuminating a foggy night in Amsterdam. I knew I'd never forget it for as long as I lived. The fact that I was still even holding the wine bottles without them falling from my grasp and smashing to the ground was commendable.

The elevator was taking too long, so I took the stairs, skipping over steps to get to her faster. Before opening the door, I inhaled deeply and closed my eyes, vowing to just go with the flow. I didn't even know whether she was really offering anything or teasing me. I just knew I was game for anything behind that door.

Kendall opened.

My mouth spread into a smile as I took her in and waited for her direction.

"I saw you looking at me," she said. "Are you interested?"

Play along.

Fuck yes.

My voice was thick with desire. "Yes." I swallowed.

"Come in."

Just play along.

"What's your name?" I asked.

"Kendall. What's yours?"

"Carter."

"Hi, Carter."

"Hi, Kendall." Slowly inching closer, I said, "Can I just tell you something?"

"Yes?"

"I've been walking these streets all day, searching in vain. I have never seen anyone in these windows who is more beautiful than you. I finally found exactly what I've been looking for. Thank you for letting me inside."

She seemed to blush, probably sensing that my words meant more than just some lines in this little skit. "You're welcome."

As I walked toward her predatorily, she teasingly took steps backwards with an impish grin.

"So, tell me, Kendall. I've never done this before. What happens now?"

"We negotiate. You tell me what you want, and I'll tell you what I'm willing to do." She leaned against a ledge near the window, slightly parting her toned legs. The streetlights outside were shining behind her.

Pulling on one of her braids, I said, "I want it all. So, you're gonna have to be the one to set some limits." I rubbed my fingertips along her cheek and down her neck. "How about we just touch for a while, until you figure out what you're comfortable with."

Closing her eyes and letting out a shaky breath, she said, "Do you want me to take off the rest?"

"Only if you're okay with it."

She stood up and moved in closer to me. "I am."

We were nose to nose when I asked, "Can I undress you?"

She nodded. "Please."

I unsnapped her bra from the front and took a moment to admire her beautiful breasts that reminded me of two perfect teacups. "You're so beautiful."

"I want to see you, too," she whispered.

Slowly lifting the shirt over my head, I felt like she should have been able to see my heart beating through my chest. I had no clue how I was going to continue to exercise restraint.

Just take one moment at a time.

Savor this.

I unbuckled my belt and threw it aside then pulled my trousers down and slipped out of them.

We were both just in our underwear now. I ran my hands down her neck and cupped both breasts in my palms, massaging them slowly. Trying to maintain some control over myself, I tightened my abs to keep my dick in check.

"Can I touch you?" she asked.

Relaxing my body, I begged, "Please."

Kendall rubbed her petite hands up and down my chest and around my biceps. I loved the way her nipples puckered in reaction to the contact.

Touching her while she was touching me yet having to restrain myself was by far the most erotic thing I'd ever experienced. It was so hard keeping my mouth off of her. I licked my lips over and over again to keep myself from losing control and ravaging her.

I'd been looking into her eyes when I felt her hand slip into my boxers and wrap around my cock. So sensitive, I winced at the contact. She began to pump it slowly into her hand as she continued to look at me. Shutting my eyes in ecstasy again, I bent my head back as Kendall jerked me off, twisting her little palm around my cock over and over. She used her thumb to spread the precum around my tip. The room was so quiet, our frantic breathing the only sound.

I was going to come.

Ready to explode, I placed my hand on hers to stop her.

"Stop or keep going, Kendall. You tell me. But I'm not gonna last much longer. It's been way too long."

As much as I loved that she was giving me this fantasy, I couldn't ignore that there was still a slight hesitation in her eyes.

I was certain that she wanted me as much as I wanted her, but she wasn't ready. Tonight wasn't the night.

That didn't change the fact that I needed release like a motherfucker.

I needed to take charge.

"I want you to keep jerking me while I rub you. We're gonna come together, nothing more, nothing less."

A look of relief replaced the uncertainty on her face.

The talking ended there.

We kissed hungrily as she stroked my slick cock up and down between us while I worked to take her underwear off. Massaging her clit with my index and middle fingers, it wasn't long before the muscles between her legs began to pulsate. Her breath hitched, and I knew she was coming. God, she was even more hard-up than I was. Hearing her moan out in ecstasy was enough to trigger my own orgasm as I shot loads of cum into her hand.

It wasn't exactly how I'd imagined our first real physical contact. It was messy and frantic, but perhaps that was in line with the unpredictability that's followed us around from the very beginning. You just never knew what was going to happen from one moment to the next.

Wrapping my hands around her tight ass, I said, "That was hot. I wanted to do so much more, though."

"I would have given you more."

"While I really appreciate this surprise you gave me tonight, you weren't ready, Kendall, and you know it."

"How do you know me so well?"

"I've spent enough time looking into your eyes to know how to read you. You're still not sure, and I won't take you fully until your eyes have not even an ounce of doubt left in them. Even what we did was pushing it."

"Well technically, I was jerking it, not pushing it."

"You can do that again later if you want, by the way."

After picking her panties up off the floor, I lifted them to my nose and muttered, "God, I missed your smell."

"When have you smelled me before?"

Shit.

"Um..."

"Carter..."

"That first day at Maria's. I might have thrown your panties over my face while I whacked off in the tub."

"That is so twisted...but kind of sweet and hot at the same time. Just like you."

"See...you *get* me. You accept me for the panty sniffer I am. This is why you can't leave me. No one else will have me." I kissed her hard then spoke into her neck, "Don't leave me, Perky. Don't leave me in Dubai. Come home to Florida with me...one more leg of the adventure. Then, you make your big decision...after Boca. What do you say?"

"Going home with you is a bit different than jet-setting around the world. Let me think about it on the flight back to Dubai, okay? I'll have seven hours to reflect and then I'll give you my decision about Florida."

As much as I wished that she'd given me an instant yes, I had to respect her wishes without argument.

That night, I held her tightly as we slept in a more intimate position than ever before—with my engorged cock pressed against her ass through the fabric of her nightshirt. My dick was begging for more just as much as I was.

The worst part was the pain in my chest that went along with a particular Beatles song that kept playing in my head.

The song wasn't quite loud enough yet, more like faded background music that my mind wasn't sure it was ready to turn to full volume. I wasn't ready to believe it. Nevertheless, the song was there.

And I Love Her.

CHAPTER 13

kendall

I FELT LIKE A SIXTEEN-YEAR-OLD GIRL, crazy over the boy who wore a leather jacket and was always getting detention in high school. That might have had something to do with the fact that I was getting felt up in the corner of an airport magazine stand when Carter thought no one was looking.

"Stop," I whispered in warning, but couldn't stop myself from smiling. Carter stood behind me as I faced a magazine rack, one hand discreetly slipped under my shirt as he fondled my left breast.

"I totally get the appeal of traveling without a bra now. In fact, I insist you never wear one again when we're together. Being able to reach up and cup this luscious tit..." He squeezed. "...whenever I want, is fucking amazing. Burn your bras, Perky."

I chuckled. An older man walked up to the rack and stood beside me. Rather than remove his hand from my shirt, Carter decided to pinch my nipple. Hard. A cross between a moan and an ouch came out, and I tried to cover it by faking a cough. "Excuse me," I said when the man looked at me.

I elbowed Carter in the ribs when the guy walked away. He groaned, yet somehow managed to get a last tweak of my nipple in before pulling his hand out of my shirt. "We're in a public place. Stop that."

Carter took the shell of my ear between his teeth and bit down as he whispered in my ear. "You love it, and you know it."

He was absolutely right. I did love it. Although Carter was the type of man you could never let know that. He'd have no qualms with a public groping session. And if I'd learned one thing about how I react to him physically, it was that I should be careful what I start because once we get going, it was next to impossible to stop myself.

"I'm going to hit the head before we board. Pick out your magazines. I'll be right back." He reached in to the rack and pulled a paperback copy of *Fifty Shades of Grey* off and handed it to me. "Let's buy this, too. You can highlight the dirty parts, and then when you decide to come home with me, we can act out some scenes." He winked.

I was just finishing up picking out the last of my magazines for the plane ride when Alexa approached. *Captain* Alexa. I hated that just seeing this woman could make me feel so unsettled.

"Kendra. How nice to see you. Have you lost Trip already?" *Bitch.*

"It's Kendall, and Carter will be right back." I picked up a magazine and did my best to ignore her, returning my full attention as I thumbed through.

She stood next to me for another moment before speaking again. God, the bitch even smelled good. "Você leu holandês?" she said.

"Umm...Huh?"

She laughed. No, actually, she didn't laugh. She cackled.

I walked to the register confused, until I looked down and realized I had been pretend reading a Dutch language *People* magazine.

Carter appeared when it was just the two of us left in line. Captain Bitchface was standing behind me. "Alexa. I've been looking for you."

"Oh?" Her voice perked up.

He wrapped his arm around my waist possessively. "Would you mind giving me about ten minutes once we're ready to board? I want to show Kendall the cockpit. Give my girl a tour."

"Ummm...sure."

The minute we walked away from the newsstand, I stopped Carter. Throwing my arms around his neck, I kissed him long and hard in the middle of the terminal. When we finally broke, both of us breathless, he smiled and said, "I'm not complaining, but what was that for?"

"Nothing. Can't *your girl* just kiss you whenever she wants?"

ABOUT THREE HOURS into the flight, I decided to put my seat back and try to get some sleep. I'd pretty much done nothing but obsess about what I should do once we landed since Carter mentioned he wanted to take me home with him to Florida. I closed my eyes, but should have known my brain would never be able to shut down and rest. Instead, I began visualizing what it might be like at home with Carter in a sort of half-awake-half-sleep daydream.

What would the place he lived in look like? I'd never been to Boca, so I wasn't sure of the architecture or the layout, but somehow I pictured him in a tall, sleek, modern, high-rise. Maybe even the penthouse suite. We'd walk through the impressive glass and steel lobby, say hello to a uniformed guard, and head straight to the waiting elevator. Carter would slip a keycard in the slot on the elevator panel and we'd shoot straight to the top floor without stopping. He'd smile at me in the reflection of the shiny silver doors, and I'd smile back, excitement coursing through my veins as I waited to be in the privacy of Carter's home. Arriving at the top, the doors would slide open—giving us direct entry to his apartment.

In my semi-conscious dream state, I took a deep breath in and prepared to step inside. It was then my dream turned into a nightmare. Standing just inside, in front of the floor to ceiling windows of the sunken living room, stood three flight attendants. All three were naked from head to toe, except for navy stilettos and little pillbox-style hats tilted to the side.

My eyes sprung open. *Oh God.*

No matter how hard I tried to remember the man that I spent time with, the man who was sweet and attentive, never looking at another woman when we were together, my fears just kept coming back to haunt me. Is this how it would always be if Carter and I somehow managed to keep in touch? What would happen to the man with the insatiable sex drive when I was big and fat, seven months pregnant and carrying a baby that wasn't his? Would he want me? Could we even make things work if I move forward with my plans?

I didn't even realize I was crying until I felt the teardrops fall from my face and wet my hand. What was I going to do? How could I continue this journey with this man and fall even more? Worse, an equally harder question was, how could I not?

Miraculously, I fell asleep a little while after that. I woke up to a hand at my cheek. "Hey, beautiful. A little less than an hour left."

I stretched my hands up over my head. "Carter. Why aren't you in the cockpit?"

"I needed to see your face. It's been driving me fucking insane the last six hours knowing you were sitting back here thinking about what was going to happen next between us."

I smiled. He looked like he was hoping I'd give him my decision, but I still had no idea what I was going to do. "I'm sorry. I don't have an answer yet."

"It's okay. I need to go back. But I wanted to tell you something before we land, and you made up your mind."

"What's that?"

He took my hand. "After Lucy died, I decided I wanted to go to school to be a pilot. But I was scared I wouldn't be able to hack it. I was partying all the time and screwing around, basically acting like an immature jerk. I got accepted into the aviation program and wasn't sure what to do. Flying a plane is a big responsibility, and I doubted I was capable. So I did something I'd never done before. I dug out the old poems Lucy had written for me when we were together and re-read them. I'm not sure what I was looking for, or what I expected, but it felt like something I needed to do. Anyway, I read them all—there must have been fifty of them—unsure of what I was even looking for. It didn't become clear until I read the last one."

"What did it say?"

"I don't remember the exact words, but the ending went something like this: *Your wings already existed; now you must learn to fly.*" Carter shrugged. "It's silly, but I took that to be a sign. I mean, what are the chances Lucy's poem would be about learning to fly when I was trying to decide to become a pilot?"

"I don't think it's silly at all. I truly believe that sometimes God directs us to read signs to guide our decisions. They're always there, but He makes us see things at certain times in our lives. I think that's what I was hoping would happen on this trip when I started out. I'd find the signs that would guide me to make the right choice."

Carter grinned. "I'm glad you feel that way. Did you happen to read the article about one of those Kardashians in your tabloid magazine?"

I furrowed my brow. "I think I did. Something about one of the twins meeting a rapper?"

He kissed my lips. "I gotta get back. Take another look at the article. Maybe it's your sign."

Confused, I chuckled. "Okay."

"See you on the ground, beautiful." He stood and began to walk away when I called after him.

"Carter?"

"Yeah?"

"Do any flight attendants live in your building?"

He gave me a sexy half smile. "Definitely not."

"Is there a uniformed doorman?"

"Nope."

"Do you live in a penthouse?"

His half smile widened to a full-fledged grin. "Not even close."

"So naked women don't meet you at your door when you get home wearing stilettos?"

He laughed. "Thank Christ, no. You have no idea how funny that question is. If you decide to come home with me, remember what you just asked."

"Okay."

After Carter disappeared back into the cockpit, I took out my magazine and flipped through the pages until I came to the story about one of the Kardashian kids. Curious as to what he thought could be a sign for us, I reread the entire article. The story was about Kendall, so there was that commonality, but that was about all I could seem to find that could possibly point me to anything. She had met a new guy, that was sure as heck nothing new, and the article had a few pictures of them kissing and roller skating. Apparently they were on a trip to Miami, so there was a faint Florida connection, too. Unable to break his cryptic message, I figured I'd ask Carter about it when we landed. But then I closed the magazine and his *sign* hit me right smack in the face.

The cover had various quotes. In the top right-hand corner, there was a picture of Taylor Swift and underneath it read. *Taylor: Music is better than sex.* I laughed to myself thinking there was no way in hell *that* was a sign he wanted me to read into. Down at the bottom of the cover was a picture of Kendall Jenner. The words underneath hit me hard, and I knew exactly what Carter had been hoping I'd see as a sign. *Kendall: I fell in love in Florida.*

WHEN WE LANDED in Dubai, I waited in my seat until the plane was almost empty. After the last person passed, I stuffed my *Okay* magazine into my bag and made my way to the cockpit where Carter was standing. For the first time ever, he looked nervous. Gone was the smiling, confident, cocky pilot I knew, replaced by something that looked a hell of a lot like vulnerability.

We said nothing until I was standing in front of him. Then, he extended his hand to me hesitantly. "What do you say, Perky? Come home with me?"

I kept a solemn face as I reached up on my tippy toes to almost see eye to eye with him. "How can I possibly go against the advice of a Kardashian?"

FLYING WITH CARTER next to me was so much more fun than having him be in the cockpit where I couldn't stare at his handsome face. The flights from Dubai to Florida were on a code share, which meant we were on a sister airline and weren't subjected to Carter's usual harem of flight attendants for the torturously long flights. We spent fifteen hours flying and changing planes, yet between sleeping with my head on Carter's chest and playing touchy feely underneath the skimpy flight blanket, I actually enjoyed every moment of the flights. In fact, I felt refreshed when we exited the terminal in Miami.

We hopped a shuttle bus to long-term parking, and when we walked to Carter's car, I realized just how much I was going to learn about the man by seeing him in his familiar surroundings.

"This is me," Carter said as we walked to a large, black Suburban. He opened the back hatch and lifted our luggage inside, then walked around to the passenger door, opened it, and helped me hop up and get in.

I turned and checked out the inside while he walked around to the driver's side. "This thing is huge. I can fit two of my cars inside here. I think I pictured you more in a little sporty two-seater than this bus. Yet somehow, this fits you, too."

"Used to have exactly that. A little red 1972 Porsche Targa. Loved that thing. Traded it with a friend last year for this beast. He had back surgery and was having trouble hopping up into the high seat, and I needed something bigger for hauling crap around."

"Hauling crap around?"

Carter put the car into drive and pulled out of the lot. "Yeah. I'm always loading this thing for one reason or another."

"How long is the drive to your place?"

"About a half-hour. Goes quick, it's mostly highway."

During the drive, I went through my emails. There was one I had been avoiding for a few days—responding to my mother. I knew she was at least half loaded when she wrote it, just from her run-on sentences. My well-spoken mother tended to lose her boarding school upbringing after a pint of vodka. Rather than explain what I was really up to, I took the easy way out and emailed back telling her I was traveling with a friend still, and I'd be in touch in a few days.

Before long, we pulled off the highway, made a few quick turns, and were pulling down a road that led to a residential community. The entrance had a large fountain in the middle of a circular drive and a welcoming clubhouse building. To the left and the right, there were entrance gates that blocked passage to what looked like hundreds of condos in a neatly planned community. Carter pulled to the left and stopped to roll down his window and key in a code. The gate slowly opened, and we drove through.

A decorative sign greeted us on the other side. *Welcome to Silver Shores. We're glad you're home safe.* An older man wearing a gray jumpsuit was driving a scooter with a basket on the front and waved and yelled when we passed. "Hey, Cap. Welcome home."

Carter waved back and smiled. "That's Ben. He was a New York City garbage man for forty years. Still wears the jumper every day. He'd be the closest to the uniformed doorman you imagined I had."

As we drove farther into the community, I looked around. It was nothing like I expected. Although it was clean and well manicured, it was the exact opposite of a sleek high-rise. Instead, the buildings were all simple two level condos, very standard and normal.

After a few blocks, we turned left and pulled into a parking spot. Carter smirked and pointed to one of the units on the first floor. "And that there, that would be my penthouse."

Chapter 14

kendall

"WELCOME TO MY HUMBLE ABODE." Carter opened his arms wide as we entered the condo.

It was a nice size, not too small, not too big. Two plush, tan-colored couches sat in the middle of the open-concept space. Palm trees blew outside of the glass door in the back that led out to a small patio area.

"This is like a little hidden paradise."

"Not exactly what you were expecting?"

"Honestly? It isn't. I was picturing something like a high-rise on South Beach."

"I know my life is pretty crazy, but when I'm home, I want peace, basically the total opposite from the fast-pace life I lead when flying."

My stomach growled. "Goodness...sorry about that."

"You hungry? I'll make you breakfast."

"Maybe a little. Yeah. That would be great."

Carter opened his stainless steel fridge. "Let's see what we got. Looks like there are some containers of food."

"That stuff can't be good. You've been gone too long."

"No. This was just made today." He pointed to a label. "See the date?"

Someone had stuck a sticky with today's date on top of the Tupperware. It said, *Hot stuff for my hot stuff. —Muriel.*

He took another Pyrex out. That one had a label that said, *Try this. It's better than Muriel's.*

My heartbeat accelerated. "What the hell is this? You have women cooking for you?"

"My neighbors. They have my return dates on their calendar and drop off food. They have keys to my place because they feed my cat and change the litter box."

"You have a cat?"

"Yes. Her name is Matilda. She hides when she smells a new person. That's why you haven't seen her."

"Of course your pussy is a female."

"I'm hoping that *my* pussy is standing right in front of me, because there is no other pussy I want." The look on his face was totally serious when he said, "I can't wait to eat it, too."

Having to clench the muscles between my legs, I cleared my throat and changed the subject. "Who are these female neighbors?"

Shaking his head, he said, "It's not what you think."

"What is it, then?"

"They're old enough to be your great-grandmothers, Kendall."

Relieved, I squinted my eyes. "You have old ladies cooking for you?"

"Yes. They insist on it to pay me back for helping them out from time to time."

"That's actually pretty sweet."

PLAYBOY PILOT

"Thank fuck they do it, because I can't cook for shit."

After a breakfast of sampling both Muriel and Irene's casseroles, I ventured to Carter's bathroom to take a hot shower.

Upon opening the door, I jumped at the site of Matilda the cat hissing at me. Claws out, she wouldn't even let me in the door.

I yelled out toward the hallway, "Carter! Your kitty looks possessed. Help! She won't let me pass."

"Shit. Be right there!"

I looked back down at Matilda. "Calm down, kitty. I'm not gonna hurt you."

Carter appeared seconds later. "Didn't realize she was in here. She usually hides under my bed. She's very possessive." He lifted the plump gray cat off the ground, and she meowed.

Matilda was just another one of Carter's crazy bitches to contend with. My heart skipped a beat when he buried his face into her fur, showering her with kisses. I tried to quickly dismiss the fleeting thought that Carter might make a good daddy someday. It caused physical pain to think about that for some reason. Maybe that was because my gut still told me that our futures were not going to intertwine.

"Don't take too long in the shower. I want to show you around. We have a big day. The first day back here is always a busy one."

"Why busy?"

He smirked. "You'll see."

What did that mean?

After I emerged from the shower, Carter opened the bathroom door, and I instinctively grabbed the towel to cover myself.

He held out his hands. "May I?"

Not even really understanding what I was agreeing to, I simply nodded.

Carter took the towel from my grasp as his eyes travelled down the length of my wet, naked body. He began to gently wipe every drop of water from my skin. His hand lingered over my crotch as he took his sweet time rubbing the towel between my legs. I was supposed be drying off, but I was getting wet instead as my clit started to throb.

The towel fell to the ground, yet Carter's hand remained, rubbing me back and forth until I felt myself suddenly start to climax. "Come. It's okay. Come," he whispered. "I want to watch your face."

My eyes rolled back as I allowed my orgasm to roll through me. It was the quickest one I'd ever had, but it was seriously intense.

When my eyes finally opened, Carter was pointing to his crotch, bringing his hardness to my attention. "Fuck. This might have been a mistake," he growled.

His cock was stretching through his jeans. I looked up at his hair, which was still tousled from playing with the cat. He looked so damn sexy. I had an intense urge to just kneel down and take care of him, but before I could make a move, he backed away.

"God, it's just too much to take sometimes," he said before suddenly exiting the bathroom, leaving me completely aroused even though I'd just come.

When I came out fully dressed, Carter no longer had an erection, which made me wonder if he'd gone to his room and jerked off. That thought turned me on even more.

After he'd taken his own shower, he emerged from the bathroom, looking delicious with his wet hair slicked back and donning cargo shorts and a fitted T-shirt. "Ready for the neighborhood tour?"

"Sure." I smiled.

The Florida sun was shining brightly as Carter and I walked about a block until we came upon a line-up of about fifty Segway scooters parked along a fence. He bent down and unlocked two of them.

"What is going on?"

"These scooters belong to everyone in the neighborhood. They give us a key that unlocks them. It's what most people use to get around."

So strange.

Carter was so big that he looked kind of ridiculous as he got on one and started down the road to demonstrate how it worked. He turned around after a short time to help me onto mine until I was comfortable with how to ride it.

Unable to contain the smile on my face as we scooted along, I listened as Carter pointed out important features of the gated neighborhood, such as a lake that ran alongside it, a small community center and an in-ground pool. The area was massive; it was starting to make sense why people travelled around on scooters.

As we continued riding, something else became abundantly clear. We hadn't passed anyone under the age of seventy-five. Also, everyone who scooted past us had either blue hair or no hair at all.

"There sure are a lot of senior citizens in your neighborhood."

Almost as soon as the words had exited my mouth, Carter nearly fell off the Segway. He stopped and began to laugh hysterically. It wasn't a normal laugh. It was a full on laughing fit.

He held his stomach as he said, "I was waiting for you to catch on, Perky."

"Catch on to what?"

"You're so cute." He hopped off the scooter and kissed my nose.

"Why are you laughing at me?"

"It took you long enough."

"What are you talking about?"

"There aren't just *a lot* of senior citizens here, Kendall. Pretty much everyone is. This is a community for active seniors over the age of sixty-five. Most of the residents are actually in their seventies and eighties."

Wait.

What?

"What the hell are you doing living here then?"

"That's the question of the year, isn't it?" He gave me a quick pat on the ass. "Come on. Get back on the scooter. I'll tell you a little story."

As we zipped along, Carter began to explain. "Okay, so a couple of years ago, my grandmother passed away."

"I'm sorry."

"Thanks. Anyway, my condo was actually hers. She and her cat Matilda lived here for many years. After she died, I was surprised to learn that she'd left me the condo in her will."

"Why you and not your sisters?"

"I think she didn't want to have to choose between the two of them. They're very competitive. She'd left them some money and gave the condo to me. I'd had every intention of selling it. But when I flew down to clean it out, I realized with each day spent down here that I'd never been more at peace in my life. It didn't matter what I looked like, what I did for a living…no women my age to have to worry about fucking over. It was like a total escape and hideout."

"So, you stayed."

"I did."

"Are you the only young person here?"

"As far as I know, I am. But the thing is...even if I wanted to leave now, I'd feel a little guilty."

"Why?"

"This is gonna sound strange..."

"Strange?" I quipped full of sarcasm. "There's nothing about this situation that's strange!"

"Many of these people have come to depend on me. For the most part, I live a pretty selfish life when I'm flying. But when I'm here, I leave my ego in the sky. You know? Helping these people out, whether it's driving them to run errands or lifting something...it makes me feel good."

Then, it hit me. "Oh my God. The Suburban. That's why you have such a big car, isn't it?"

"Yeah." He chuckled.

"You're like that van that shows up at the supermarket trucking the elderly around."

"Basically, a few times a month, I am."

"Wow. I guess there are a whole lot of things I didn't realize about you, Carter."

"There's a lot more I hope to show you, baby. Trust me."

"Don't even try to act sexy on that fucking thing," I said as we continued to roll along.

"This would definitely be the first time I've ever tried to seduce someone on a Segway."

"Where are we going anyway?"

"We're almost there."

"Where?"

"My father's house."

"Your father? I thought your parents were in Michigan?"

"They are."

"I'm confused."

"You'll get it pretty quickly. Remember what you told me back in Amsterdam...to just play along?"

"Yes."

"That's what I'm about to ask you to do."

CARTER HAD A KEY to enter one of the other units. A man who looked to be in his eighties sat in front of an older television set.

"It's about time, Brucey! My fucking feet are killing me."

Brucey?

Carter glanced over at me with a smile. "Don't embarrass me in front of my friend, old man."

"What are you doing with Michelle Pfeiffer?"

"It's not Michelle Pfeiffer, Pops."

"Who is it, then?"

"Her name is Kendall."

"Ken Doll?"

Carter raised his voice. "Kendall...Kendall."

"Whatever. Come cut my toe nails."

"They haven't been done since I was last here?"

"Who else is gonna do them?" the man grumbled.

"True. Where did you put the clippers?"

"Fuck if I know."

"You're gonna send me on a scavenger hunt again?"

"Get me some prune juice while you're up. Been backed up for days," he said before letting out a big fart.

Oh.

Okay.

"Oh, that one sounded wet!" Carter joked before nudging his head for me to follow him down the hall.

"Who is he, Carter?"

Carter spoke low, "Name's Gordon Reitman. He was a friend of my grandmother's. In her will, she asked me to keep an eye out for him. He has nobody else. His wife kicked off a few years before Grandma passed. He gets a visit from some nurses a couple of times a week, but it's not really enough."

"Why does he call you Brucey?"

"Bruce was his son's name. Only child. The kid died in a car accident as a teenager. When Gordon started losing his mind, he started to think Bruce was still alive and that I was grown-up Bruce. I tried to correct him once, and he didn't believe me. Got belligerent. So, I just went with it."

"He really believes that you're him, or he just *wants* to believe it?"

"I think he really does believe it at this point, yes."

Wow.

Carter fished through some drawers in Gordon's bathroom and finally located the small plastic bag containing the clippers. He also placed two rubber gloves over his hands.

"Why do you need those to cut his nails?"

"You'll soon find out."

Back in the living room, Carter sat down on an ottoman in front of Gordon's feet before pulling the old man's socks off. His toenails were yellow and crusty. It became abundantly clear now why Carter was using the latex gloves.

While he began to tend to Gordon's toes, I walked over to a mantle that displayed pictures of a young boy in a baseball cap. There was another picture of the same boy as a teenager. Then, on the far end of the mantle was a picture of Carter, kneeling down next to Gordon.

"Ow, fucking hell!" Gordon yelled, prompting me to turn around.

"Hold your foot still and watch your language in front of my girl, Pops, or I'll have to tickle your feet." Carter proceeded to tickle the bottom of Gordon's foot briefly as a warning, and the old man let out an uncharacteristic cackle.

"There'll be more where that came from," Carter said.

"Bout time you brought a girl home, son."

Carter looked over at me. "Well, this one is special."

Had he never brought a woman to this place?

"I loved you in *Grease*," Gordon said.

I looked at Carter in confusion. "Hmm?"

"Apparently, he still thinks you're Michelle Pfeiffer. Just go with it." Carter put the clippers back in the bag. "All set."

To my amazement, Carter then started to pump some lotion into his hands and began rubbing Gordon's feet. The old man bent his head back on the chair and closed his eyes. He started to moan out in ecstasy. After several minutes, the moaning turned to snoring. Gordon was out like a light.

Carter got up, and I followed him into the bathroom. He suddenly turned around and lifted his lotion-covered hands teasingly. "Let me cup your face."

"Gross!" I laughed. "Take off those gloves!"

"Come on, you know you want some of what I have."

"Carter, seriously, no joke. Clean your hands off if you ever want to dream of touching me again."

He inched closer teasingly and wriggled his brows. "Nothing wrong with a little fungus."

"Carter!"

"Alright. Alright."

Carter removed the gloves before washing his hands. He then turned around, slowly backing me against the wall and planting a warm kiss on my lips.

Running my fingers through his hair, I looked into his eyes. "You know, I've been slowly learning to trust you, seeing the person beneath the playboy pilot façade. But this, what you've been doing for this man—not just the feet stuff but letting him feel that he has some family—really shows me who you really are. It reminds me of how much I loved helping Wanda all those years ago and inspires me to be a better person. You're selfless, Carter."

He inched closer. "Well, at this particular moment, I'm feeling the *opposite* of selfless...very greedy."

"Is that so?"

"Have I ever told you how beautiful you are, Perky?"

"I think so, yes."

"No, I mean, really *told* you. I don't think I've ever really made it clear aloud how badly I want you, and I need you to know that, before you try to leave. I know I've been on my best behavior, but I'm gonna be honest. Ever since we landed here in Florida, it's getting harder for me to hold back. If you told me right now that you'd let me fuck you right this second, I'm pretty sure I wouldn't be able to resist any longer. So, I'm just letting you know, that I've reached my breaking point—my *dick's* reached it's breaking point. I need to fuck you, need to be inside of you."

"Here? In this old man's bathroom? With his dentures practically staring at us from the sink?"

"If you told me you wanted it here... fuck yes. I'd fuck you right here. I wouldn't waste another second of our precious time. But seriously, the ball's in your court. I have a spare bedroom. You sleep in there tonight, alright?"

"Wait. I don't get it. Now, you're telling me you *don't* want to sleep with me?"

"No. Not anymore. I can't sleep next to you anymore with

my dick pressed against your ass, unless you let me inside. A man can only take so much."

"Okay. I can understand that."

"And while I'm being honest with you, I'm gonna say something else, because things might get a little crazy tonight, and I might not have a chance."

"Alright..."

"We only have a few days here. I know you have to spend some of that time deciding what to do. I feel at the very least, we've become close friends. So, as your friend, I need to let you know that I think you'd be making a huge mistake going ahead with the artificial insemination in Germany."

"Okay, tell me why."

"It's a fuck of a lot of money at stake. I get that. But money isn't everything, Kendall. Some day, when the panic of this deadline has passed, you'll look back and regret giving up your beautiful baby. And believe me, that baby *will* be precious if it's coming out of you. You can't play around with human life. Not to mention, money can't truly make you happy, either. I think your childhood is proof of that. It may not be millions, but that's my two-cents. Pun intended."

I just stared into his eyes, absorbing his words before asking, "What makes you happy?"

"You," he said without hesitation. "You're the only thing that's made me happy in a really long time. And I don't want to even imagine losing this feeling."

"Thank you. I feel the same, and your opinion on everything is noted. Believe me, I heard it loud and clear."

Carter let out a deep breath and looked down at his phone. "We'd better get out of here before he wakes up and makes me wash his ass."

"Say what? Has that happened before?"

"He's got a bad back...has trouble reaching behind himself. I'll come back tomorrow and check in on him."

"God, you're a saint."

"Nah. Just doing what any good son would do." He winked.

"Earlier you said we had a busy night. Is something happening tonight?"

He looked way too amused for my comfort. "I'll let you guess, but before you ponder it, just remember where you are."

"Give me a hint."

"It starts with a B."

"Blowjob?"

"Fuck. Why did you have to say that? Now, I'm gonna be scooting down the road with major wood."

I concentrated and repeated to myself, "Where we are... where we are...I know! Barbecue!"

"Good guess, but no. I'll give you another hint. You might get lucky tonight."

I laughed. "Ball gag."

"Bingo!"

"That's it? I'm right? Ball gag?"

"No, Perky. *Bingo*. That's the answer. It's Bingo night."

Chapter 15

kendall

"COME IN!" I YELLED over my shoulder as I stood in front of the mirror in the guest bedroom finishing tying up my hair into a ponytail.

The door creaked open. "Come in? *Fuck.* You gotta stop talking dirty like that to me when we're about to go out and be in front of a hundred senior citizens."

I laughed, "*Come in* isn't dirty. It's your brain that's dirty, Carter."

He walked and stood close behind me, speaking to my reflection. "I think you should avoid using certain words tonight, like *come* and maybe a few others."

"What others might that be?"

"Off the top of my head? Blow, suck, jerk, hole, ride, bend, swallow, inside, meat, nuts, slurp, taste, munch, lick, pull, yank, hot, warm, wet, nibble, throb, bang, cherry, box, eat, ache, stroke, push, pull, ram, screw, messy, plow, thrust, and fill."

My eyebrows shot up. "*All of that* was off the top of your head?"

Carter looked down and groaned. "*Fuck*. Better add *head* to that list, too."

"I think you've gone insane." Finishing my hair, I turned to face him. Since he had been standing behind me in the mirror, I hadn't noticed what he was wearing. "You're wearing your uniform? To Bingo?"

Cocky Carter seemed to blush. "The ladies ask me to wear it."

I covered my mouth and cracked up. "Oh my God. You're old lady eye candy."

"Shut up." Carter was embarrassed. It was the first time I'd seen him be modest about his looks, so I couldn't help but goad him.

"You're their bingo bitch."

"Pipe down, Perky."

"The cougar caller."

He shook his head, but I could see the corners of his mouth twitch.

"You're their PILF."

"PILF?"

"Pilot I'd like to fuck. Like a milf, but with a hot pilot instead."

Carter grabbed my ponytail. "Keep talking, big mouth. Every time you tease me, I'm gonna tease you back." He gave my hair a good strong yank, exposing my neck to him. Then he proceeded to lean down and slowly lick from my collarbone to my ear. When a small mewl fell from my lips, he whispered into my ear. "You're going to have to lock this door if you decide to sleep in here tonight."

MY LIPS WERE STILL SWOLLEN when we arrived at Bingo ten minutes late. The room erupted in cheer when Carter walked to the front of room. Some of the men walked to greet him, slapping him on the back and shaking hands. The women all buzzed in their seats. It was the craziest thing I'd ever witnessed. Carter was a rock star...to a group of elderly people in a retirement community.

I watched amused from the back of the room until an older woman approached me. "You must be Kendall?"

"Yes. How did you know?"

"Carter texted me earlier asking me to take care of his girl tonight. And...well..." She looked around the room. "You're the only one who didn't have to sling your breast over your shoulder for the walk over to the bingo hall."

I smiled, and she offered me her arm. "Come on. I'm Muriel. I saved you a seat between me and Bertha."

Muriel and Bertha each had at least a dozen bingo cards spread out in front of them. Both had also set up their tables with personal items. Muriel had a small silver frame with a picture of three small children, a water bottle, three different colored ink stampers and a small candy dish filled with jellybeans. When she caught me looking, she lifted the frame. "This is Seth, Rachel, and Emma. My son's kids. He married a bitch on wheels but she gave me the gift of grandchildren, so I tolerate her."

"They're beautiful."

"Thank you. You and Carter want to have kids some day?"

My heart sank at the mere mention of me and a baby. "I don't know. We haven't known each other that long."

PLAYBOY PILOT

Bertha leaned over and interjected, "I'd have his babies if I could. Pop out all those little mini pilots with dimpled chins."

Muriel whispered to me. "Ignore her. She hits the sauce before coming to Bingo. We don't complain because it makes her unable to mark up her cards right, which means better chances for the rest of us to win."

Bertha yelled. "I can hear you, you know!"

Muriel shrugged and waved her off. Bertha had a straight line of four 7-Ups at the top of her table area and offered me one. "You want a 7 and 7, Barbie? Water bottle's got Seagram's for you to mix it with. Gotta disguise it because some of the uptight board members decided Bingo night should be alcohol free."

Muriel snickered. "Tell her *why* they made that rule, Bertha."

Bertha gulped from her red cup. "My pants were too tight. I opened them while I was sitting here and forgot to snap them back up before I got up. These people all act like they've never seen a little ass before."

Muriel added, "First, it hasn't been a little ass since 1953. And second, she's leaving out the part where she tried to walk with her pants down around her ankles, tripped and fell, and pushed Mr. Barthman on her way down. He cracked a tooth when he landed."

"It was a denture, not a real tooth."

Muriel and Bertha then proceeded to bicker over me, both leaning in to yell in a different ear. When I looked up, Carter was watching from the front of the room and cracking up. He held up one finger, and then plugged in his microphone and tapped it before speaking. "How are all my Bingo Babes doing tonight?"

The women around the room hooted and hollered.

"Is everyone ready? We're going to kick off tonight with a favorite that I'd like to dedicate to my guest here with me this evening. The first game will be any horizontal line. Just mark off any five spaces across your card to win." He looked directly to me as he continued and winked. "Any which way you want to lie down horizontally will earn you a prize from me."

I rolled my eyes. Bertha gave me one of her cards, a stamper, and slid one of her fuzzy-haired, freaky trolls in front of me wishing me luck before the games started.

Carter stood at the front of the room behind a folding table that held a wire cage filled with small white balls. He cranked a lever at the side, which started the balls jumping round. Stopping it, he reached in and pulled out the first ball. "Today we're starting off with one little duck."

The room quieted, and everyone picked up their stampers and began stamping. I had no idea what was going on, but Muriel seemed to be stamping the number two. When she saw I was confused, she explained. "One little duck...it's a bingo term, it means the number two. The two looks like a duck."

I didn't have a two on my card, but I watched as Carter's eyes scanned the room. He was making sure everyone had enough time to stamp their dozens of cards. Eventually, he cranked the lever again. This time, when he pulled out the ball he said, *Grandma's getting frisky* into the microphone.

Muriel translated again, "G60. Frisky rhymes with sixty."

Again everyone went to work at stamping their cards. It seemed I was the only one who needed a bingo lingo dictionary. While they were all busy checking their cards, Carter began to hum into the microphone. I recognized the tune, but couldn't put my finger on it.

PLAYBOY PILOT

A few more calls later, Carter looked down at the ball and then winked at me, "Anyway up. A favorite of mine."

I didn't need Muriel to translate Carter had just called O69. Throughout the night he continued to hum that same song. I'd initially assumed it was the Beatles, but then when he began to sing the first line about knowing when to throw in the cards, I recognized it as Kenny Rogers, *The Gambler*.

Curious, I asked Muriel. "Does he sing Beatles songs while he's up there ever?"

"He used to. Until we took him to the Kenny Rogers concert for his birthday."

"You took him to see Kenny Rogers?"

"Yep. Most of us hadn't celebrated our birthdays anymore until Carter moved in. But now, we look forward to them. On his birthday, we chip in and introduce him to something from our generation. On our birthday, he surprises us with something from his."

I was blown away at how deeply connected Carter was with these people. "What did he give you for your birthday?" I asked Muriel.

Her eyes lit up, and she turned, lifting her foot to show me her shoes. "Reebok Pumps. My back was killing me when I went out for my daily walk. You pump these crazy sneakers he got me up...no more back pain."

"I didn't even know they still made them."

By the end of the night, I realized I'd had a great time. Muriel had written down the recipe for Carter's favorite meal, and Bertha, who was halfway sloshed, told me dozens of dirty jokes all centered around pilots. There I was, sitting in a Bingo hall full of people the same age as my grandparents, and there was nowhere else that I wanted to be. It was in that moment, as I watched from afar while Carter cleaned up and talked to a few of the other residents, that I realized how hard I'd already fallen. Muriel noticed me in deep contemplation.

"Confused about the man?"

I sighed. "How did you know?"

"I know that look. Been there with my Connor. Met him at eighteen, and he scared the bejesus out of me. The man could quite literally talk your pants off. Had that way about him, like Carter does. I tried to keep away. Didn't help that he was gorgeous and a police officer who was rough around the edges, either."

I smiled. "You said *my Connor*. I guess you eventually stopped running away from him?"

Her face fell. "I did. But, unfortunately for me, it wasn't until I was nearly thirty-five."

"What happened?"

"I was eighteen, and he was twenty five. I was a Jewish girl from the east, and he was an Irish boy whose parents were off the boat. My heart said yes, but my brain said no. As did my father. I made the mistake of listening to my brain over my heart. Eventually, I ran one way. He went the other. Lost almost twenty years with the love of my life before we caught up with each other again."

"Wow. Is he...does he...live here with you?"

"Died in eighty-two. Random traffic stop gone bad when he pulled over a man who happened to have a trunk full of guns. Shot him point blank and left me a widow at thirty-seven. Found out I was pregnant with my son a few days after his funeral."

I clutched my chest. "Oh my God. I'm so sorry."

She nodded. "Thank you. But I didn't tell you my tale of woe to bring your head down. Told you to remind you life is short. Half of the people in the world will tell you to follow your head, half will tell you to follow your heart. My advice, follow the one that isn't confused. The stronger one will eventually convince the other to fall in line."

Carter walked over wheeling a man in a wheelchair. "You ready? Just need to help Mr. Hank get into his car on the way out."

I thanked Muriel by pulling her into a hug. "Thank you. For everything."

She understood what I was saying. "You're welcome, sweetheart. You take good care of our Captain, and I'll make sure Bertha doesn't come knocking on your door at 7AM tomorrow wearing that skimpy robe she thinks will land her a young pilot."

Carter kissed her cheek. "Night, Muriel."

After everyone was out of the Bingo hall, Carter locked up with a key on his key ring and we headed back to his place. He took my hand while we walked.

"Can I ask you something?" I said.

"Anything."

"How did you know all those Bingo terms? That O-eighty-three was time for tea or that I-twenty-three was thee and me?"

"They told me a few of them. I saw that they got a kick out of it when I used the lingo. So I looked more up on the Internet and memorized the terms and some games." Carter shrugged. "Long stretches of time to learn new stuff on overseas flights." He chuckled. "Although I think my co-captain thought I was losing it when I had him quiz me the whole trip from Germany to New York."

"I don't know what to make of you, Carter. One minute you're dirty talking in my ear and the next you're taking me to Bingo."

"Not exactly the date you're used to, I'm guessing."

"Definitely not."

"Tomorrow night I'll take you out on a real date. Just me and you to some fancy restaurant."

I stopped on the sidewalk. "I didn't mean it like that. This might have been the best date I've ever been on."

"Really?"

I nodded. "The whole purpose of dating is to get to know the other person. It's sad, but I don't think I figured that out until tonight. I'll be honest, dating for me was always about what restaurant some guy would take me to. I judged men based on what they spent and the designer they wore. Their last name meant more to me than how they treated the people who'd passed down that name. But seeing you up there tonight, I had an epiphany."

"An epiphany, huh?"

We were still stopped on the sidewalk, holding one hand. I reached out and took Carter's other hand into mine. Taking a deep breath, in the middle of a retirement community, I decided it was my moment of truth. "I'm crazy about you, Carter Clynes. I'd rather be with you in a Bingo hall sitting between Bertha and Muriel as they argue, than be in a five-star restaurant with a descendant of the Rockefellers. You sing Kenny Rogers because you know they love him, clip your fake father's toenails, and buy women sneakers to help their bad backs." I stepped to Carter and wrapped my hands around his neck. Taking one more deep breath, I spoke directly into his eyes. "I'm crazy about you, Carter. There is nowhere else I'd rather be than standing next to you, wherever that might take me."

Carter leaned his forehead to mine and closed his eyes. He was silent for a moment before he spoke. "Perky, you have no idea how much it means to me to hear you say that. I feel the same way, maybe even more. I don't have all the answers, but I want to be the one to help you find them."

Tears streamed down my face. "I'm happy, Carter. So damn happy. And I'm terrified at the same time."

His thumbs at my cheeks caught my tears. "So am I, beautiful. So am I."

Just then, a small red car slowed to a stop, and the window rolled down. "You need a lift, Cap?"

Carter lifted his hand. "I'm good, George. But thanks."

The old man waved back. "I look younger in here, don't I? The babes dig my car."

"You look great, George. Go slay 'em, old man. But watch out for that hip."

The car slowly pulled away and then something dawned on me. "Was that, by any chance...a Targa?"

"It was."

"That's your car, isn't it? The car you traded to a friend who had surgery?"

"He needs it more than I do, anyway." Carter slung his arm around my shoulder, and we started walking again. "Apparently, I don't need the car. I can pick up hot little blonde chicks at a Bingo hall."

Chapter 16

carter

IT WAS A TYPICAL FLORIDA NIGHT, breezy with a hint of drizzle in the air. But there was nothing typical about the moon tonight; it was spectacular—magical, even. There was also nothing typical about the way I was feeling, like my heart was about to beat out of my chest; like I was stepping into territory that I'd never ventured into before with Kendall. Like something big was about to happen.

The girl I was crazy about had just looked at me with tears in her eyes and told me she was crazy about me, too. I never wanted this feeling to end, never wanted this night to end. I was on cloud nine. Fuck that...I was on cloud sixty-nine.

The entire time at Bingo, I hadn't been able to take my eyes off of my girl, couldn't wait to get her alone again.

As Kendall and I continued our walk hand in hand back to my condo, I intentionally trailed slightly behind her, unable to resist staring at the way the thin silk material of her dress clung to her beautiful ass crack. I felt like the luckiest man in the world to be taking her home.

Adjusting my pants to combat my almost painful hard on, I glanced over at the lake in the distance. Since it was pretty much bedtime in these parts, I knew we'd have it all to ourselves. My neighbors barely ventured out to the lake even in the daytime.

Needing to prolong this night, I asked, "Wanna head down to the water? Go for a swim?"

Head.

There was my dirty mind again. I just couldn't shut it off tonight.

"I don't have a swimsuit. This dress is dry clean only. I can't get it wet."

Wet.

Fuck.

I raised my brow. "I was thinking we'd swim without clothes, actually."

"Oh...*that* kind of swim." She bit her bottom lip and smiled. "Sure, Captain. I'm up for anything tonight."

Anything.

Kendall squealed as I suddenly lifted her off her feet and ran toward the lake while she wrapped her hands around my neck. Unable to remember the last time I'd been this horny, I felt like a teenager. I also couldn't remember the last time I'd felt this *happy*. Perhaps, it was sometime before Lucy died. All I knew was there was no mistaking how happy Kendall was making me feel tonight.

When I planted her back down on her feet, she looked up at me. I was still wearing my pilot's uniform as I towered over her. She watched every movement of my hands as I slowly unbuttoned my shirt and threw it onto the grass. We were far enough away from the nearest house that I knew no one would catch us naked at this hour. I wasn't holding back.

After whipping my belt out of my pants, I unzipped and stepped out of them, then placed my hands on my hips while staring down at her ogling me.

Her eyelids were heavy, filled with lust as she looked down at my engorged cock that was practically bursting out of my boxer briefs. I fucking loved the way she was looking at me. It only made me harder. Not even trying to hide my arousal, I wanted her to see what she was doing to me.

"I assume you can swim, Perky?"

She finally looked back up and met my stare. "Yeah. I can do a mean back stroke."

Stroke.

Fuck.

My dick twitched.

Walking slowly toward her, I said, "I can stroke pretty well myself."

She cleared her throat. "Or stroke *yourself* pretty well?"

I wrapped my arms around her waist. "Yeah...that."

"I bet you can. What about the breast stroke?" she muttered, clearly affected by my touch.

Kissing down her neck and over her breasts, I said, "What about it?"

"Would you like to stroke yourself between my breasts, Carter?"

Fucking hell.

My dick was throbbing now.

"I've been dreaming about coming all over those beautiful, perky tits since the airport lounge. You're killing me, dirty girl. I'm drowning, and we haven't even gone near the water yet."

"Don't worry. If you drown, I know mouth to mouth." She smiled against my lips.

Tugging at the strap of her dress, I asked. "Can I take this off?"

She nodded silently. I lifted her dress over her head then unsnapped her bra from the front, letting it fall. I couldn't resist taking her nipple into my mouth and ever so gently tugging on it with my teeth. I let out an unintentional growl, starting to feel myself come apart.

As I gripped her thong and slowly slipped it down her legs, I took notice of how wet it was. That proved our dirty talk had gotten to her just as much as it had gotten to me.

There was a slight chill in the air, and when she shivered, an enormous need to warm her up prompted me to pull her naked body closer into me. Things spiraled out of control pretty quickly from there.

When two people are connected in the way that Kendall and I were, words aren't always necessary. Her nails were digging into my back. Her heart was pounding against mine. With every fiber of her being, she was telling me that she was ready to surrender to the enormous pull that had existed between us ever since that very first encounter in the airport. There wasn't a shred of resistance left between us.

Right there, under the magnificent moon, I knew in my gut that we weren't even going to make it down to that water. I was going to take her right here on what was technically private lakefront property.

Holding her face in my hands, I kissed her with everything in me as she raked her fingers through my hair. We collapsed onto the dewy grass as I bore down onto her with all of my weight, covering her body with mine.

Through the fabric of my boxers, I desperately grinded my cock against her clit over and over as she writhed under me. She was soaking my underwear with her heat, and the need to feel that wet pussy wrapped around my cock was unbearable. We were rubbing against each other like two oversexed teenagers. Her hips bucked. Without using words, she was begging me for more.

I broke our kissing just long enough to say, "Can't hold back anymore, Kendall. You keep that up, I'm gonna come all over you when I'd rather come inside of you."

"Come inside of me then."

"Seriously, tell me to stop. Otherwise, I'm about to fuck you on some old person's grass."

She responded by pulling me harder into her and wrapping her legs around my back as she worked to pull down my boxer briefs.

Frantically, I patted my hands out in search of my pants. I'd slipped a single condom in the back pocket, which I'd carried for some time. I never quite knew if I would lose it at any given moment with her; I needed to be prepared and thanked fuck I'd remembered to bring it with me tonight. That condom had followed us around since Rio.

Fumbling with the wrapper, I'd never opened one so fast in my life. Sheathing it over my cock, just the thought of what I was about to feel for the first time was enough to make me explode before it even started.

Sinking into her was euphoria. Her tight pussy stretched for me with every inch deeper that I moved inside of her. Unable to resist, I fucked her hard at a desperate pace. It was the rawest, most spontaneous sex I'd ever experienced. It was desperate in part because even as I lay naked on the grass, balls deep inside of her, I still had no idea if I was going to lose her in a matter of days.

That terrified me.

The thought made me fuck her even harder, more possessively.

"Open your legs wider."

She willingly obliged as she grabbed my ass to help control my movements. We were like two animals in heat, mating in the still of the night. I thought about all of the small planes that fly low overhead around here. If it were daylight, what a sight they would have seen from above: my bare ass ramming into Kendall in the middle of what was basically someone's back lawn.

I needed to come so badly, but I only had one condom and needed to make this last because the walk home was too damn long. It was quiet except for the sounds of our breathing, our bodies joining together, my balls slapping against her ass and the wetness as I moved in and out of her. It was sexual sensory overload, and I was drowning in it—drowning in her.

Kendall was more petite than I was used to in a woman, so much so, I worried I might have been hurting her. It was a challenge to fuck her the way I wanted with all of my weight on top of her. She surprised me when she suddenly pulled away then flipped over, sticking her fucking beautiful ass in air. She wanted me to take her from behind. It was as if she'd read my mind.

Pulling on her blonde hair, I relished the feeling of entering her again. The sight of her tight ass as I pounded into her was too much to handle. Within seconds, I unexpectedly started to shoot my massive load.

"Fuck, Kendall. I'm coming. God…this is so…" My words trailed off as I lost the ability to speak.

"Me, too," she said as she slammed her ass back into me over and over, milking my dick for all it was worth.

It felt like a neverending orgasm—a fitting end to days upon days of neverending physical and mental foreplay. My body trembled until every last drop had emptied into the condom.

I immediately wanted more.

After carefully pulling out, I flipped her around to face me. We stayed kissing on the grass while she rubbed her wet pussy against my abs. It was driving me insane.

"I'm hard as a rock again, baby. I've got to get off of you, otherwise I'll end up inside of you again, and I don't have anything else with me. We need to get back to my house, stat."

"Okay." She kissed me harder, causing me to collapse down onto her again.

"Remember that fancy dinner we were supposed to go to tomorrow night?"

"Yeah." She smiled.

"I think we need to order it in, because I don't think I can keep my hands off of you long enough in public. Is that okay?"

"Sounds like a plan."

Forcing myself off of her, I said, "Let's get out of here."

"I just need to wash off really quickly in the lake."

She went ahead of me, and I ran to catch up. We ended up frolicking in the water for several minutes. I lifted her up, threw her down, spun her around, and we kissed over and over. I'd been to a lot of places as a pilot, travelled around the entire world, but nothing had been more spectacular than this night with Kendall by the lake.

Some flashing lights in the distance caused us both to take notice. We ducked down into the water and held each other while we kissed quietly until whatever it was passed. I couldn't tell if it had been a car or someone walking by with a flashlight. It would be just my luck to get into some kind of trouble that would spoil what was literally the best night of my life. I couldn't let that happen.

"Are you ready, gorgeous?"

"Yes. Take me home, Captain."

When we returned to our spot, Kendall slipped on her dress, while I looked around for my pants.

"Where the fuck are my pants?"

She squeezed out the water in her hair. "You can't find them?"

"No. They're gone. My underwear, too."

"Is this a joke? Does it have something to do with those lights we saw?"

"Someone apparently decided it would be hysterical to take only my clothes."

Kendall covered her mouth. "Oh my God. I don't mean to laugh, but this is nuts. Do you want me to walk back to your house and get you some pants?"

"That would be great, except for the fact that my house key was inside my pants!"

"Shit." She threw her thong at me. "Here."

"What are you doing?"

"Put it on."

"That little thing is not gonna cover half of my junk."

"It's better than nothing."

Rubbing my temples, I tried to think. My house was over a half-mile away.

"Let's run to Gordon's house. Compared to my place, he's pretty close to here, just around the corner. He's probably sleeping, but he keeps a key in the plant pot outside his door. I'll go in there and get some pants."

Kendall and I couldn't help laughing our heads off as we ran. With one of my hands holding hers and the other covering my ass, we finally made it to Gordon's doorstep. She waited outside for me.

Gordon was snoring as I entered his bedroom. His closet door creaked as I opened it, causing him to jump awake.

"Dad," I whispered. "It's me. It's okay."

"Brucey?"

"Yes."

"What are you doing here?"

"I need to borrow some pants."

"What kind of trouble did you get into?"

"I was skinny dipping with a girl, and someone stole them."

"Michelle Pfeiffer?"

"Yeah." I smiled in the dark.

"Atta-boy." He then simply rolled over and began snoring again.

Securing Gordon's loose trousers with a belt, I returned outside to rejoin Kendall. We couldn't stop cracking up as we made our way back to my house. The pants were loose yet ridiculously short on me.

After breaking through a window, I carried Kendall into my bedroom and without even putting her down, reached into my drawer for a condom.

"Please tell me your taking those pants off."

I laughed against her mouth and nodded as I unbuckled, letting Gordon's giant trousers fall to the floor. I ripped the condom with my teeth and somehow managed to get it on without putting her down. I gasped upon sinking into her. She was already fully wet.

"Fuck. I can't ever let you go now, Perky. You know that, right? This feels too good. Too damn good." I was already addicted, and there was no way I could fathom not having this in my life anymore—not having *her* in my life.

"Carter..." she moaned.

I thrust in to her. "Kendall."

Again. "Kendall."

Again. "Fuck, Kendall. How am I gonna fly planes ever again when all I want to do is *this* for the rest of my life?"

She suddenly started to spasm around my cock, and I immediately came in response. Her back slammed against the door as I pumped in and out of her, still needing more when there was nothing left to give.

Beads of sweat were pouring off of us. Speaking against her limp body, I said, "I feel like I've lost my damn mind over you. I've never felt this way about anyone. I don't know what tomorrow will bring. I don't even know where my fucking pants are! All I know is I can't let you go, baby." I held her close. "I can't let you go."

My heart was racing faster than it ever had after sex. I knew that was because for the first time in my life, it wasn't *just* sex; it was so much more.

Chapter 17

kendall

THE SMELL OF BACON wafted through the air. Wrapping the sheet around my naked body, I followed my nose to the kitchen. I stopped at the doorway to take in the scene before me. Carter was completely naked, his taut ass swaying back and forth as he stood in front of the stove frying bacon while belting out the Beatles *I Got a Woman* along with the radio. It was seriously an astounding sight. The epitome of Carter Clynes' magnetism was on full display—gorgeous, confident, playful, loving, a little crazy, and a whole lot magical.

When he caught me leaning against the doorway, I felt his smile inside of my chest. My heart swelled watching him walk to me, take one hand in his, and wrap the other around my back. Carter pulled me close and lead with a strong hand as we slow danced together.

He sang the words of the song with his mouth at my ear.

I got a woman.

I got a woman.

It was one of those beautiful moments in life that felt like a dream. I wanted it to last forever. I wanted *us* to last forever.

The song ended, and Carter pressed his lips to my forehead. "Morning, beautiful."

God, there couldn't possibly be a better way to start a day, could there? "How long have you been up?" I asked.

"Not long. Maybe a half-hour."

Smoke was billowing from the frying pan behind him. "Umm...I think you're burning the bacon."

"Shit." He rushed to the stove and twisted the dial to turn down the flame. The sizzling bacon made a loud crackle, followed by a snap, right before a burst of hot oil splattered hitting Carter in the abs. "Ouch. Shit! Damn it."

I giggled. "You might want to think about putting some pants on before you burn the good parts."

Waving the spatula at me, he said, "The good parts, huh? You mean my hands?"

"Well...those are pretty good. But not what I was worrying about you injuring."

He pointed to his lips and grinned. "My mouth? That must be what you're worried about."

"That's definitely good, too. Especially that little thing you do with your tongue where you swirl it around and then flutter."

His pupils dilated, and his voice was low and gravelly. "You like that, huh?"

My cheeks flushed thinking about how he'd brought me to orgasm more than once with his mouth. I nodded.

Without taking his eyes off of me, he reached back, turned the flame completely off, and slid the pan from the hot burner to the cool one to the right. "I don't even remember what we were talking about anymore."

"I had suggested you cover up a certain body part so it didn't get burned with bacon grease splatter."

"Oh I'm gonna cover it alright." He took a few long strides to where I was still standing and surprised me by scooping me up and tossing me over his shoulder in a fireman's hold. "Gonna cover it with your gorgeous pussy in about ten seconds."

He swatted my ass as he headed toward the bedroom.

"What about the bacon?"

"Fuck breakfast. I'm going to eat you."

IT WAS EARLY AFTERNOON before we even thought about real food again. Carter had just microwaved one of the Tupperware containers in his fridge, and we were sitting in bed eating goulash by passing the container back and forth between us. He slurped an egg noodle into his mouth while making his eyes go cross. It was something a six year old might do, and that made me wonder what Carter might have looked like as a young boy.

"Do you have any photo albums?" I asked.

"Not with recent photos."

"Do you have any of you as a boy?"

"I do, actually. When I moved down to Florida, my mother made me an album of old family photos. I found it with a letter when I was unpacking. She wrote that she wanted me to remember how much I was loved and asked me to look at the album at least twice a year—on my birthday and hers."

"That's so sweet."

He handed me the almost empty container, and I declined my turn at stuffing my face. "I'm full. You can finish it."

"I like eating with you. You only eat half, and I get to finish off the rest."

"Better watch it. Might wind up with a pot belly eating two dinners all the time."

"We'll work it off and then some."

I had no doubt we would. Carter handed me the water bottle we were sharing and I took a sip. "Do you do what your mom asked in her letter? Look at the album twice a year?"

"I do."

"When is your birthday, anyway?"

"July Fourth."

"Are you kidding?"

"No. Why?"

"That's my birthday, too."

Carter mumbled. "And eventually the pieces fall into place."

"What's that?"

"Nothing. It's something my mother always said."

"What did you do on your birthdays growing up?"

Carter finished off the last of the noodles in the Tupperware and stood from the bed. "I'll show you."

He came back a minute later with a thick photo album and sat with his back to the headboard. Adjusting me so I was positioned next to him, he opened the album on his lap. The first page had two pictures of a chubby naked baby that was probably about three or four months old.

"Is that you?"

"Yep. Look at the size of my balls. Why are they so big? Are all baby's balls that size, or did I just have to grow into mine?"

I laughed. "I don't know. But you were so cute! And chubby, too."

The next page had pictures of two girls who were probably about six or seven and a boy of maybe four who was most definitely Carter. The chin dimple was a dead giveaway even if it hadn't looked exactly like him. "Are those your sisters?"

He nodded. "Catherine and Camille."

They looked about the same age. "Are they twins?"

"They are. Fraternal. My mother is a twin, too."

Carter, Catherine, Camille. "What are your parents' names?"

"Mom is Calliope and dad is Carter."

"So you're one of *those* families, huh?" I bumped shoulders with him. "All your names begin with the same letter?"

"Five people, all our initials are double C. Hated it when I was a kid for some reason."

He flipped a few more pages, and I watched Carter grow up before my eyes. He was a cute baby and an even cuter little boy, but God, did he grow into his looks in his teens. We laughed at the progression of his hairstyles over the years. The last few pages of photos looked like they were recent, in the last few years. I slipped a photo of Carter holding a little girl who was probably about two out of the slot. They were sitting in front of a Christmas tree. "Who's this? She's adorable." She had platinum blonde pigtails, and Carter's captain's hat was covering half her eyes. Her toothy smile was outlined in chocolate and she held a squished chocolate covered éclair in one fist.

"That's Corinne, Camille's daughter. Don't let the face fool you. She's a holy terror."

"I bet she's sweet. Wait...Another C name?"

"Yep. Catherine has a son. Wanna take a guess?"

"Charlie? Chance? Cash? Christopher?"

He pointed at me. "Christopher."

"Will you keep up the tradition someday? Maybe a little Carter or Claire?"

His entire demeanor changed. Carter's eyes held a seriousness that I hadn't previously seen from him. "I don't know. I never really gave it any thought before." He seemed to be contemplating something for the longest time. Eventually, he said, "Wasn't even sure I wanted kids. I'm gone twelve days out of the month. But now, I'm starting to wonder if maybe that is something I want. I think the right woman can change what a man thinks he wants out of life. I guess it depends on her. On us."

I swallowed. "That makes sense."

He looked down at the photo album. The last picture was of him, his parents, and his two sisters. They were all smiling broadly and had their arms around each other's shoulders. He brushed his fingers over the page. "My sisters like to bust my balls about having kids. They act like I'm pushing fifty instead of thirty. For years, my mother has been saying this thing that I thought was just something she read on a Hallmark card somewhere."

"What's that?"

"She said I'd have a family when I was ready to stop traveling all over the world searching for something and realized what I was looking for was already at home." He continued looking straight into my eyes. Since the first time my gaze landed on Carter Clynes in that airport lounge, my heart had been beating a million miles an hour. But in that moment, I felt it happen. My heart slowed, took a deep breath, and let out a giant sigh. Just like that, it gave in, unable to fight it anymore. I had no idea how long we had or how things were going to play out, but I knew without a doubt that I was in love with Carter.

THINGS LIGHTENED UP between us in the late afternoon. Carter went to check on Gordon and then when he came back, we had sex in the shower, followed by sex on the bedroom floor. I got the feeling that my ass print was going to be all over the man's condo by the time we left in a few days. Even though my body felt like I'd just taken a strenuous yoga class followed by running a marathon, Carter apparently was no worse for the wear.

"How about if we head over to the gym for an hour and then I take you out to a nice dinner tonight?"

I was lying on the bed with my head dangling upside down off the edge watching a rerun of *That 70's Show*. "Seriously? You want to go exercise after all that sex?"

Carter chuckled, walked over to the bed, flipped me over, and swatted my ass hard. That seemed to be a thing for him. "Oww...." I rubbed at it.

"Come on, lazy. I still have a lot of energy to burn off. We don't go to the gym, you won't be able to walk for a month."

We decided to walk to the fitness center, even though it was on the other side of the development. The lake from last night was on the way, and Carter wanted to see if his uniform pants turned up in the daylight.

"Where the heck could they have disappeared to?" I asked. Scouring the lake, there was no sign of his pants anywhere. It was the most bizarre thing.

"No idea." Carter shrugged. "But I'm glad I'm due to pick up my annual replacements next month. I've lost half my uniforms over the last year."

"Lost? Do you leave them behind at hotels when you're traveling?"

"That's the strange thing. I lose them at home. Last month, I could have sworn I had a hat at Bingo, but I couldn't find it afterward. Think the forgetfulness of some of the residents is starting to rub off on me."

I DECIDED TO GO ALL out for dinner. I slipped into a tight, little black dress and a pair of the tallest, sexiest high heel shoes I had with me. They were open-toed and had silk ribbons that wrapped half way up my calves. A good push-up bra gave me an abundance of faux cleavage that strained from the low V of my dress. Remembering how much Carter had liked the slutty look when I'd styled myself in Dubai, I blew my blonde hair with some extra body, lined my blue eyes with thick black and painted my lips blood red.

The extra effort paid off when I walked out of the bedroom.

"Jesus Christ."

I circled. "You like?"

"You look like every wet dream I had growing up."

"I'm not sure if that's a compliment or creepy."

"It's a compliment. Any boy or man would love to jerk off to you." He winked, and I laughed.

Outside, Carter opened the door to his SUV and helped me inside. Before shutting the door, I said to him, "You know, I think you get away with saying anything you want just because you're so good looking."

"Is that so?"

"It is. I think you make people delusional with your looks and charm, and we start to think that things like 'any boy or man would love to jerk off to you' is normal."

"It is normal. It's only natural. Any man who doesn't think of what you look like tonight as future whack off material is full of shit. I just tell it to you straight."

I laughed. "Again. That sounded charming, but I'm pretty sure if someone else said it...totally creepy."

Carter drove through the development slowly, although it's not like he had much of a choice. There were a hell of a lot of speed bumps in his retirement community. As we made our way toward the front gate, we passed at least a half dozen couples power walking in tracksuits. They all waved, and Carter called a greeting out the window to each by name. I still couldn't get over how entrenched he was in this retirement village.

The exit of the development was next to the clubhouse where Bingo had been held, and the parking lot was packed again. "What's going on tonight?"

"Singles square dancing night."

"Are you kidding me?"

Carter smiled and shook his head. "Nope. A lot of widows and widowers in the area so they try to mix things up a bit in activities."

"That's awesome."

We pulled up at the gate, and Carter dug his keycard out of his pocket to scan so that we could exit. While we were waiting, a small car pulled into the last handicapped spot in front of the clubhouse. "Isn't that your old car?"

Sure enough, George, the old timer Carter had traded cars with, was getting out of a little red Porsche. We both watched him walk around the car and open the passenger door. Extending a hand, he helped a lady out of the car. "What the..." Carter trailed off.

"Is that...is that what I think it is?"

Carter looked stunned, his mouth was literally hanging open. "I think it fucking is."

The two of us watched, completely speechless, as George got out of Carter's car and walked his date into square dancing...dressed in a full pilot's uniform. *Carter's pilot uniform.*

Chapter 18

carter

I WISHED FOR A STORM as I watched the news on the small TV in the kitchen. A hurricane, tropical storm, tornado, cyclone, whatever the hell would cancel my flight tonight. Since the day they pinned my wings, I never wanted to be grounded. Not once. Yet this morning, I hated being a damn pilot. The thought of leaving her for the start of a seven-day trip was making me feel physically sick. Knowing what was looming, an ache in my chest had been building since yesterday.

I was pretty sure Kendall felt the same way. We'd decided to stay in today, rather than go out again. For five days, we'd both danced around the elephant in the room without any direct conversation about what she was going to do. We needed to have *the talk*. Yet I was scared shitless of what the end game might be.

Inside my heart, I knew I was in love with her. I think my mind even had begun to accept it. What I feared had nothing to do with what might happen to me if I admitted it. My fear was what my love could do *to her*. What if I told her I loved her, but then I realized it was something other than love a year down the road? Or I fell out of love?

Lucy.

I couldn't fuck up Kendall's life unless I was sure. More than sure. I'd done enough damage throwing false promises around.

And what if I told her, and it influenced her decision?

Money or love? Sounds easy, doesn't it?

It's not.

Although the solution that had been on my mind the last twenty-four hours seemed so simple. Why couldn't she have both? I could give her everything, couldn't I? My love. A child. Her rightful inheritance.

A child.

Our child.

Kendall was in the shower. I heard the water turn off and looked at the clock. Twelve hours. I needed to decide. We needed to talk.

Tick-tock.

Tick-tock.

Tick-tock.

Twelve hours was basically the entire day before I had to be at the airport tonight for my flight to Venezuela. I didn't care what we did today as long as we were together for every last second of it.

When Kendall emerged from the bathroom, I couldn't help just staring at her with a smile on my face.

She squinted her eyes, "What?"

"Can't I just look at you?"

She came around and straddled me. "I can't believe you have to leave tonight."

Suddenly, it felt like the load of unanswered questions I'd been harboring were starting to choke me.

My tone was abrupt. "What are your plans, Kendall? I need to know."

She leaned her head on my shoulder and said, "I'm going home to Texas. I need some time away to really think. I owe Hans and Stephen a final answer."

I pulled back to look her in the eyes. "Those are their names? The dudes in Germany?"

"Yes. I can't string them along much longer."

Nodding to myself for a bit, I said, "I think that's a good idea then. Take some time to think things over. As much as I love being around you, neither one of us can think straight around each other."

"I need to go online and get a ticket. I'm gonna try to get onto something that leaves out of Miami so we can depart from the same airport around the same time."

Slapping her ass playfully, I said. "Why don't you do that, get it over with. I was thinking we'd stay home, but after you're done, maybe we should hit the beach, get some sun and fresh air, just chill there for the rest of the day until we have to get ready."

A half-hour later, Kendall and I headed to Deerfield Beach. Even though the water was calm and perfect, we both opted to just lie down on the sand, taking in the sound of the ocean and the crystal clear blue sky.

As relaxing as the beach should have been, we were both still tense. At one point, we were lying on our stomachs, and she wouldn't let go of my hand. Our faces were turned toward each other. When she finally flipped around, I followed suit and let go of her hand to place mine on her taut stomach. I rubbed my thumb along her perfect navel, and a surge of jealousy and possessiveness overtook me. The answer was becoming clearer to me.

I wanted her to belong to me and only me.

I didn't want her to carry some other man's baby. No fucking way.

I wanted her to carry *my* baby.

Not just because of some crazy inheritance shit, but because I *wanted* a baby with her—a future with her.

While having a baby right *now* wasn't ideal, there was no doubt that I wanted it. So, given the urgent situation, why wait?

Lucy.

That was all I could think of. It was the fear of hurting Kendall, like I'd hurt Lucy. It lingered like a black cloud over me—that fear of letting Kendall down. It was ever present, but damn it, it wasn't strong enough to overshadow my need for her—my love for her.

This situation was all or nothing.

Now or never.

I wanted time with her for myself, but I also had to respect her deadline. She would lose everything if we didn't act fast. No matter what happened, it was win-win as far as I was concerned. I made enough to support both of us even if the money were to fall through in the event we had a girl. The thought of a little blonde version of Kendall who called me Daddy made me smile. I wanted to do this. I wanted to father her baby.

Our baby.

My heart started to pound. "I love you, Kendall." The words came out easy. It was the first time I'd ever said them to anyone but Lucy and my immediate family

She turned to me, looking stunned as she lifted her hand to her forehead to shield her eyes from the bright sunlight.

I continued, "Before you say anything back, I have a lot more I need to say."

"Okay," she whispered.

"This is crazy, right? Falling in love so fast? But I'm convinced that's how it happens when it's the real thing. You just know when it feels right. Kendall, you make me so incredibly happy. And while ideally, I'd want you all to myself for a while, I understand that loving someone also means taking their needs into consideration."

"What are you saying?"

"I'm saying that I don't want to share you with anyone. That goes for your body, too. I don't want you carrying another man's baby. I want to be the one. I want to get you pregnant. But more than that, I want to be a *father* to that baby, to love it, because it would be a part of you and me. I want it *all* with you. I don't care if we've known each other ten minutes or ten years. When you know, you know." Cupping her face in my hand, I said, "I know where my head and my heart are. They're on the same page, but I guess you have to figure out whether *you* want the same things I do."

She leaned in and planted a soft kiss on my lips. "I love you, too, Carter. I really do. I have no doubts about that, but I really wasn't expecting you to offer what you just did. Having a baby is one thing, but *raising* it is another. I guess you've just given me another thing to think long and hard about."

An intense relief coursed through my veins, relief that she didn't tell me I was crazy, relief that she seemed to be considering my offer.

"You don't think I'm nuts for wanting to knock you up?"

"Isn't this whole situation nuts to begin with…in a good way? Anyway, if I didn't know you so well, maybe it would seem a *little* nuts. But you're my loveable, crazy captain, and nothing about our entire experience together has been conventional. Not one single thing."

"Believe me, I'm scared. I never want to let you down like I let Lucy down. But I think for the first time in my life, something has mattered enough for me to take a chance. I'm way more terrified of losing you than I ever could be of trying and failing. And I can assure you that if we had a child together and somehow ended up apart, I would never turn my back on my kid. There is nothing more important than a child or their best interests. That baby—our baby—will be my priority. If that means finding another career because you can't handle me being away, then so be it."

"I wouldn't ask you to do that, Carter."

"Well, I guess I just want to drive the point home, that I take this very seriously."

"Understood." She looked up the sky. "Would you mind if we left the beach? I'd really just like to spend the last couple of hours back at your place."

I lifted myself off of our blanket and offered my hand to help her up. "Let's get out of here."

We spent the rest of the afternoon making love in my bed with a slow intensity that hadn't existed before our talk. With my offer and admission of love, our relationship had just moved to another level, and I had to trust that her being away from me wouldn't change anything between us.

As much as I was ready to dive head first into everything with her, there was still a small part of me that worried that today could be the last time I saw her. Crazy, right? After everything we'd been through. Maybe that was the part of me that still felt like I didn't deserve to love this intensely when Lucy couldn't.

The sun had almost completely set as we drove to the airport. Kendall wouldn't let go of my hand. It felt so strange not taking her with me to Venezuela. It was as if I couldn't remember what it was like to fly without her.

When we arrived at Miami International, I parked in the spot that the airline reserved for me. Neither one of us moved to exit the SUV as we just stared at each other until I finally cupped her cheek and pulled her into a passionate kiss.

"Perky, please don't forget this, how right this feels."

"I won't. I couldn't ever forget it, Carter."

Her flight was two hours after mine, so she'd have to leave me at the gate for my airline and linger around the airport until it was time to head to her flight on a different airline.

One of the stewardesses, Renee, passed by us. "Good to see you're back on, Trip." She then winked at me.

I knew *exactly* what Kendall was thinking, and she was right. That flight attendant had been just another notch on my belt some time ago. It sickened me, especially now that I knew what it felt like to have meaningful sex with someone. I looked at Kendall and wanted to scream, *"Stop looking at her. She doesn't matter!"* We just didn't need this right now. It only added to the stress of our separating.

After a quiet few minutes of silence, I pulled her into a hug and whispered in her ear, "I have to go."

Her tears moistened my pilot's shirt as she said, "This feels surreal."

"I know, but it's only temporary. We'll be back together again soon."

She sniffled. "Okay."

Lifting her chin to meet my eyes, I said, "P.S. I love you."

She could tell from my expression that there was more to that sentiment than just me stating the obvious.

"A Beatles song?"

"Yes. But that one *really* matches this life moment, probably more than any of them."

"I love you, Carter."

"I love you, Perky. Promise me we'll talk on the phone and figure out when we'll be back together next."

"I promise."

"I'm gonna be thinking about you the whole flight. You know that, right?"

She playfully grabbed my collar. "You'd better be."

"I'll miss you."

"Sing a song for me, Captain."

"You can guarantee that." I hugged her one last time, squeezing her tightly. "Fuck. I can't let go."

She pushed back and wiped her eyes before waving me away. "Go. You'll be late."

I started on my way through security. When I turned around, she was still standing in the same spot watching me. I blew her a kiss before continuing down the hall. Right before I was about to turn the corner, I turned back one last time, but she was gone.

When the jet hit cruising altitude that night, I saw something I'd never seen while flying before: a shooting star. I took it as a sign that things were going to work out.

Don't let me down, Perky.

I picked up the intercom.

"Good evening, Ladies and Gentleman. This is your Supreme Commander, otherwise known as Captain Clynes. I'd like to take a moment to welcome you onto this beautiful Boeing 757. Our flying time from Miami to Caracas is approximately three hours and thirty minutes. We anticipate a smooth ride with little to no bumps. So, sit back and relax. Again, welcome aboard International Airlines Flight 553 to Caracas, Venezuela. As I often like to do to welcome my passengers aboard, here's a little rendition of a Beatles song that's fitting for tonight—fitting because I've entrusted my heart to someone whom I left back at the airport. She's taking it with her to Texas. I'm sure some of you can relate to this feeling. So, the song for tonight is called, *Don't Let Me Down*."

Chapter 19

kendall

MY MOTHER REEKED of alcohol as she spoke into my face, "You can't be serious!"

I'd made the mistake of filling her in on my trip to prepare her for the possibility that nothing would be going according to plan anymore. My mother had always strongly encouraged me to go ahead with the insemination in Germany, mostly for her own selfish reasons.

"I normally wouldn't be telling you any of this, especially not when you're half-drunk, but given the circumstances, you need to know where my head is at and that the Germany plans may not happen."

"And what are those poor guys supposed to do now that you've changed your mind?"

"I haven't closed the door one hundred percent, but I never promised them anything. I haven't even met them in person, and I'm not the last woman on Earth with a womb. They would find another way."

"Yeah, well, you're gonna lose them as an option if you keep stringing them along."

"Do you think I don't know that? I spoke to them this morning and told them I would let them know my decision no later than next week."

"You're gonna end up with no one, and we're gonna end up destitute!"

My blood was boiling. "Is that all you care about?"

My mother pointed her finger at me. "I shouldn't have to worry about what I'm entitled to. Your whacky grandfather put us in this position—not me."

"Stop being so selfish. We are talking about human life here."

"No, we *were* talking about human life—you giving the gift of human life to a nice couple in need and getting us *set* for life. Now, we're talking about some ridiculous love child scenario that is destined to end badly."

"And exactly how do you know that?"

"Kendall, will you look at yourself for a moment? Think about how crazy this sounds from the outside looking in. You go on a trip, fall for the pilot of your goddamn plane... who now wants to father your child? Oh, and I'm sure it has nothing to do with the fact that you just told him you're about to inherit millions of dollars! Sweetheart, wake up!"

"Carter is not after the money!" I screamed, startling the horses outside.

"Well, that's what you want to believe, and quite frankly, I would've thought you to be smarter than that." She stumbled back into her seat then said, "You have been planning a meticulous strategy for months with these nice men overseas. If you went along with the original plan, you wouldn't have to worry about raising a baby that you don't want. It would be in a good home. We would be set for life. Everybody would win. And yet...you're considering doing the total opposite of everything we talked about just because some pilot stuck his face between your legs."

"You are so vile."

"Vile, maybe, but I speak the truth."

"Well, I'm not so sure I want any of this anymore. I might just walk away from the ranch and the money for good. Maybe you'll never see me again."

"Don't talk like that, Kendall. You wouldn't do that to yourself."

"I'm serious. This inheritance bullshit has caused me nothing but stress from the moment I found out about it. Don't act like you really give a shit about me, Mom. You don't see anything but dollar signs when you look at me now. It's pathetic. I'm your daughter, not your meal ticket."

"I'm only trying to help you get what's rightfully yours."

"So, I suppose you wouldn't mind if I had a legal document written up saying you're not entitled to any of it?"

Dead silence.

I nodded slowly. "That's what I thought."

Unable to handle any more of this conversation, I stormed out of the house and drove toward the city. Wiping tears from my eyes, I blasted the music to drown out the thoughts in my head.

When I finally stopped the car, I realized I really needed Carter. I immediately dialed him. Thank God he picked up.

His voice was low and sexy. "How did you know I was thinking about you?"

"Carter..."

He could tell that I'd been crying. "What's wrong, baby?"

"I should've never come home."

"Why are you upset?"

"My mother. She's saying things to try to brainwash me."

"Things like what?"

"She thinks I'm crazy for considering your offer. She thinks you're only after the money."

There was a long moment of silence before he spoke. The anger in his voice was penetrating. "I can't even begin to tell you how irate that makes me. First of all, I wish this money situation never existed. Second of all, I'll sign whatever is needed to prove I have no interest in that money. To be honest, the money part sickens me a little. I just want a life with you, Kendall. I'll sign any dotted line to get that." His voice cracked, "Just tell me where to fucking sign, Perky."

I let out a long breath into the phone. "Just talking to you makes me feel better. I miss you so much."

"You want me to come there? I'll tell the airline it's a family emergency."

"I don't want you to lie to get out of work."

"I wouldn't be lying. You *are* family to me now, the most important thing in my life."

That made my heart melt.

"Thank you for offering, but I think I still need a little more time alone."

"Okay, but if you start to feel like you need me, just tell me. I'll be there in a matter of hours."

"Thank you. That makes me feel better to know that you would do that for me."

"I'd do anything for you, Perky. Anything."

"Oh, I know. Even knock me up."

"No, that would be for *us*. The more time that goes by, the more I want it. And I sure as hell am looking forward to working on it. God, that's gonna be so much fun."

When I laughed, he said, "Is that a smile I hear?"

"Can you even *hear* a smile?" I giggled.

"We'll get through this together. I promise. And in case you didn't hear me back in Florida, I'll say it again. I love you. And if we have this baby together, nothing will matter more to me. I would never turn my back on my child."

"Okay…I hear you."

"Maybe give yourself a break from thinking about it for a couple of days. Sometimes, when you're trying hard to figure things out, overthinking it makes you more confused. You need to stay away from your mother, go some place quiet and relax. The answer will come."

Carter was right. I needed away from the ranch.

"I think that's a good suggestion."

"Guess where I am?" he asked.

"Where?"

"On the beach in Caracas. Missing the hell out of you and drinking our drink."

"What's *our* drink?"

"You don't remember?"

"No?"

"Caipirinha. It may not be Brazil, but it's a popular drink here, too."

"Oh yes! Our drink from Rio. Say it again in your Portuguese accent, Captain."

"Caipirinha."

"Mmm."

"I miss that little moan. You're making me hard."

"Hopefully, you'll get to hear it again soon in person."

"I'm living for the promise of that, baby."

I ENDED UP TAKING Carter's advice and staying for a few days at a hotel in Plano. It helped to get away from my mother and her strong opinions on the matter.

I knew in my heart what I wanted. I wanted a life with Carter, but would I agree to let him get me pregnant, or should I just abandon the inheritance altogether?

Why couldn't I have it both ways—Carter and the money? It almost seemed like that was too good to be true, like it was *too* simple of a decision. At the same time, it felt like I would always be waiting for the other shoe to drop under that scenario. Nothing is perfect in life.

I'd stopped at one of the outdoor shopping plazas near my hotel for some ice cream and sat on a bench outside of one of the stores. I needed a sign from God.

Please give me a sign that the decision in my heart is the right one.

I continued to stare into space as I licked around the circumference of the ice cream over and over, forming smooth lines around the ball of soft serve.

When I got up to throw away the last of the cone, I looked up. Staring me in the face was a gigantic advertisement for baby clothes. It featured a large, chubby baby boy with rolls of fat on his legs. He looked exactly like the baby picture of Carter that he'd shown me. My heart seemed to expand with every second that I stared at the baby's joyful smile. If this weren't a sign, I didn't know what was. In fact, I couldn't think of a better one if I tried. That is, until I looked up at the name of the children's clothing store.

Carter's.

PLAYBOY PILOT

I WAS FOLDING MY purchases from the day when my cell phone rang. Frank Sinatra's *Come Fly with Me* made me smile from ear to ear. I'd changed Carter's ringtone after hearing that song in the car this afternoon. *Another big sign.* I couldn't recall ever hearing that on the radio. Maybe on my grandfather's CD player, but definitely not on any station I listened to. Yet today, there it was.

After throwing out my ice cream cone, I'd wandered into Carter's to look around. It was honestly only the second time I'd ventured into a children's clothing store. The first was for my cousin Harper who got pregnant when she was eighteen by her thirty-nine-year-old, married college professor. Us Sparks' high society women truly were all smoke and mirrors.

"Hey, handsome," I answered.

"You sound better than when I spoke to you this afternoon."

I sighed. "I feel better, actually."

"Any particular reason? Not that I'm complaining. But I'd like to know what it took to turn your mood around. Store that in my mind for a day that I might need it again."

"It was you, actually."

"Go on. I'm liking the sound of this story so far."

I laughed. "Well...today I was doing some heavy thinking. And let's just say that there were some ways that you were present with me." I folded the little outfit I'd bought today into my suitcase. Not only had the store been named Carter's, but inside I'd found a tiny navy suit with piping down the sides of the pants that looked almost exactly like Carter's pilot uniform. I couldn't help myself. I was at the register before it even *registered* in my brain that I was buying clothing for a baby I had just decided I wanted to try to have.

Outside the store with my bag in my hand, the sun seemed to shine brighter. The air breathed a little easier. My head and heart that had spent weeks in turmoil, finally came into perfect alignment. *Oh my God.* I was going to have a baby. *A baby.* With a man I was crazy in love with.

Feeling freed, I did what every well-bred Texas debutante would do. *I went shopping.* The strip mall had a dozen other stores, and I hit each and every single one of them. My bags were almost too heavy to carry by the time I reached the last store—an Army Navy store where I found a set of antique Airman wings.

Looking down at the folded suit with the wings pinned to the lapel, I could actually visualize a little dimpled boy wearing it as his Daddy held him proudly. *His Daddy.* Lost in dreamland, I almost forgot Carter was on the phone.

"Perky, you still there?"

"I am. Sorry. But I'm thinking that I'm going to hold off on telling you anymore about my day. I would much rather *show you* what reminded me of you."

"Does that mean I'm going to be seeing you soon?" I heard the hope in his voice, and it made my palms sweat with excitement.

"It does actually. I was hoping we could meet up." I finished zipping my suitcase and plopped down on the bed.

"Say the word. Where and when? I'll divert my flight to Dubai in the morning if I have to. Hijack a 757 full of Arabs to Texas if you have some good news for me."

I knew he was kidding, but there wasn't much I would put past this crazy man. "Where will you be on Monday next week?"

"Hang on...let me check my phone."

Thirty seconds later, he was back. "I'll be in Miami Monday."

That had to be another sign. "The airport we met in?"

"That's right. I have a layover for the night, and then I'm heading back to Brazil again. Sounds like fate to me, beautiful. What do you say? Is it a date? Meet me in Miami. Same bar it all started at. I'll book you a ticket that gets you in as close to when I land as possible?"

I took a deep breath of courage in and let out the rest of my fear. "Yes. I need to see you. I have a few things I want to talk about. But I also miss you like crazy."

"You got it. You'll have a ticket by morning."

We talked for another hour after that. I didn't tell him about my purchases or the decision I was pretty sure I made. All of that needed to be done in person. But toward the end of the call, I said, "I bought something today that reminded me of you."

"Oh yeah? What's that?"

"It's a surprise."

"You know, I probably shouldn't tell you this, but I have something that reminds me of you, too. I didn't buy it though. I sort of stole it from you before you left."

I was lying across the hotel room bed diagonally, staring up at the ceiling and flipped over to my stomach. "What could you possibly...." Then I remembered what I thought went missing in the dryer when I'd washed my dirty clothes at home. All of my bra and panties were sets, and my red bra seemed to have been missing the matching underwear. "Oh my God...you didn't."

Carter took a deep breath in over the phone, and I *knew* he was sniffing. My hand flew to my mouth. *Oh my God.* "You have them over your face right now, don't you?"

His response was a cross between a moan and a groan.

"Oh my God, Carter!" I giggled. "You're certifiable. I *cannot* believe you stole my underwear!"

"Really? I would have thought it would be something you would come to expect by now."

"I suppose that's true." I bit my lip. "Do you..."

"What are you asking me?"

"You know..."

"Damn right I do. But I want to hear you ask me anyway."

Carter was definitely much more aggressive in the dirty talk arena than I was. That was something I probably needed to work on if I was going to be in a long-term relationship with a pilot, and we would constantly be separated. So I pushed past my normal comfort zone. My voice was low, it actually sounded kind of sexy. "Do you...touch your cock when you smell me?"

He literally growled. "God, the word cock from your mouth is going to make me explode hard."

"Really?" I wiggled around the bed. "I was thinking your cock *in* my mouth would make you explode hard."

"Kendall..." he warned.

"What? You started it."

"Yes... and you can't play with me like that."

"I wish I *could* play with you right now."

He chuckled. "I'm going to need to start traveling with some lotion for our nightly calls."

"I think that's a very good idea. Why don't you pick some up at the airport store in the morning, and since I'm heading back home tomorrow, I'll be able to have Jack for our call tomorrow night."

"Jack?"

"It's my name for my little rabbit vibrator."

"Did we just make a date to *jack off* together tomorrow night?"

I laughed softly. "I think we did."

"I'll call you as soon as I'm checked into my hotel."

"Okay. That sounds good."

Carter's voice grew serious. "I love you, Kendall."

"I love you, too, Captain. Four more days, and we'll be together again."

Four more days.

Chapter 20

kendall

I WAS NEVER SO excited in my life.

I'd arrived at the airport three hours early even though I was taking a domestic flight, and Carter had booked me a first-class ticket that had its own line that always breezed through security. I couldn't stop smiling. The little girl in front of me had on one of those black Mickey Mouse ear hats and could hardly keep still while her mother checked them in for their flight to Orlando. Her anticipation dulled in comparison to how I felt.

If everything went on schedule, I would be back in Carter's arms in a little less than six hours. His flight was due to arrive an hour before mine, and he'd assured me the eager Captain would be landing his *sweet ride* on time.

Just being in the airport, seeing all the International Airlines' uniforms that were similar to Carter's, made me feel better than I had in days. It was pretty screwed up that the Dallas airport brought me more comfort and felt more like home than going to my real home this week did.

PLAYBOY PILOT

After I'd made my decision about what I was going to do, I decided not to share it with my mother. There was absolutely no good that could come of it. She would only put a damper on my excitement. I'd always known that my mother put finances toward the top of her priority list. I just didn't want to believe that my happiness wasn't above her desire to maintain a certain lifestyle. The last week had forced me to see things clearly for the first time. Or maybe I'd always seen her for what she was; I'd just chosen to turn a blind eye to it all.

Even though I didn't admit to my mother that I'd made my decision, I think she knew. When I woke up this morning, I'd found a manila envelope on the dining room table with my name inked across it. Inside was a lengthy co-parenting agreement—one that spelled out that Carter had no legal financial claim to any of my or any future child's inheritance. All I'd need to do was fill in Carter's name and have him sign it. When Mom woke up around noon with her daily hangover, she'd find the envelope exactly where she'd politely left it for me. Except the agreement was sitting on top of the envelope, and it was also ripped in half. Figured I'd make my point a little less subtle than she did.

I stopped at a newsstand, picked up some magazines and snacks, and headed to my gate. There was a gaggle of flight attendants sitting across from me. I hated that I immediately wondered if Carter had slept with any of them. It wasn't that I didn't trust him, because oddly enough, I completely did. But I found myself extremely territorial when it came to Carter. The thought of him being with anyone else caused an ache in my chest. Even though I knew it was ridiculous—we'd both been with other people—I couldn't help feel that way.

The plane boarded almost a full hour before takeoff, which was always a good sign. I had priority boarding since

I was in first class, yet I waited until the gate had almost completely emptied out before heading down the jetway to board.

I was sitting in row 2A, an aisle seat. Stowing my bag overhead, I quickly got myself organized and took my seat. I smiled at the woman next to me as I buckled. The flight attendant quickly came over to offer us a pre-flight drink. She glanced down at her cabin list. "Can I get you something, Ms. Sparks?"

"That would be great. I'll take a glass of merlot."

She then spoke to the passenger next to me. "How about you, Cass? Milk, water, orange juice?"

"I'll take a water. Thanks, Lana."

When I glanced over at my seatmate again, she offered an explanation. "I'm a flight attendant on this airline. Flying standby and was lucky enough to get the big seats." She smiled.

I'd only had my wine for less than five minutes when the captain came over the loudspeaker and said we were going to push away from the gate. Needing something to calm my nerves for so many reasons, I guzzled down the full glass knowing the flight attendant would be by to collect it any second.

The woman next to me sighed audibly. "What I wouldn't give to do what you just did."

"Guzzle a full glass like a sailor and hope no one notices?"

She patted her belly and grinned. "Exactly. I'm four months along."

"Wow." I looked down at her practically non-existent belly. She was barely showing. "I would never have guessed. You're so tiny."

"The bulk of the weight seems to have gotten confused and swung around back. My ass is tremendous already."

"I doubt that's true. You look thin all over. But even if it is, big butts are in now, so you'll be in style."

"I'm hoping I gain some up top eventually. My boobs are so small, and this little guy's daddy is a boob man." My mind wandered to my own body. Would my breasts be big when I was pregnant? Carter had always said he liked my perky B cups, but something told me he wouldn't be upset if I had a little boob gain myself.

After the flight took off and leveled out, Cass, which I found out was short for Cassandra, took out a pair of Beats headphones and instead of putting them over her ears, slipped them over her small baby bump. She was playing music to her stomach. When she caught me looking, she said, "I read somewhere that babies might be able to hear in the womb, so I started to play him classical music."

"Him? It's a boy?"

"I'm not sure yet." She rubbed her belly. "But I really think it is."

There was so much I was going to have to learn. Since I didn't know this woman, I decided to let her in on my little secret. "Can I ask you a personal question?"

"Sure. Go ahead."

"Did it take you a long time to conceive? I mean were you trying for long? I'm asking because my boyfriend and I..." I hesitated before admitting it out loud for the first time. "We decided we're going to try to get pregnant."

The woman gave me a genuine smile. "That's great. Congratulations." It was the first time anyone had seen anything positive about my plan to have a baby. And it felt good. Everything was starting to fall into place.

"Thank you."

"Actually...it didn't take us long at all. I got pregnant the second time we were intimate."

"Wow. That's amazing."

"It is, isn't it? This little guy was definitely not planned. But I think he was meant to be. He's the glue that is going to bind the three of us together forever."

"Will you be able to work much longer? The airlines have rules against flying too far along into a pregnancy, don't they?"

"Yep. Another twelve weeks or so, and then I'm going to be grounded. Most of the airlines won't even let passengers fly after twenty-eight weeks, no less their flight attendants. Too much risk for early labor. They'll give me a desk job. Probably checking people in and out or working the gate. I'm hoping I can transfer to Florida anyway, so the change will be good timing."

"You live in Texas now?"

She nodded. "I live in Allen. But I'm originally from Florida, and most of my family is still down there. Plus, the baby's dad lives in Florida, so I'm probably going to relocate."

"Do you think you'll go back to work after the baby's born?"

"I hope not. All I ever wanted to do was get married, have a bunch of kids and stay home. It's not easy these days to make it on one salary. Gotta make sure you snag yourself a good one like I did."

Her intonation soured me a bit. *Snagging* a good gravy train. It was probably because it was something my mother would say.

After my second glass of wine, I started to come down from my adrenaline high, and exhaustion was beginning to creep in. Knowing Carter was going to be insatiable when we reunited, I figured I would get some sleep while I still could. I didn't wake up again until the captain was speaking overhead telling us that we were going to be landing in just a few minutes.

I stretched in my seat. "Wow. I was really out."

"You were. Had to take the headphones from the baby to drown out the little snore you had going on."

I covered my mouth. "Oh my God. I'm so sorry."

She uncapped her water bottle and finished the little bit left. "I'm just teasing you. You were snoring, but it didn't bother me any. I think I'm too nervous to sleep, or we would have been doing a duet together"

"Nervous about the baby?"

"No. I'm seeing the baby's dad tomorrow. We haven't seen each other in a while."

"I know how you feel. I haven't seen my boyfriend in a week, and I'm a nervous wreck. If I hadn't inhaled those glasses of wine, I would never have slept. I'm so excited."

"It's been a little longer than a week for us."

"Oh? How long?"

"Three months."

"Wow. That's a long time. He hasn't even seen your new pregnancy body yet."

"Yes, that's true. Although that's the least of my worries."

My brows drew down so she explained. "He doesn't even know I'm pregnant yet."

"Oh. Wow. Oh my."

"Yep. Now you can understand why I wanted to guzzle that wine."

"I certainly can."

"Do you...do you think he's not going to be happy about becoming a father?"

"I have no idea how he's going to react. He's a bit of a wild one. Not sure he planned to ever be tamed. But down deep, I think he's a stand-up man, and he'll do the right thing."

I wasn't sure I wanted to know what the *right thing* even was. The entire conversation was beginning to turn my stomach. What kind of a woman doesn't tell a man she's pregnant for months? Although I suppose there could be a lot of reasons for that. Maybe he's not the greatest guy, and she considered not even having the baby or something. It really wasn't my place to judge. Especially with all the crazy stuff I had been planning on doing. You never really know anyone's true story unless you're standing in their shoes.

Landing was bumpy, but I was thrilled to have arrived a few minutes early. I wanted to use the airport restroom to freshen up before I met Carter at the bar we were going to meet at.

As we taxied to the gate, I began to clean up my magazines and tossed my garbage into my bag. Smiling, I turned to Cass. "Good luck. Are you going to get to see your boyfriend soon?"

"Tomorrow," she said. "He's got a flight in the morning that I'm going to join him on. Although he doesn't know that yet either."

The plane came to a stop, and a ding came over the loudspeaker indicating it was safe to get out of our seats. I began to unbuckle. "Does he travel a lot for work or something?"

"He does. All the time, actually. He's a pilot."

I stood and opened the overhead, grabbing my bag. "Oh, that's funny. So is my boyfriend."

The cabin door opened quicker than any flight I was ever on before. The gods just seemed to be smiling down on me today—a smooth flight, pregnant traveling companion, on time arrival. Stepping into the aisle, I said, "It was nice meeting you. Best of luck with your pregnancy and everything."

"Thanks. You too. I hope you get pregnant as easily as I did."

PLAYBOY PILOT

I was just about to walk off the plane when I heard the flight attendant saying goodbye to Cass who was right behind me. "Good luck, sweetie. Give me a call later, and let me know how Trip takes the news."

I froze mid-step. My mind had to be playing tricks on me. Turning around, I asked. "Did she just say Trip...how Trip takes the news?"

Cass smiled, thinking nothing of it. "Yes. It's a nickname for my baby daddy. His name has three of the same letter so they call him trip for triple."

I felt the blood rush from my face. "What three letters?"

"C. His name is *Captain Carter Clynes*."

Chapter 21

kendall

MY LUGGAGE WAS THE LAST left on the conveyor belt. How long had it travelled around in circles before I finally noticed it? How long had I even been standing here?

The joy I'd felt over the past twenty-four hours had completely transformed into a mixture of shock, panic and sadness. I couldn't remember the last time deep sadness completely consumed me like this. My emotions had left me a frozen shell of myself as I stood in baggage claim.

I'd lost track of Cass sometime after she revealed the name of her baby's father. To be honest, I barely remembered exiting the plane and arriving at this spot.

Finally lifting my suitcase off of the belt, I looked around at the crowds of people making their way through the airport. A part of me wanted to just run, but a bigger part knew that I had to hear it from him—that he knew her, that he was the father of this baby.

Was there a chance she could've been making it up? I quickly banished the thought from my brain, refusing to give myself false hope.

My head felt like it was going to implode between the intermittent intercom announcements, the sounds of the people rushing around me, and the fearful thoughts in my head. Everything seemed loud. Looking down at my phone, I realized I was late in meeting Carter at the airport lounge.

One foot in front of the other.

Go.

You have to face him.

The escalator slowly descended into what I was pretty sure was going to be my own personal hell.

When I got to the lounge, I closed my eyes to grab my bearings before entering. When I opened them, I spotted him in the corner. He was all decked out in his pilot's uniform and looking up at a sports channel that was playing on the television. Just inside the entrance, I stood there with my heart pounding and admired his tall stature without him noticing me, for the sheer reason that it might have been the last time I could do it.

He suddenly turned around. My heart dropped when I noticed he was holding a large bouquet of flowers. When our eyes met, Carter's mouth curved into the biggest smile. My heart was breaking with every step he took toward me. And with each step, his smile slowly faded once he realized that I was crying and that they weren't tears of happiness.

He mindlessly threw the flowers onto a nearby table. "Perky? What's wrong? What's happening?"

Unable to speak, I gripped his shirt for balance.

"Did something happen on the flight?"

Still unable to form words, I nodded.

He pulled me into a hug, and I was too weak to resist. Crying into the crook of his arm, I could feel his heart beating a mile a minute against my cheek.

When he pulled back and examined my eyes again, he said, "Tell me what's going on." When I continued to remain silent, he begged, "Please."

Closing my eyes, I prayed for the strength to get through this, then finally spoke.

My voice was shaky. "I sat next to a woman on the plane. She was four months pregnant."

"Okay. It freaked you out?"

"No."

"Did something happen to her?"

Grabbing a chair for balance, I sat down and looked up at him.

He didn't move. "Tell me what happened, Kendall."

"She was an off-duty flight attendant."

"Alright. I'm not following."

"Her name is Cass. Do you know her?"

He started to open his mouth to say something then froze when realization hit. "I do know her, yes."

"You dated her."

"Yes. How many times have we gone over this? It didn't mean anything. It was before we met and..." His eyes widened, and a look of panic flashed across his face as he put two and two together. "Wait. You don't think that *I* got her pregnant?"

"It's not that I *thought* it. It's that she *told me* that in her own words. She says you're the father of her baby, Carter. She was flying to Florida to come tell you in person. She's supposed to be on your flight tomorrow."

He shook his head in disbelief then yelled, "What? No!" He knelt down to where I was seated in order to look me in the eyes. "No, Kendall. No."

"Can you look me in the face and tell me with absolute certainty that it's not possible that you are the father of her baby?"

His eyeballs moved from side to side as he struggled to make sense of this. He ran his hand through his hair. This news was out of left field for him too, and I had no doubt that he was in total shock.

I repeated, "Is it a possibility?"

He finally stood up and took a seat across the table from me, seemingly still too stunned to speak.

I rephrased my question. "Did you, or did you not sleep with her four months ago?"

"Yes," he whispered. "I did."

"So, it's technically possible."

The light drained from his eyes as it truly hit him. It *was* possible.

He couldn't deny it.

Leaning his head into his hands, he asked, "We don't know anything. What if she's lying about the pregnancy?"

"She didn't know who I was, Carter. She had no reason to lie to me."

Still holding the sides of his head with both hands, he just continued to look up at me. The fear within me was expanding with each second that I witnessed the fear in his eyes growing. I had wanted him to tell me Cass was delusional. I had wanted him to tell me it was all a lie. I had wanted him to make me feel safe, and he couldn't. He simply couldn't prove anything one way or the other.

My mother's voice rang out in my head. *"You're gonna end up with no one, and we're gonna end up destitute!"*

Carter's own words from the past also came back to haunt me. *"I would never turn my back on my kid. There is nothing more important than a child or their best interests."*

My head was spinning. "I'm sorry, Carter."

"Sorry? What are you saying?"

"I have to leave."

He grabbed my hands. "Perky, no. Don't do this. Whatever happens, we can get through it. I prom—"

"I can't." Shaking my head with tears streaming down my cheeks, I repeated, "I can't. I'm so sorry."

"Can't what?"

"I can't be with you."

Something I never expected from him happened as he continued to stare at me. His eyes began to glisten. Being the man that he was, he fought back the tears as he stared at me incredulously.

Unable to stand seeing him so hurt, I forged a lie. "I was going to tell you that I decided to go ahead with the insemination anyway. So, I suppose this timing is just as well."

His eyes were red. "That's bullshit."

"No."

"Don't lie to me," he spewed.

I needed to rip the Band-Aid off. My eyes were still filled with tears as I suddenly got up and walked over to my suitcase.

"I have to leave."

He followed closely behind me. "Kendall, don't do this."

"I have no choice."

"What if this is a lie, or if it's not…what if the baby isn't mine? We don't know anything yet," he pleaded.

"What if it is?" I screamed.

"Then, it won't matter. I belong to you. This doesn't change anything."

"It changes everything, Carter! *Everything*. I've never felt more pain in my life than I do in this moment. I can't handle it. If you ever really loved me, please just let me go."

My tears were now blinding me when I whispered one last time, "Let me go."

My words seemed to have gotten through to him. He stood there frozen as he watched me walk away. I focused on the rolling sound of my suitcase, fighting the urge to turn back around to look at him one last time.

I didn't.

I needed to get out of the International Airlines gate as fast as possible.

Fifteen minutes later, I found myself at the Lufthansa Airlines ticket desk.

"When is your next flight to Munich?"

After searching the computer, the attendant said, "We have one that leaves in an hour with a stopover in New York."

I closed my eyes to shun off the immense sadness creeping in as I realized what I was about to do. Everything was flashing before my eyes: Rio, Dubai, Amsterdam, Boca. The love that grew more and more with each step of our journey. I still loved him, and I knew I always would, but I couldn't risk losing everything. More so, I couldn't handle the pain. Carter fathering another woman's baby was just too hard to accept. I loved him too much and couldn't witness him living out a part of our dream with someone else. I had been looking for signs to help me make a decision. I would say landing that seat next to Cass was just about the biggest sign I could've gotten.

Before I had a chance to change my mind, I let out a long breath and finally answered the attendant. "I'll take it."

Chapter 22

ELEVEN MONTHS LATER

carter

"LAST WEEK, WE EXPLORED your past, what happened with Lucy. We didn't have enough time to revisit the situation you alluded to, that brought you here to seek help. So, I think we should delve into that today, if that's okay with you. I'd like you to tell me about her," Dr. Lemmon said.

"Alright."

"Take your time."

Suddenly, it felt like I couldn't breathe. The words just wouldn't come out.

"Sorry. This is just not easy for me. I haven't spoken about her with anyone. I've spent the past several months basically running, spending even less time at home than before because, even though she was only there with me a short time, it's the place that now reminds me of her the most because it's where we..." I hesitated, "Consummated our relationship."

"Tell me about her," she repeated.

"Her name was Kendall. Uh, *is* Kendall. I mean she's not dead. She's still out there somewhere."

"How did you meet?"

"At the airport."

"Not too unusual for a pilot, I suppose."

"Yeah, but our story was anything but usual."

The next twenty minutes was spent describing the weeks that Kendall and I fell in love. The words flowed freely until I came upon the hard part.

"So, she called you and said she was meeting you at the airport. It sounded good. You assumed that she was going to take you up on your offer to father her baby. You felt ready to be a father..."

I closed my eyes. "Yes. Yes, I did. With her...I did."

"What happened that day?"

I continued my story, painfully recalling the last moments with Kendall inside the airport lounge before she revealed her run-in with Cass and walked out of my life for good.

Dr. Lemmon took off her glasses, seeming affected by my story. "That must have been a very difficult moment."

"I still can't wrap my head around it, how everything just crumbled so fast."

"Do you blame her for leaving so abruptly?"

"No. No, I don't. I might've done the same thing in her shoes."

"What did you do after she left?"

"I stayed at the lounge in disbelief. It took me a couple of hours to work up the energy to go home. I had a friend pick me up, because I'd had a lot to drink, so I passed out on my bed and slept the entire night until it was time to wake up for my flight the next day."

"How was that?"

"Just as Kendall had warned me, Cass showed up. She worked the flight and told me she needed to talk to me about something important once we landed. After we got to Brazil, she told me everything...that she was pregnant and carrying my baby."

"What was your reaction?"

"I was despondent, too heartbroken to even think about the big picture. At that point, all I could think about was losing Kendall. Nothing else mattered. I told Cass I would help support the baby if it turned out to be mine, but that I wouldn't be able to give her anything more. I made it clear I would insist on a blood test once the baby was born."

"Was she okay with that?"

"She wasn't happy with my lack of interest or excitement, but there was nothing I could do to change that. I didn't want that life with her. All I cared about was Kendall and had no energy to deal with anything else."

"What ever became of Kendall?"

"I wish I knew."

She looked stunned. "You don't know?"

"To this day, I don't know. She said she planned to go along with the insemination, but whether she really followed through is a mystery."

"Have you tried calling her?"

"Yes. Several times. She either disconnected her phone or changed her number, but I haven't gotten through. I remember her telling me her mother's name once. I mailed a letter to an Annabelle Sparks in Dallas but still don't know if it ever got to Kendall. I can't find her on social media. I don't know what else to do, or if she even wants to see me if I did locate her."

Dr. Lemmon jotted down some notes before looking back up at me. "Tell me what happened...with the baby."

"I was at the hospital when he was born. She named him Aidan. I didn't know how to feel, because a part of me still didn't believe he was mine. At the same time, I felt guilty for not feeling more."

"Is he yours?"

"Two weeks after he was born, she finally had the blood test done. The days waiting for the results were torture."

"And?"

"He's not my son." I let out a long breath. Anytime I relived that moment of truth, I couldn't help feeling the same relief as the first time all over again.

Dr. Lemmon repositioned herself in her seat. "Wow."

"Yeah."

"How did you feel about that?"

"It was an odd mix of anger and relief—relief because it absolved me of any responsibility in a situation I never chose, but anger because of all that I'd lost as a result. Things I can never get back."

The woman I'd never get back.
The family I'd never get back.
The life I'd never get back.

"What has your life been like since finding out the truth?"

"It hasn't changed much, to be honest. Working as many hours as I can. Going through the motions. What I've always done."

"You use your job as a means to hide from your demons. First it was Lucy. Now it's Kendall."

I raised my voice in defense. "What do you suggest I do?"

Aren't I paying you to tell me what the fuck to do?

"Until you know what's become of Kendall, you won't find that inner peace. Coming here was a good first step, but there is nothing I can do to keep this from haunting you."

"I told you. I tried to contact her. I don't know where she is."

"You said you have a potential address in Texas. Why not go there, see if you can find out what's happening in her life?"

I couldn't bring myself to respond, even though I knew the truth; I was scared shitless. Scared of what she'd been through, scared of upsetting her, scared of the unknown. One thing was for certain; if I knew she wanted to see me, I would be there in a heartbeat.

THE THERAPY SESSION had left me drained. Instead of feeling better, it felt like the floodgates guarding my sanity had burst open.

That night, back at my condo in Boca, I was hanging up my uniforms that I'd picked up from the dry cleaner when my eyes landed on white fur at the back corner of my closet. It was exactly where I'd tossed it away months ago.

I'd bought a teddy bear in Venezuela and planned to give it to Kendall if she'd taken me up on my offer. I took the bear and stared at it as I sat on the edge of my bed.

"I should have tossed you in the trash. Then, I wouldn't have to look at you right now."

Great. Now, I was talking to inanimate objects.

"What do you think? Should I go to Texas? Try to find her?"

You're fucking nuts, Carter.

"What do I have to lose? I've lost everything, right?"

Bringing the bear closer to my face, I said, "I'm letting you make the decision. If you continue to remain silent, I'm going to assume that you don't object."

I placed it on top of my dresser and stood back, crossing my arms and still staring at it.

"Speak now or forever hold your peace," I said before lying on my bed and opening my laptop.

With three days off before I was due to fly to Rio, I used my miles and booked a flight to DFW Airport.

Turning to the chest of drawers, I pointed to the stuffed animal. "If this blows up in my face, I'm blaming you."

THE SPRAWLING RANCH was at least eight acres. There were a few horses grazing, but it seemed pretty desolate and unkempt given the size of the property.

The infamous Sparks Ranch.

I'd always wanted to see where Kendall grew up; I just didn't expect to be visiting this place without her.

A blonde woman who looked like she might've been beautiful twenty years ago opened the door. She had a cigarette hanging from her mouth and smelled like booze. "Can I help you?"

"Do you live here?"

"Yes, this is my property."

"Are you Annabelle?"

"Yes. Who are you?"

"I'm looking for your daughter, Kendall. My name is Carter Clynes. I used to know her."

She took a long drag then blew the smoke out, pointing her finger at me. "Oh my God. It's you. You're the pilot."

"Yes. She spoke of me?"

"She did."

That pleased me.

"Is she here?"

"No. My daughter hasn't been here in months."

Filled with dread, I asked, "Where is she?"

"Beats the hell out of me. Kendall made it clear she did not want me to know her whereabouts."

"When was the last time she was here?"

"She'd taken a trip to Germany. Wouldn't tell me what happened there. Trip lasted about two weeks. I only found out she'd gone there from the ticket on her luggage, otherwise she wouldn't have even given me that much."

"How long was she here for after returning from Germany?"

"A couple of days. She said she was just grabbing her things and leaving again. She told me not to worry about her."

"She didn't say whether she was going through with the insemination?"

"No. My daughter much prefers to torture me, changed her phone number, making it impossible for me to find her. She would prefer to leave me here suffering, wondering if I'm gonna lose everything or not. We don't have much time left. If she hasn't given birth to a male baby, everything will be gone soon. It'll be the end of my world as I know it."

This woman was unbelievable. It took everything in me not to tell her to go fuck herself. But I needed her not to kick me out just yet. "I would say that's being a little dramatic, Ma'am. You know, there *is* the option of downsizing and getting a job. It's hardly the end of the world just because you can't maintain this property or lifestyle. At this point, I think you should be more concerned about your daughter's well-being."

She chose to ignore my comments. "What is it you want?"

"I need to find her."

Annabelle walked over to an ashtray and put the cigarette out. "I'm sorry. As I said, I can't help you."

PLAYBOY PILOT

Looking around the vast living space, I asked, "Does she have a bedroom here?"

"Yes."

"Would it be okay if I took a peek inside to see if I can find any clues as to her whereabouts?" When she seemed to hesitate, I said, "It could benefit both of us if we can locate her."

She lit another cigarette, took a long puff and shrugged. "Go on ahead. Second door on the left up the stairs."

Nodding my head once, I said, "Thank you."

The door creaked open as I entered Kendall's room. The sun was pouring into the space, casting a shadow on her light yellow bedspread. Everything was so clean, delicate and feminine, just like her. My heart felt heavy as I traced my fingers along her personal items.

My hand stopped along a framed picture of Kendall with an older man that might have been her grandfather. It was a few years old. Seeing her beautiful smile again only made me more determined than ever to find her.

After scouring the room, nothing of informational value turned up. I felt defeated. Opening her half-empty closet, I lifted a few of the remaining dresses one by one, smelling each one, hoping for any recognition of her scent.

My hand landed on something unusual. I froze. Hanging in the leftmost corner of the closet was a tiny suit made for a baby boy. It was navy with piping down the sides and looked like a little pilot's uniform. I looked at the tag. The name of the brand was *Carter's*.

Holy shit.

I took it down from the rack, and that was when I saw it: a pair of pilot's wings pinned to the front of the suit. Filled with painful longing, I closed my eyes and remembered her words from one of our last conversations before everything was destroyed.

"I bought something today that reminded me of you."

This must have been what she was going to bring me. It was proof that she had been planning to take me up on the offer. She wanted the baby, too, just as much as I did. I clutched the suit to my chest.

She lied about having decided on Germany. But the truth of the matter was, she *did* end up going there. I needed to know what happened, where she was. I needed to tell her that I still love her and accept whatever decision she'd made.

Would I still love her if she gave birth to another man's baby?

Yes.

Goddammit. Yes, I would.

I needed to find her.

Think.

Think.

Think.

Could I get the FBI involved? The police? She'd willingly left. They weren't going to spend time looking for her. I could hire a private investigator, but would that make her angry if she found out I'd done that against her will?

Then, I had a light bulb moment. In two days, I would be in Rio again. If there was anyone who might help solve this mystery, it was *her* crazy ass. This wasn't a job for the police.

This was a job for Maria Rosa.

Chapter 23

carter

IT WAS ALMOST MIDNIGHT by the time the taxi dropped me off. A boarder answered the door and went back to his room. I followed my nose, which led me straight to the kitchen. Maria was stirring a large pot on the stove with one hand while feeding Pedro a slice of mango with the other. She didn't turn around, and I hadn't called ahead to let her know I was coming, so I assumed she thought I was someone else.

"Venha comer. Conversaremos, então." *Come eat. We'll talk.*

"É Carter, Maria." *It's Carter, Maria.*

She still didn't turn around. Instead, she took a bowl out of the cabinet next to her and scooped out some feijoada. When she turned and placed the bowl on the table, she wasn't the least surprised to see me. She'd known I was coming all along.

"Comer! Comer!" *Eat. Eat.*

She was psychic enough to know I was coming, yet I caught her off guard when I dropped my bags and hugged her. For some reason, being there made me feel something I hadn't felt in almost a year—hope. I didn't let go of her for the longest time, but when I did, she squeezed my face and kissed both of my cheeks. After, we sat and ate together in comfortable silence. By the time we were done, I was beginning to get anxious about what I wanted to talk to her about. I'd never asked her anything about my future. She would just randomly come out with things when she looked at me sometimes. I wasn't even sure if she *could* answer my questions. Was being clairvoyant an on-demand ability?

After we cleared the table, I was starting to work up the nerve to ask, when she suddenly took both of my hands into hers. I never had to ask a single question. It wasn't necessary since she told me to sit and began to tell me all about my future.

Three hours later, I was in my room, and my head was spinning. I tried to fall asleep, but it was almost impossible because the only room available was the one that Kendall and I had shared. I could still feel her spirit even after eleven months.

Eleven months.

What would she look like pregnant? Her perky tits heavy with milk and her ass a little fuller. Was I that hard up that the thought of a very pregnant Kendall was making me hard? *Fuck.* She was the only thing that could even get me hard anymore. Eleven months of celibacy. It was the longest stretch of my life since I was sixteen.

I'd decided on the long flight over that I truly didn't care if she carried another man's child. In a fucked up way, I almost wanted her to. Having her get everything she wanted would make the time we'd spent apart count for something at least. Because the thought of both of us wasting the last eleven months of our lives for no damn good reason was enough to make my chest constrict.

I thought about everything Maria had said tonight over and over in my head. As usual, her messages were cryptic, and it was difficult to decipher what it was she was even trying to tell me. But I was determined to listen to her advice no matter what it was. The problem was, I wasn't sure what she wanted me to do.

A resposta está no céu. A resposta está no céu.

She just kept repeating the same phrase over and over again.

The answer is in the sky. The answer is in the sky.

SINCE IT WAS MORNING before I finally crashed, it was late afternoon when I woke up. My flight wasn't until the following day, so I had plenty of time to try to figure out what Maria was trying to tell me. She was out at the market when I went looking for her, so I went for a walk on the beach in an attempt to clear my head.

After about a mile of walking in the blaring sun, I came across a lone chair sitting at the water's edge. It dawned on me that the last time I'd walked this beach was with Kendall. Almost at this exact spot, we'd come across *two* random chairs. I hoped that this wasn't a sign...that I'd only need *one* chair from now on.

Feeling forlorn, I sat down to try to make some sense of my crazy life. Leaning my head back, I closed my eyes and let the sun shine down on my face while I recalled what had transpired the last time I sat in this very spot with Kendall. It played out in my head like a movie. Our chairs were facing each other, and we were playing footsy in the sand. I asked her why she was on the trip, and she had initially been vague. I'd soon find out that she was avoiding telling me her secret because she was embarrassed to admit the truth. She thought I would see her as shallow and desperate.

But the real truth was, before I met Kendall, *I* was the one who was living my life shallow and desperate. Going from woman to woman, never wanting to stay in one place too long. The woman who thought she was desperate turned out to be what I was in desperate need *of*. True love.

Not only had Kendall told me her secret in this spot, but I'd also opened up about Lucy. It was the first time I'd ever told anyone about Lucy. I'd never really even spoken to my parents about everything that had happened. Yet I'd shared my demons with Kendall, and despite it all, she'd opened up her heart anyway. At least I thought she did.

The sun felt so good heating my face. The sound of the waves lightly meeting the surf lulled me to relax. I let out a deep breath and allowed the beach to wash away some of my stresses. There was no point tearing myself up over the past anymore. The only thing I could control was the future now.

My future.

A resposta está no céu. A resposta está no céu.

Maria Rosa's words kept playing in my head over and over.

The answer is in the sky. The answer is in the sky.

What the hell was she trying to tell me?

The answer is in the sky. The answer is in the sky.

Using my hand to shield my eyes, I looked up into the sun. Suddenly, the answer struck me in a moment of clarity.

The answer is in the sky.

Lucy in the Sky with Diamonds.

Maria was trying to tell me to go see Lucy. How could I have been so dense?

I'D CALLED IN A FEW FAVORS to make it happen. Considering I took every available flight that anyone asked me to take over the last five years, it wasn't as difficult as I thought to get myself coverage for five days. After my flight back to the states today, I'd be flying standby back to Michigan. It had been more than a year since I was home and even longer since I'd visited Lucy. In fact, the last time I'd gone to Lucy's grave was...*never*.

The time had come.

I didn't know how or why, but Maria knew. *The answer is in the sky.*

IT WAS A TYPICAL late March morning in Michigan. Snow covered the ground, and ice covered the snow. My footsteps crunched beneath me as I walked on the frozen grass to row sixty-eight in the Crestwood Section of the Fairlawn Cemetery.

When the numbered stakes in the ground reached the designated row, I looked around and took a deep breath. Luckily, there was no one in sight as far as I could see. I was relieved because I was definitely not ready to run into Lucy's family. Seeing anyone today was more than I could handle.

Lucy's row had about twenty headstones. I walked slowly, reading the names on each until I came across hers.

Lucy Langella
July 10*th*, 1986 – September 7*th*, 2004

Pain sliced across my chest. I sucked in a jagged breath before reading the epitaph carved in script beneath her name.

Sometimes love is for a moment.
Sometimes love is for a lifetime.
Sometimes a moment is a lifetime.
Ours for a little while.
Wings for eternity.

It had been twelve years, yet time hadn't closed the wound that was ripped open by Lucy's death. It still hurt like hell. Fresh pain. Only today, instead of chasing it away, I welcomed it.

I read the beginning of the inscribed words again.

Sometimes love is for a moment.

Sometimes love is for a lifetime.

Is this what Maria wanted me to see? I tried to make sense of it. Was Lucy my moment and Kendall my lifetime?

Wings for eternity.

Was she trying to tell me I didn't deserve either? That I was destined to fly around the world for eternity and never settle down?

The ache intensified. I squeezed my eyes shut as the taste of salty tears hit my nasal passage. Was this my punishment? Lucy had loved and lost. I'd done that to her. It made me realize that my life was easier to live before Kendall ever walked into that airport bar. They say that it's better to have loved and lost than never to have loved at all, but right now, I was thinking that's a bunch of bullshit. Wouldn't Lucy and I both have been better off if we'd never loved? I wouldn't have realized that my life sucked before Kendall and Lucy would... still be here.

My shoulders started to shake long before the sound came. When it all hit me, I had to sit down in the snow, or I would have fallen over. As much as I tried to fight it, I couldn't anymore. The sobs rose from deep within me, and I cried for all of the losses. For Lucy's parents who never got to experience any of the joys that my parents had. For Lucy and Kendall, for letting them down because I couldn't keep my dick in my pants. And for the realization that...

Sometimes a Moment is a Lifetime
...and that's all you get.

Chapter 24

carter

FIVE DAYS OF R&R didn't help. I'd decided to forego visiting my parents even though I was only a short drive to their house. I was a mess, and if they'd seen me in this condition, it would only make them worry.

Sadly, I couldn't wait to get back to work. Being in the air had become my home, and I was going stir crazy anywhere else. I arrived at Detroit airport three and a half hours early for my flight. The crew check-in hadn't opened yet, so I headed to the Sky Lounge to get some breakfast while I waited. I'd just ordered a turkey and Swiss omelet and sat down to read the paper when a familiar voice called my name.

"Hey, Trip."

Alexa Purdy was definitely not dressed in the standard-issue Captain's uniform. She looked more like she was going to the beach than about to command a commercial flight. Her toned legs were long to begin with, but the short shorts she had on coupled with high heel sandals made her look like she could be a New York City Rockette.

"Alexa." I nodded.

"Where you heading today?"

"New York. You?"

She gave me an I'm-going-to-eat-you-for-dinner smile and purred, "New York."

"Flight plan had Ken Myers listed as my second."

"Oh. I'm just a passenger. I was supposed to meet my friend in the city for a few days. But she cancelled on me at the last minute." She pouted and flirtatiously swayed back and forth. "Now I'm all alone."

I cleared my throat. "It's a busy city. I'm sure you'll find lots to do."

Without being invited, she sat down across from me and tilted her head. "Do you still have that little blonde girlfriend? What was her name? Kylie?"

I didn't bother to correct her because saying her name hurt too much. "It ended."

Alexa didn't even pretend to hide that my answer made her happy. "And how long are *you* in New York for, Trip?"

"Just the one night. Have a flight out to Copenhagen tomorrow evening."

"One night, huh?"

I was grateful when the waiter came with my omelet. Even though I wasn't really hungry, I dug in to occupy my mouth so I wouldn't have to keep talking.

Alexa opted for a yogurt parfait and black coffee. With her tall, thin frame, long dark hair, and big brown eyes, she really was a beautiful woman. Although everything about her was pretty much the polar opposite of what Kendall looked like. If I remembered correctly, she was also the polar opposite of what Kendall was like in bed, too. While Kendall had a healthy sexual appetite, she liked for me to take the lead and play the dominant partner role in bed. Alexa, on the other hand, was aggressive and liked to remove the mystery of what made her tick by telling her lover very specifically what she wanted. At the time that had worked for me. It ensured there was a quick and easy happy ending for both of us. Since my time with her had been limited to a few layover romps, I was only anxious for a release followed by some good shut-eye.

Thinking about Alexa in that way made me feel angry with myself. But it also made me angry with Kendall. Over the last five days, I'd realized that her being pregnant with another man's child wasn't enough to make me run the other way. I now knew I would stick it out with her regardless of her being pregnant. It would be messy, but in my mind, she was worth whatever it took. Yet she'd left me before she was even certain I *had* a child. I'd gone from sad to angry and back a few times over the last few days. And my mood was currently in the angry zone.

For the next hour, Alexa and I caught up on some of the places we'd spent time and talked about who'd retired. Anything work related brought me a sense of comfort. *Because it was all I fucking had anymore.*

"Do you have a place booked for your layover yet?" she asked.

I hadn't actually reserved anywhere because I hadn't checked my flight assignment until I woke up this morning. "I'll probably just stay at the JFK Radisson. I think that's where they still put us up."

"I have a room at the Plaza. What do you say, you come into the city with me and spend the night. We can go out dancing? Or if you're not in the mood, we can skip the dancing and just go straight to bed." She arched an eyebrow. Alexa was nothing if not a straight shooter.

Although I really had no desire to, I figured I might as well jump back into my life. This was going to be it for me. I hadn't been with another woman in more than eleven months. If I was jumping back into action, it might as well be with a woman who I knew I was compatible with and also had no expectations for anything more than just fucking. What the hell? It was better than being alone anymore. "Sure...why not."

AFTER WE LANDED, I HAD to wait around for one of the local International Airlines mechanics to come by. One of the plane's gauges had stopped working mid-flight. It wasn't critical to safety, but our policy required us to stay until we met with the service technician so that we could explain the problem first-hand. I told my second officer to leave, and I'd stay behind and wait. Unlike me, *he* had a family waiting for him at home. I also had Alexa to keep me company while I waited. Apparently, there was a backup in service calls, and I was going to be sitting around for up to an hour. Alexa joined me in the cockpit to wait.

"Remember that time we almost got caught in Berlin while we were on weather delay? I was sitting on your lap riding you, and the door was open to the cockpit, and we didn't hear the announcement that they were finally going to start boarding?" She was sitting in the chair next to me and rubbed her fingers up and down my arm as she spoke.

I nodded, unable to answer vocally because I knew my voice would come out full of disgust. I remembered the day she was talking about, although the thought of it made me feel ill at the moment. *Loveless fucking*. What had happened to me that I wasn't really interested anymore? I was positive if I had told her to get on her knees right at that moment as we waited for the mechanic, she would have done so happily. There was a time when getting head in the cockpit was better than any high. Would I ever get back to those days where I felt like that? It sure as hell didn't feel like it at the moment.

"We have an hour to kill. We could put the sun shield up and pregame it?"

"I'd just rather get this taken care of and head to the hotel."

She was quiet for a moment. "What's going on with you, Trip? You don't seem like yourself."

"Nothing. Just tired from the flight." I wasn't going to insult her and tell the truth—that I felt like I was waiting to go before the firing squad rather than looking forward to being inside of her again. No reason to hurt her feelings. The shit I was going through was all my problem.

She must have sensed that my mind was elsewhere. "What happened to you and the little blonde, anyway? Rumor around the crew was that someone had finally grounded Captain Bigcock?"

My brows drew together. "Captain Bigcock?"

"Don't pretend you don't know what the flight attendants call you. It's no secret that you like to fuck, and you're well equipped."

I shook my head, disgusted with myself. *God, I really was an asshole before I met Kendall.*

When I didn't respond, she pressed again. "What? Were you in love with her or something?"

Head over fucking heels.

"I don't want to talk about this with you, Alexa."

"Why? I was married once. I was in love. I could be a friend, too, you know. There's more to me than just a place to stick your dick once in a while. You just never had any interest in getting to know me before."

I stared at her. She was absolutely right. Before Kendall, I wouldn't have agreed with her, but now I knew what it was like to let someone in—to open myself up to more than just sex—so I was able to see things clearly. I'd never given her a half a chance. "I'm sorry about that, Alexa."

She let down her tough guard and, for a second, I saw a vulnerable side of her that I'd never seen before. "That's okay. I took what I could get from you."

Luckily, the mechanic showed up quicker than expected and ended our little heart to heart. After I showed him the broken gauge and ran though a checklist of other questions, I was done and released from my duty. Alexa and I disembarked, and we headed into the terminal and began our walk to the airport exit.

As we made our way through the concourse, my mind was racing. Was this the right way to go about making myself feel like the old me again? Mindless screwing with a co-worker? Why did it feel wrong now? Kendall was gone, it had been more than eleven months, and there was no reason for me to stay faithful to a ghost.

As we passed a Hudson News stand, I thought I actually saw a ghost. A woman was browsing magazines, her back facing me, but from behind she looked exactly like Kendall. My heartbeat started to accelerate more in that quick flash than it had in a long time. Seeing the ghost of Kendall had me more worked up than the thought of what I was about to do with Alexa. I stared at the woman as we passed. Realizing she was wearing a flight attendant's uniform for a sister airline, National Elite, I felt deflated and forced myself to look away. I was really starting to lose my mind.

A conscience I didn't realize I even owned had started to kick in by the time we reached the exit. There was no way I could do this with Alexa. As much as I hated myself for not being able to move on, I just wasn't ready. The taxi line had only one person waiting. We got in line, and a cab quickly pulled up. When the driver got out and opened the trunk, I waited until he took Alexa's luggage.

"Alexa. I'm sorry. I appreciate the invitation, but I can't do this."

"Do what?" She seemed sincerely perplexed.

"Go with you. To your hotel. I'm not ready."

"Not ready? You mean..."

"No, not like that. It's not a physical problem. I'm just... my mind is somewhere else, and that's not fair to do to you."

She stepped closer and grabbed the lapels to my uniform. "I don't mind."

I forced a sad smile. "I'm sorry. But I do."

She sighed loudly. "Is there anything I can offer to convince you?"

Can you make a ghost turn into reality?

"No. I'm sorry." I opened the back door of the car and waited for her to get in.

She slipped inside and looked genuinely sad, rather than angry. "If you change your mind, you know where to find me."

"Thank you. Take care of yourself, Alexa."

I shut the door and rapped my knuckles on the top of the yellow car to let the driver know he could pull away. Then I stood there for a full ten minutes staring at nothing but the sidewalk. I didn't know what to do with myself. I could go check into a hotel, but that thought depressed me even more than the incident with Alexa did. So I did the only thing that seemed to make me feel better lately—and headed back into the airport.

PLAYBOY PILOT

The Sky Lounge food wasn't half bad, and it would kill some time before going to my depressing hotel by myself. I headed through the security I'd just exited and back down the National Elite concourse. As I passed gate thirty-two, I caught a glimpse of what I thought was the blonde Kendall ghost walking down the gangway to board her flight. She really looked like her from behind. The swing of her hips was even similar. I stopped to watch her walk the entire way down, not moving until she'd disappeared out of sight. Again, my heart was beating out of control just seeing a woman who looked *similar* to Kendall.

What the *fuck* was wrong with me?

I shook my head, blinked a few times, and forced myself to continue walking. I'd made it two or three more gates when I suddenly turned back around. "*I'm losing my fucking mind*," I grumbled to myself. It was ridiculous, I knew. But my heart was still racing, and I'd never be able to sleep tonight if I didn't at least ask.

I waited in line behind a woman who wanted to change her seat. When it was my turn, I made sure my captain's hat was on my head. "Hi, I'm Carter Clynes with International. I could have sworn I just saw an old friend that I used to work with go down the gateway.

"You mean Captain Reisher?"

"No. A flight attendant. We used to work together."

"Let's see. We have Melissa Hansen, Nat Ditmar and..." The woman turned to her co-worker. "What's the new flight attendant's name again? The blonde?"

My heart started to pound with anticipation.

"The one that just finished training last week?"

"Yeah, that's her. She just boarded today's flight."

"Oh. Her name...is Kendall."

I froze. It couldn't be. "Did you say Kendall?"

"I did. Is that who you thought it was?"

It has to be one giant coincidence.

"Kendall...is her last name Sparks?"

"Yeah, that's it. She works the shuttle from New York to Boston now."

Am I imagining what I'm hearing? Have I lost the rest of my marbles? Or can it really be possible that Kendall had become a flight attendant and was right down that hall?

The thought seemed insane.

I looked up at the flight board. It showed Boston, but was flashing delayed. "What time are you supposed to leave?"

"Our wheels up time is in fifteen minutes, but they're telling us to expect at least an hour delay due to high winds."

"Is the flight full?"

She keypunched a few things. "There are a few seats left right now."

"I'll be back." I took off as fast as I could, running to the ticket counter where I could buy a seat.

SINCE IT WASN'T MY AIRLINE, I had to wait in line with everyone else, and I was starting to get antsy. I'd checked the time on my phone a dozen times in the fifteen minutes I'd been waiting. The guy in front of me must have noticed.

"You look like you're worried you're going to miss your flight, mate." He had what I thought might be an Australian accent.

"I'm trying to get on a delayed flight. There aren't many seats left though."

"You're a pilot, aren't you?"

I nodded.

"Don't they give any preffy to the big boy at the head of the plane? What are you waiting on line like us cattle for?"

"It's not the airline I work for."

"Ah. Well you can go ahead of me, if it helps any. I'm three hours early for my flight." The guy had a large dog carrier crate in front of him.

"You early to check-in your dog or something?"

"Or something." He chuckled. "My wife and I were visiting here in New York. She won't leave Mutton here home alone. The damn thing goes wherever we go."

"Mutton?"

He leaned in and whispered, "That's a goat I got in there." Then he held his finger up to his mouth giving the universal sign for shhh. "Don't tell the people at the airline. My wife thinks they won't notice."

I leaned over and peered into the crate. Sure enough, the guy had a small goat inside. "You don't think they'll know it's a goat?"

"You haven't met my wife, Aubrey. She went to hit the head. But by the time we're done at this counter, they'll be offering Pixy here Milk-Bones. She can sell wood to a forest. Come to think of it, you're best going ahead of me. Because if they try to make this thing fly with farm animals, we're going to be here for a good lot."

I shook my head, amused. The guy was so charismatic and good looking, something told me he could sell the ladies behind the counter that the goat was a kitten if he tried. We talked for a few minutes, inching up a little at a time.

"So where you heading? Taking an adventure of some sort?"

"I hope so," I said.

When the flight attendant called out 'next', the Aussie told me to go ahead of him. I extended my hand. "Thanks. Good luck with your...pet."

"Thanks. Hope you find that adventure."

I hope so, too.

CHAPTER 25

carter

IT WAS HER.

My chest tightened.

Holy shit. I wasn't imagining all of this.

As I sat in my seat at the rear of the plane, I squinted my eyes to see every movement that Kendall made as she worked the front of the Boeing 737. It was surreal to see her in this role. It was like my worlds were colliding in the strangest way.

Somehow, she hadn't seen me board. That was a blessing because I needed time to process. She'd been helping an old man stow something away in the overhead when I snuck past her in disbelief.

I debated confronting her right then, but this was neither the time nor place to deal with all we had to talk about. My greatest hope was that she didn't freak out when she inevitably noticed me.

Getting her fired was also something I really wanted to avoid. I knew the deal. There were plenty of people waiting in the wings for flight attendant positions. A majority who go through the training never even end up getting hired by the airline. Even though I didn't understand how she came to be here, clearly, it was something she wanted. I wasn't going to risk taking that away from her.

The confusion swirling around in my head was mind numbing.

Did she have the baby or not?

Flight attendant training was only a couple of months. Technically, she could've trained while pregnant then flew up until a certain point when they stopped allowing it. What actually happened to her all of this time was a total mystery.

The flight to Boston would only be an hour. Thank God. There was no way I could have lasted longer being stuck in this spot and unable to get answers.

Beads of sweat were forming on my forehead. My heart was beating so fast that for the first time ever on an aircraft, I actually got a little panicky. I never particularly liked flying unless I was controlling things from the cockpit anyway.

Kendall assumed her position up front for takeoff. Once we were airborne, she would likely be heading down to the galley at some point. There was no way I would be able to hide unnoticed until the end of the flight. The thought of coming face to face with her in front of all these people made me ill.

Working as a pilot had prepared me to deal with dozens of potentially catastrophic scenarios. Despite that, I didn't feel prepared in the least to face Kendall.

I studied her as best I could from afar. She was wearing a gray pencil skirt and a light blue blouse with three-quarter inch sleeves. There was a darker blue stripe that ran down the middle. Her normally unruly hair was tied neatly into a low bun.

She seemed guarded and mechanical when interacting with the passengers. The smile I remembered that used to light up the room, now seemed fake with a hint of darkness beneath it. Kendall reminded me of myself before I met her. There's no better profession than flying for people who want to run from their problems.

It scared me to think of *what* she might be running from at this point.

Did she have the baby and feel guilty over giving it up?

Fuck.

The urgent need to know what happened was making my skin crawl.

Kendall had been talking to one of the passengers when she suddenly began to make her way down the aisle toward the back of the plane.

She spoke to one of the other flight attendants. "I need a bandage for the passenger in 6C. Where do we keep those again?"

"I'll grab it," her co-worker said.

She happened to look in my direction while she was waiting for her colleague to fetch the Band-Aid.

Our eyes locked, and there was no turning back.

Looking like she'd seen a ghost, Kendall grabbed the back of one of the seats for balance. We just stared at each other for the longest time. The look on her face gave me the impression that if we weren't thousands of feet in the air, she would have run away from me, not toward me. Actually, it looked more like she was debating whether to jump.

Even though she was right in front of me, she seemed miles away, far from being ready to face me. Perhaps, she truly thought she would never see me again. I'd often wondered if that would be the case myself.

"We need to talk," I said in a low voice before silently mouthing, "Later."

Before she could respond, the other attendant returned. "I've got the bandage."

Kendall didn't move. She was still looking at me, blinking, flustered.

The woman waved the bandage to garner her attention. "Kendall…"

Breaking her stare, Kendall cleared her throat and took it. "Oh, thank you."

Her walk back to the front was slow and almost wobbly. She held onto the back of each seat as she made her way down the aisle. I knew my showing up would be a shock, but clearly it had really done a job on her. Sweating profusely, I was in no better shape.

By the time the plane landed, I'd had no further interactions with Kendall.

Her voice came over the intercom once. "Please remember to take all of your belongings before deplaning."

I waited for all of the passengers to empty out of the aircraft before slowly walking toward where she was beginning to clean up. I stopped short at the sound of the Captain addressing her.

"Kendall, you feel like getting a drink with us downtown?"

My fists instinctively tightened. I knew all too well what he was up to. He was a fucking snake. This was the pot calling the kettle black, of course; I was a viper myself at one time.

"No. Thank you. I'm kind of tired. I'm gonna head home."

Home?

Was she living in Boston?

She wasn't looking at me as I passed by them to the exit. With everyone's eyes on her, I couldn't risk causing her to break down here in the plane. Instead, I simply walked with a lump in my throat down the jetway to the terminal and waited.

Ten minutes later, Kendall emerged, flanking the two pilots and the rest of the crew. She was rolling a small black suitcase. When she stopped, the Captain turned around.

"Are you sure I can't convince you to come?"

"I'm sure. See you next week."

"Alright."

I gave him the evil eye. When they were out of earshot, Kendall finally turned to me.

Sucking in my jaw, I stood there facing her, still barely able to breathe let alone talk.

I managed to say, "Hi, Perky."

Her eyes slowly filled with tears that didn't fall. "What are you doing here?"

"What do you think? I needed to see you."

"You should've left well enough alone."

I took a few steps closer. "I needed to know you're okay."

She stepped back a bit. "I'm fine."

"No, you're not."

"How did you find me?"

"I'd stopped looking, and then it happened."

Understandably, she looked confused. People were passing us by, but we just stood motionless in the same spot.

"I need to know what's going on with you, Kendall."

Shaking her head, she cried, "Well, I don't want to know what's going on with *you*. Because I can't handle it."

I raised my voice. "You can't handle the thought of my fathering a child with another woman because you still love me." Inches from her face now, I said, "I hate to break it to you, but you left for nothing."

"What do you mean?"

"The baby's not mine. He's not mine, Kendall! A DNA test confirmed it. She was trying to trap me."

"Whose is it?"

"Fuck if I know."

Thinking about that whole situation was making me incredibly angry all of a sudden.

She lifted her hand to her mouth. "Oh my God." We were quiet for about a minute straight as a woman's voice rang out over the intercom to announce that someone was lost.

When the noise stopped, I continued, "All this time we could have been together. I could have been the one to share in it with you. Where is it?"

"Where is what?"

"The baby! Did you do it? Did you go through with it?"

She shook her head slowly and whispered, "No."

A headache split through my head. "No?"

"No."

"You mean to tell me, that all of this..." I paused to compose myself. "Happened...for nothing?" Rubbing my temples, I said, "I don't even know what to say to you. I'm numb." I looked down at the floor incredulously before meeting her gaze again. "You couldn't get pregnant, or you couldn't go through with it?"

"Can we go somewhere else to talk about this, away from all these people?"

"Where do you want to go?"

"I have a car parked in the garage."

"Alright." Grabbing my travel bag, I followed Kendall to the spot where her older Ford Explorer SUV was parked.

We got in and sat in silence until she started talking.

"I went to Germany, spent some time with Hans and Stephen after I left you at the airport lounge. I was supposed to go home, get my things and go back. I did end up going back to Dallas and packing some stuff. I had a return ticket to Germany, but while I was at the airport, I just decided that I couldn't go through with it, couldn't bring a baby into this world for the wrong reasons. Moreover, I couldn't bring a baby into this world and give it up. The money stopped mattering long before that point, I think. The inheritance didn't mean anything anymore."

"Why didn't you come to me at that point?"

"I was afraid. I didn't think I could handle what I thought was happening with you and that woman. It was just so devastating."

I'd chosen not to tell her I visited the ranch in Texas. I didn't want to divert from the issue at hand, which was finding out what the hell she'd been doing for the past eleven months.

"So, you didn't go to Germany. Where did you go?"

"I was feeling so lost. It felt like it was the lowest point of my entire life. The only place I felt like going was back to that beach in Rio."

My heart started to beat faster. "You went to Rio?"

"Yes. I stayed with Maria Rosa."

What?

"What?"

"Yeah."

"She never told me."

"I know. I made her swear to never tell you I was there. There was a boarder who spoke English who was translating for me the entire time. Even though it scared the shit out of me, I asked Maria to read me, to tell me what I should do with the rest of my life."

"What did she say?"

"It translated to *the answer is in the sky.*"

Holy shit.

With my jaw dropped, I let her continue.

"I thought long and hard about what that could possibly mean. The first thing I assumed was that she was telling me to go back to you. But I couldn't do that. On my flight back to the states, I thought about how I didn't really feel like I belonged anywhere. I became envious of you, because for the most part, your job didn't require you to be in one place. That was exactly what I needed at that point in my life. I needed to fly, to travel, to live…to find myself. But I also needed enough money to survive. Then, it clicked. *The answer is in the sky.* A few days later, from a hotel room in Texas, I started researching flight attendant school, entering training a month later. After six weeks, I was hired, and because I'm newer, they stuck me on the commuter route from New York to Boston. I keep an apartment here in Everett, but I don't spend a lot of time in it. I fly standby whenever I can to visit other places. I basically wander."

Wow.

"Forgive me Kendall, but this is just a hard pill to swallow. You left me in an airport lounge, with my heart ripped to fucking shreds, so that you could basically fly around all day, like a shell of a person running away from life. Jeez…that sounds awfully fucking familiar to me."

"I've basically *become* you."

"Have you fucked that pilot?"

"No!"

The thought of her with anyone gave me murderous urges. Something in the air shifted as we stared at each other, and in that moment, I just needed to touch her, to feel her lips against mine before any other words were exchanged.

Without thinking it through, I placed my hand on her knee and squeezed it. She closed her eyes and bent her head back upon the simple touch. Her breathing quickened, and I took my hand and placed it around the back of her head, pulling her into me and devouring her mouth.

The kiss was fervent and desperate, different from all of the others we'd had before. This one was releasing nearly a year of pent-up emotions and sexual starvation—for me, at least. I prayed it was the same for her—that she hadn't been with anyone.

Even though I was still so angry, I needed to have her like my life depended on it. I pushed my seat back as far as it would go and lifted her on top of me. Too worked up to even speak, I told myself I would let her breathing and body continue to guide me, to let me know it was okay to do this.

When Kendall began to grind desperately over my painfully hard cock, I knew there was no going back. When she suddenly lifted her skirt so that it was up by her waist, I unzipped my pants and within seconds she bore down onto me. The feeling of sinking into her hot, wet pussy after all this time, was like nothing I'd felt before. I hadn't ever gone this long without sex, and I'd never been separated from someone who I truly loved. Those two things combined made this different from anything I'd ever experienced.

It was frantic.

It was unstoppable.

It was totally inappropriate in an airport parking garage.

It was beyond hot.

It lasted under a minute.

When I felt her spasm around me, I shot my load inside of her, hoping that she was on the pill but not caring enough about the risk to stop. It felt too good. She stayed on top of me for a while before making her way back into the driver's seat. Still panting and exhausted, we both leaned our heads back and stared at each other with looks that screamed, *"What the fuck just happened?"*

She was the first to speak as she adjusted her clothing. "I needed to figure out who I was, Carter, aside from rich bitch Kendall Sparks from Dallas, Texas. I wasn't ready for a baby. I wasn't ready for anything. I needed to grow up. When you met me, I was still such a confused person. The time alone has helped me to grow. I've been miserable. And that has taught me that this *isn't* the kind of life I really want long term. But for now, it's served its purpose. What I also know is that there hasn't been one moment where I regretted having no money. That inheritance all went to charity as my grandfather promised it would. And you know what? I couldn't be happier about that. The money wouldn't have made me happy. It wouldn't have changed anything. The only thing it would have done was keep my mother's ass at home when it should be out working like everyone else."

I needed to know. "Have you been with anyone all this time?"

"No. No, I haven't." She swallowed. "Have you?"

"No. I couldn't. Even though I thought you were gone forever, I still couldn't. But I'm so fucking angry, Kendall. I'm angry that you left me, that you didn't believe in me enough to stick it out. I'm angry that the past eleven months of hell were basically for nothing. But what angers me the most is that despite all that…I get it. And I still fucking love you so much." Cupping her cheek, I finally admitted, "I went to Maria Rosa, too. Just like you, I was desperate. The message she gave me was, *'A resposta está no céu.'* You know what that means?"

"No."

"The answer is in the sky."

Kendall's eyes widened. "Are you kidding?"

"No. I took it as having something to do with *Lucy in the Sky with Diamonds*. Because of that message, I went to Lucy's grave, cried my eyes out. I'd never visited her once. As much as it was painful, it gave me the bit of closure that was desperately needed. The timing of that trip, which broke up my normal routine, put me in New York at the exact same time that I spotted you in the airport. I would have never seen you otherwise."

"We both got the same message."

"Neither of us would be here right now if it weren't for those words. Maria gave us a road map back to each other. We interpreted it in our own ways, took different routes, but ended up here. It's up to us now to figure out the next leg of the journey, whether that's together or apart."

CHAPTER 26

kendall

WE'D BOTH BEEN QUIET the entire drive to my apartment. It was only ten miles, but traffic gave me more than a half-hour to think. Carter was looking out the window, seemingly lost in his own thoughts. After our parking lot frenzy, I'd asked him if he wanted to come home with me. It surprised me that his immediate response wasn't yes. He'd actually suggested that perhaps it was better for him to stay at a hotel in order to give us both some time. But I'd talked him into spending the night at my place. And now…I was beginning to realize it wasn't the smartest thing to do. My head was spinning thinking about everything that had transpired over the last two hours. Especially what it meant for us from here.

I pulled the SUV into my designated parking spot and broke our silence. "It's not as homey as Silver Shores, but this is where I live."

Carter looked at the sign on the lawn. "The Charleston Chew Lofts, huh? Pretty sure no one at Silver Shores can eat Charleston Chews. Those things were always killer on the teeth. I chipped a baby tooth eating a frozen one once. Probably tougher on dentures."

"The building is actually the old Charleston Chew Candy factory. It was converted into condos but still has a lot of the original factory details, like exposed brick and wooden beams. My place is small, only a studio that I can barely afford now that I'm a working girl, but the building has a great rooftop deck that I spend a lot of time on." I pointed up to the top of the building. "I've spent hours staring up at the sky and thinking over the last few months."

I had been looking up at my apartment building, and when I turned to Carter, I realized he had been staring at me. "What?" I asked.

He shook his head. "Nothing."

Carter took our bags, and I led the way to my place. In the elevator, it felt almost surreal to be standing next to him again. Over the last year, I'd often dreamed of him being here with me. So it wasn't surprising that I was currently feeling like I was in the middle of a hazy fantasy rather than reality. Which is probably why when the elevator doors opened on the third floor, I didn't move.

"Is this your floor? You pushed three when we got in."

"Oh. Yes. Sorry."

I fumbled with my keys when I unlocked the door to my apartment. Once inside, I spun around holding my hands out. "This is your tour. You can pretty much see most of the place from here."

Carter set our bags down and looked around. "Very nice. It's modern but warm. It suits you."

"Thank you. My neighbors on both sides work at the airlines, too. Gabby is in 310; she's a flight attendant at Delta. Max in 314 is a pilot at American. We barbeque together once in a while on the rare occasion that our schedules are in sync."

I caught Carter's jaw tense. "A pilot lives next door?"

"Yes."

He nodded.

The fact that he was restraining his comment made me offer more. "He just turned fifty-three and is thinking about retiring to Florida. Maybe when he gets a little older, he can be *your* neighbor."

"Wiseass."

I kicked my shoes off and walked to the refrigerator, grabbing us some drinks. "Speaking of Florida. How's your posse? Muriel, Bertha, Gordon?"

Carter's face fell. "Gordon's not doing too good, actually. Had a stroke about four months ago, and the physical therapy isn't going as well as they hoped. He lost complete use of one arm, and his speech is still pretty slurred."

"That's terrible. I'm so sorry. Does he have any family at all near you?"

"None. I took a few weeks of vacation after it happened to help him out. But when I'm gone for four or five days, he doesn't get out much. Muriel and Bertha take turns looking in on him, but they can't lift him. The physical therapist comes to the house to do his exercises, but other than that, it's been tough on him."

"He's lucky he has you."

"You mean Brucey." Carter smiled.

"Yes, his wonderful son, Brucey." I hesitated before continuing, unsure if I should be so forward. Ultimately, I decided what I wanted to say was about Carter and not us, so I said it. "You know…that first time we went to visit Gordon, and I realized that you were not only taking care of a man who was once a stranger to you, but you were letting him call you Brucey and filling the void of missing his son, that was the moment I admitted to myself that I was in love with you. Because you weren't just this beautiful man on the outside who was fun to spend time with, you were just as beautiful on the inside."

Carter stared at me. When he spoke, his voice was hoarse. "If you really loved me, how could you have left me, Kendall?"

Ashamed, I looked away. "I don't know."

"Do you regret it now?"

"I've regretted it every day since I left you in that airport bar."

"So why didn't you do something about it? You knew where to find me. You knew where I worked, where I lived... you knew everything there was to know about me for Christ's sake." He raked his fingers through his hair.

Even though I'd asked myself that same question over and over for the last year, I *still* had no answer. "I don't know. I'm sorry, Carter."

After a few tense minutes, Carter spoke. "Are you hungry? Do you want to order something? Or do you want to get some sleep? You must get up early to work the shuttle."

"I'm actually really tired."

"Okay. So let's get some sleep."

I looked around the apartment, oddly unsure of what our sleeping arrangements would be, even though we'd just been intimate in the car. "I can sleep on the couch if you want. You can have the bed."

Carter walked to me, he lifted my chin so our eyes met. "I'm confused about a lot of things that have to do with us. But wanting to share a bed with you is definitely not one of them. If you're good with it, I'd like nothing better than to sleep next to you again."

"I'd love that."

His hand at my chin moved to cup my face, and he leaned down so that our noses were almost touching. "And another thing. When we wake up, I plan to fuck you on that bed we'll be sharing. Only this time, it won't last two minutes like it did in the parking lot."

I swallowed. "I'd love that, too."

"Good. Now let's get you some sleep. Because you're gonna need it."

CARTER AND I WERE sitting on the rooftop deck next to an electric heater that doubled as a light post. It was a little after midnight, and I was curled into him on the wicker couch with a blanket over us. He hadn't been kidding around when he'd said that the second time we were intimate, it was going to last more than two minutes. After an hour and a half nap, we spent three hours going at it in my bed. I was sated and content as he stroked my hair, and we both stared up at the stars.

"I met your mother."

Well *that* got my attention. Surely, I never expected those words to come out of Carter's mouth. I pulled my head back to look at him. "Did you just say you—"

"I met Annabelle."

"Where? How?"

"I went to Dallas after I found out that the baby wasn't mine. I needed to see you."

"How did you get the address?"

"It's not hard to find people on the Internet, Kendall. I mailed her a letter, and she never responded. My therapist told me I needed closure, so I decided to take a chance and went to the address that I'd sent the letter to."

There was so much in that answer that I had more questions about. Therapist? Closure? But my curiosity about dear old mom won out. "What did she say to you?"

He shrugged. "Not much. She basically said she didn't know where you were and insinuated you left her destitute."

"I sort of did. My lifestyle wasn't the only one to drastically change by the decisions I've made. I was selfish in making my choices."

Carter grew angry. "Fuck that. You weren't the selfish one. She had no right to expect you to go through with that crazy clause your grandfather put into his will. When I thought there was a chance I could be a father, at first I did a lot of thinking about what that would mean for *me*. Then one day I was standing at the front of the plane greeting passengers and a couple boarded with a baby. I didn't know them, but I looked at that little screaming blue-eyed monster and realized how it affected me didn't matter anymore. I wouldn't have much to give my kid, but I would give him the best of me no matter what. Anyone can father a child, but a good parent puts a child's needs before his own. A parent should be selfless, not selfish. What your mother expected you to do was selfish. She should never have pressured you."

"Wow. It sounds like you were really prepared for that baby to be yours."

"I don't know about that. But I decided if that's the way it turned out, I was going to give him my all."

"Him. She had a boy?"

"Yeah."

It was dark, but I saw pain in Carter's eyes. "It hurt you when you found out he wasn't yours, didn't it?"

He nodded. "I didn't expect that. But, yeah, it did. As much as I didn't want to have a baby with her, I'd somehow started to care for the unborn child."

I lifted to my knees to look him straight in the eyes. "You're an amazing man, Carter Clynes. Someday you're going to be an incredible father."

THE NEXT MORNING came too quickly. Even though I didn't have to be at work until the following day, Carter had an afternoon flight, and he still had to get back to New York before that. I found myself looking at the time every few minutes while he was in the shower. When he came out with his airline-issued pilot's shirt and pants already on, rather than in the towel I expected to see him in, I was disappointed.

"I was looking forward to seeing your body all wet after the shower, you know."

He sat on the bed and pulled on his socks. "I can't be half-naked around you. That would wind up with me half-naked inside of you. And I need to get to the airport if I'm going to catch the ten o'clock shuttle back to New York and make my flight."

We still hadn't talked about what was going to happen after he left today. Were we back together? Was this just physical for him? I knew he still loved me, yet I had the distinct feeling that he wasn't as sure about wanting to be with me as I was about him. It would be painful if he didn't want to try again, although it might be what I deserved after running away from him when he needed me most.

I broached the subject hesitantly. "Will you be in Boston anytime soon?"

He looked at me and shook his head without saying anything. My heart sank.

"How about New York? You must have a layover in New York on your schedule."

He slipped one of his large feet into his shoe. "Haven't checked." When he was done getting dressed, he stood and zipped his suitcase. "We should probably get on the road in case there's traffic."

I nodded and somehow managed to keep my tears at bay. Swallowing them down my throat as I dressed left a large lump of emotions clogged in my chest.

Just like the drive from the airport yesterday, the trip to the airport was silent. Every single minute that ticked by was making it harder and harder to focus. We'd only just found our way back to each other, and I wasn't ready to lose him again. I didn't need a commitment, but I needed to know that this was the beginning of *something*. That we'd try to figure things out. Yet as I exited the highway into Boston's bustling airport, it was beginning to feel more like the end than the beginning.

Oh my God.

Was it the end? Was this the closure he'd talked about with his therapist? It was a good thing we were almost to the terminal drop off because I was fighting the palpitations in my chest and beginning to feel a hyperventilation-style panic attack coming on.

I parked at the curb and stared straight ahead. I knew if I looked at his face, I was going to lose it. Carter was watching me intently; I could feel it.

"Perky..."

Tears began to fill my eyes, and I refused to let them spill over. My hands gripped the steering wheel so hard that my knuckles turned white.

He continued, "I had a great time."

Hearing the start of his blow off, my sadness suddenly morphed into anger. "Don't you dare, Carter. I know I screwed up. But don't you dare spend the night with me and then give me the Captain Carter Clynes flight attendant blow off special." I finally turned to face him. "I love you. I never stopped. And I know down deep you still love me, too. So don't cheapen what we have by treating me like one of your harem...one of your flight attendant fucks. Tell me it's over if you want, but give me that much respect at least."

Carter hung his head. His voice was soft and strained when he spoke again. "I'm sorry. That's not what I meant to do."

Just then, a loud knock on the passenger window startled me. It was airport security telling us we needed to drop off and move along. Carter told him we'd be done in a minute and then reached for my hand. "I'll call you. Okay, beautiful?"

"When?"

Again, he looked away. "I don't know."

I wanted so much to savor the last kiss he gave me. But I couldn't. Everything was numb. He brushed his lips softly against mine and then cupped my face in both hands. "*Yesterday*," he whispered.

I smiled and nodded. The Beatles summed up our moment perfectly. Love coming back made *Yesterday* seem so much easier. But what would tomorrow bring?

Chapter 27

carter

"THIS IS YOUR SECOND VISIT in a week. Did something happen to bring you back here today?" Dr. Lemmon asked.

"I can't sleep."

"Is the trouble falling asleep or staying asleep?"

"Both. I have this incredible energy inside of me, and I just can't seem to get rid of it."

"How do you normally burn off excess energy?"

"That's not an option."

Dr. Lemmon nodded like I'd just given her the answer even though I hadn't said shit. "So let's talk about that. Am I wrong in assuming that in the past you used sex as a way of relaxing yourself enough to rest?"

"You're not wrong about that."

"And when you say *it's not an option*, I'm assuming that isn't in the literal sense. You're a good-looking pilot. Options must be boundless."

"No, I didn't mean there weren't any options. I meant I wouldn't be taking any of the available options."

"So it's been what, a week now since you and Kendall spent the night together?"

"One week today."

"And it's been three days since you were here."

"You want me to put this crap on a calendar for you?"

Dr. Lemmon smiled. "No, I think I got it now. Have you spoken to Kendall recently?"

"Just that one time I already told you about. When she called me."

"What night was it when you spoke to her, again?"

What the hell was with this woman and her dates today? I thought back. I'd just landed in Florida from my Dubai flight when she called, so it must have been Tuesday. "Tuesday."

"And you spoke for about an hour, if I recall correctly."

"Give or take, yeah."

"And how did you sleep that night?"

Let's see. Kendall and I had spoken the entire drive home and then while I made a sandwich in my apartment. I'd woken up the next morning still in my uniform at almost ten. "That was my last good night of sleep. But I was tired from a long flight."

"Did you fly yesterday?"

"I did."

"For how many hours?"

"Nine."

"And how many hours was the flight you were tired from when you spoke to Kendall that night you slept well?"

"About the same."

Dr. Lemmon just stared at me.

"So you're saying that I can't sleep without talking to Kendall anymore?"

"I'm saying that the two are very likely connected. You're feeling anxiety. Unsettled. Nervous. All of which is keeping you from sleeping. Is there any other reason for you to be feeling this way, other than how you left things after your encounter with Kendall?"

It annoyed the shit out of me that she was so right. "No."

"Well there you go."

"So what am I supposed to do? Call her every night so she can sing me a lullaby?"

"You already know what you need to do."

"So what the hell am I paying you for if I already know all the answers?" I let out a frustrated sigh.

"You need to make a decision to either move forward with Kendall or cut ties. We talked about this the other day. I can help you sort out your thoughts and figure out your next steps, but only you can make the decision on whether to be with the woman you love or not. You have trust issues with Kendall. It's understandable. She left you once, and you're afraid she'll do it again when things get tough." Dr. Lemmon took off her glasses and rubbed her eyes. "Carter, Lucy had a disease."

"Lucy? We're talking about Kendall here, Doc."

"The two are very much intertwined. In our previous sessions, you admitted you felt like Lucy took the easy way out with her suicide. That is a common misconception of the loved ones left behind. But the truth of the matter is that people who commit suicide believe there is no other choice. Depression is a disease, not unlike asthma, measles or the Plague. If left untreated, they all get worse, and eventually the disease takes the life."

I raked my fingers through my hair. "Okay. But I don't understand what this all has to do with Kendall."

"You've had two special women in your life. Lucy, who you perceive left you when things got tough. And Kendall, who did the same. You're afraid of it happening again."

I wasn't sure she was right, but I felt drained and wanted the conversation to move on. "So bottom line, I need to make a decision on whether I can trust Kendall again, or I'm never going to sleep?"

Dr. Lemmon chuckled. "I can prescribe you something to help you sleep at night in the short term. But other than that...shit or get off the pot."

Shit or get off the pot? I was paying two hundred and fifty dollars an hour for advice my father gave me in third grade.

I WAS AFRAID TO TAKE the sleeping pills. Even though I'd filled the prescription, the warning label had cautioned against driving heavy machinery for twenty-four hours after taking the medicine. I'd say my Boeing 747 qualified as pretty heavy machinery, and since I had a flight tomorrow afternoon, I needed to find other ways to wear myself out to get some sleep.

After running five miles around the outskirts of my development, I decided to stop in and check on Gordon again. Unfortunately, the visit had only made me feel worse. I wasn't an expert by any means, but he seemed to be deteriorating a little more each day. His ankles were constantly filled with fluid, and tonight he had trouble wiggling his toes on one foot. Even though it was after hours, I'd called his doctor to give him an update. He'd basically told me that I should just try to make sure he was comfortable, that there wasn't too much more they could do for a man of Gordon's age and health.

It was late by the time I arrived back at my apartment. Feeling an intense sadness over how things were progressing with Gordon, I wanted nothing more than to pick up the phone and call Kendall. Other than Dr. Lemmon, she was the only person I'd ever really opened up to in my life. I knew she'd understand how I felt. But that wasn't fair to do to her. I needed to figure out if I can see a future for us before unloading my depressing shit on her.

The fucked up thing was, I didn't know how to see a future for us. Yet I couldn't see a future for me *without her*. I was stuck in purgatory. *Story of my life*.

At midnight, I decided to pack my bag for my flight the next morning. Muriel had washed and starched all of my uniforms, even though I'd told her it wasn't necessary a million times. What I loved about the people here at Silver Shores was that they knew they needed help at times, yet they never wanted to take it for free. It made them feel good to barter things I could use in return. They were good people.

My closet was filled with crisply pressed shirts. I grabbed three and folded them into my bag. I'd lost a little weight over the last few months, so I pushed my size extra large jackets to the side and reached farther into the closet to fish out a size large that was stashed in the back.

The hanger I'd grabbed had a smaller jacket on it alright. Only it was about forty sizes too small. In my hand was the little pilot uniform that I'd found in Kendall's closet when I'd went looking for clues in her bedroom. I'd tucked it under my shirt and taken it with me for some reason that day. After I arrived back home, it made me angry to see it every day, so eventually I pushed it in the back where I couldn't see it. Yet I never got rid of it.

I stared at the little uniform for a long time. Visions of a little tow-haired boy wearing it as he ran circles around his mother while laughing were clear as day. The boy had bright blue eyes just like his mother. And Kendall looked more beautiful than ever. I actually closed my eyes and smiled watching the scene play out in my head.

That night, I slept like a baby. I dreamt of that little boy and his mother. It was so vivid, so real, that I was confused when I woke up. For a moment I expected them to come running into my bedroom.

But they didn't.

Which caused a gnawing ache in my chest.

And that was all on me.

As I rushed to get ready for my flight, the little pilot's suit was still laying on top of my dresser. I rubbed my finger over the little wings on the lapel and remembered the face of the little boy from my dream. Unpinning the little wings from the child's jacket, I swapped it with the wings on my own uniform. They weren't that different in appearance, yet they'd made all the difference to me.

I could *see* my future.

I could *see* my family.

I could *see* the woman I loved.

Now I just needed to figure out how to make things right again.

I DECIDED TO QUICKLY check on Gordon before leaving for the airport, since it would be a few days before I would be back home again.

One of the women usually came by his house late in the morning and stayed until a physical therapist showed up, but no one was likely there yet.

Knowing he could be sleeping, I was careful to open the door slowly.

"Dad?" I called out in a low voice.

There was no answer. Gordon was always a heavy snorer, so it was odd that no noise was coming from the bedroom.

He was lying flat on his back, completely still.

"Dad?"

He didn't respond.

Sitting on the edge of the bed, I repeated louder while nudging his shoulder, "Dad, it's Brucey. Wake up."

Placing my two fingers against his neck, I checked for a pulse.

There was none.

Lowering my head, I listened for a heartbeat that wasn't there.

I kept my cheek on his chest and wept. He may have been my fake father, but there was nothing fake about the tears that were falling from my eyes.

Chapter 28

Kendall

A SIMPLE PHONE MESSAGE was about to change everything.

Rolling my suitcase through Logan Airport, I realized I'd missed a call from Carter. The phone must have gone off while I was driving to work with the music turned up.

I listened to the message.

"Hey, Kendall. I'm about to board my flight. I wanted to hear your voice before takeoff, but I guess that's not gonna be possible. It's been a very shitty morning. Um..."

There was a long pause.

"Gordon died. I found him in bed. He wasn't breathing. He must have passed away in his sleep. He was all alone."

My heart fell.

Oh no.

A long breath escaped him into the phone.

"He died all alone with no one holding his hand. It's so fucking sad. No one should have to die alone."

A tear fell down my cheek as the message continued.

"Anyway, it really brought home what matters. I miss you. I'm gonna need to hear your voice tonight to fall asleep. I'm just letting you know."

There was a bit of silence before he said, *"Shit. I have to go. I'll call you when I land in Rio."*

Standing there frozen in the middle of the terminal, I suddenly felt like a complete fish out of water in this airport. Sweating through my uniform, I knew I couldn't let this go on.

What was I doing here?

I needed to be with him.

The ball was so far in my court, that it wasn't even funny. I was the one who'd left; I needed to be the one to bring us back together.

The time apart since reuniting had been good for us, it had given us both time to think, but it was time. There was no way anything could ever work between us if I kept this job. Because of his schedule, it was difficult as it was to have a relationship. Factor in two people working for different airlines, and it was virtually impossible. At this rate, I would never see him. Something had to give.

It was my turn to give.

MARIA ROSA LET ME IN with minimal inquisition. Not that I would have understood her questions anyway. I think she knew full well what I was there for.

I nodded. "Obrigada." I'd finally learned how to say "thank you" appropriately in Portuguese.

Pedro hopped up on my shoulder, and to my surprise did not urinate on me before he fled again. Perhaps, after three visits, I was finally in with the monkey crowd.

Maria pointed me to the correct room, signaling with her index finger to be quiet since Carter was sleeping. Slowly opening the door, I was met with a sight for sore eyes.

I didn't know what Carter had been dreaming of, but clearly it was...wet. His cock was rock hard and glistening, sticking up straight in the air. He was completely and gloriously naked. So tired from my trip, I wanted nothing more than to crawl into bed with him. Stripping off every last thread of clothing, I prowled on my hands and knees onto the mattress.

Carter's eyes blinked open, and he shuddered before realizing it was me.

"Perky?"

"Yes."

"Oh my God. I thought I was dreaming."

"You're not."

"What are you doing here?"

"Shh," I said as I lowered my mouth over his cock. His words trailed off as he lost the ability to speak. Bending his head back, he gave up all control as I went down on him. Holding on to the back of my hair, he guided the movement of my mouth.

I loved listening to the low moans of ecstasy escaping him. At one point, he pulled away and lifted my body onto his.

The bed shook as we went at it. It was fairly early in the morning, and I was sure we were interrupting the other boarders, who were sleeping or having breakfast, but I didn't care. We needed this. We both came in less than a few minutes. It had been way too long.

Soaked in post coital bliss, I answered his earlier question.

"I got your phone message. I told them it was a family

emergency. As soon as I landed in New York, I booked a ticket for the next flight to Rio."

"You lied for me?"

"No. It wasn't a lie. You're the only real family I have now. And I truly needed to see you like my life depended on it. So, that's an emergency in my book."

We were still lying naked on top of each other when he asked, "How long can you stay?"

"As long as you need me."

"Fucking forever then?"

"Okay."

He pulled back to examine my face. "Okay?"

"Yes."

"You're not going back to work?"

"Flying was never for me, Carter. It was just a means to run away while at the same time, somehow in vain connecting with you. It was a good experience, served its purpose, but I need to be able to see you whenever you're home."

"What will you do?"

"You." I laughed. "I'll do *you*...until you tell me to do something else."

Running his fingers through my hair, he smiled. "I just happen to have a full-time position open for that."

"Honestly, I'll find something—something I love. For now, I just love *you*. I owe you so much, for coming to find me and for not giving up on me, even though I'd abandoned you. I've stopped running. And there's no better place to stop than where it all started."

"We have two days here. Then, I'm going back to Florida for Gordon's funeral."

"*We're* going back to Florida."

"You're coming with me?"

"If Silver Shores doesn't mind one additional underage resident?"

"This is really happening?"

"Yes. If you'll have me, I'm yours. I want to sing you to sleep in person whenever you're home."

"This is truly the happiest day of my life, Perky. I want you to know that."

Later that afternoon, Carter and I were on the beach sipping Caipirinhas just like we had done during the beginning of our journey. I thought back to how scary of a time that was for me compared to the peace I was experiencing now.

"The last time we were here doing this, I didn't know who I was. I was just a girl sitting with a hot pilot, sipping drinks on the beach in Rio. I was a confused person, ready to sell her soul and that of her unborn child."

"And now?"

"Now, I'm just…loved. I don't want anything else but to be the girl sitting on the beach with the pilot who loves me. Everything I ever needed, I actually had that day. I just didn't know it yet. And my future children will not only have me but are so lucky that they will have you as a father."

"You want to have a baby with me, Perky?"

"Someday, yes. But I want to enjoy being with you for a while first."

He looked at me for a good length of time before he said, "I kept it."

I tilted my head. "Kept what?"

"The little suit you bought from Carter's that looked like a pilot's uniform."

"How did you know about that?"

"It was hanging in your closet in Texas. When I saw it, that was how I knew."

"Then, you knew I was going to tell you I wanted to have your baby, that I lied at the airport lounge when I said I'd made my decision to go through with the insemination."

"That little suit was what I'd held onto for hope all of this time."

"I was sure when I spotted it at the store with your name that it was a sign."

"It was. We just had a few detours in the meantime."

"There are signs everywhere, aren't there?"

The sound of a small plane could be heard overhead.

Carter pointed up to it. "There's one right now."

We both looked up at the sky in unison. A banner with a message was trailing the small aircraft.

Carter huffed, "Fuck! Assholes ruined it. The banner was supposed to say, *The Answer is in the Sky: Kendall loves Carter*. I knew that guy didn't understand me!"

Instead it read: *The Answer is in Disguise: Ken Doll Loves Farting*.

CARTER AND I WERE BACK at Silver Shores following Gordon's memorial service. It was a rainy day, fitting for the task at hand. We were cleaning out his condo, choosing which items to donate and which Carter would keep.

"There's no way I'm throwing out these pictures of him and his son. I'll keep them with me for as long as I live. It's the least I could do for him."

Gordon had no family that we knew of, so if Carter hadn't kept this stuff, all of the keepsakes would have likely been destroyed.

As I was cleaning out the bedroom closet, I laughed when

I spotted the pair of pants that Carter had borrowed the night of our missing clothing mishap by the lake.

"Remember these, Captain?"

"How could I forget? That reminds me, did you happen to notice that old man George showed up at the funeral in one of my uniforms? I just can't figure out how he gets into my place and steals my shit. Turns out, he's been swindling all these ladies, telling them he used to *be* an airline pilot. He gets them tailored to fit and everything. He's lucky I don't blow his cover."

"Let him have his fun. He's an innocent old hornball."

Just then a knock on the door interrupted our laughter.

When I opened it, a man in a gray suit was standing there, holding a folder.

"Can I help you?"

"Yes, I'm looking for Carter Clynes."

Carter put down the box he'd been sifting through. "That's me. How can I help you?"

"Gary Steinberg. I'm Gordon Reitman's attorney."

"Attorney? He had an attorney? He didn't even have a cell phone."

"Yes. I've been with Gordy for years."

"How can I help you?"

"He instructed me to give you this note upon his passing. Perhaps, you should read it first, and then we can go over his will."

"Will?"

"Yes. Mr. Reitman had a significant amount of money. He left you as the sole beneficiary."

"No, you don't understand. He had lost his mind some years back. He thought I was his son. He meant to leave everything to Brucey. I can't in good faith take anything from him, knowing he intended for it to go to his son."

"You *are* Carter Clynes?"

"Yes."

"He specifically named you, not Bruce Reitman."

"I don't understand."

"Maybe the letter will explain."

The lawyer gave him the small white envelope. Carter opened it and carefully unfolded the paper inside. After he read it, he looked stunned. Then, he handed it to me.

I know.
Thank you for letting me pretend it was true.
I could never repay you, but I'm going to try.
Sincerely,
Gordon C. Reitman, III

Wow.

Just wow.

Carter shook his head in disbelief. "I don't get it. All this time he knew I *wasn't* his son?"

The attorney nodded. "Apparently so."

Kneeling down to where Carter was sitting, I placed my hand on his shoulder. "Oh my God."

The attorney continued, "As I mentioned, Mr. Reitman accumulated a considerable amount of assets over his lifetime. With no immediate family, he has named you the sole heir to his estate, which is valued at over twenty million dollars."

I felt like I was going to collapse.

What did he just say?

Carter's eyes bugged out. "Excuse me?"

"Gordon had invested considerably in real estate when he was younger and sold off his properties gradually over the past fifteen years. He had quite a bit of money put away as a result. Nevertheless, he chose to live modestly."

Carter's jaw dropped. "Wha...when did he put my name on there?"

"About a year ago, he came to me and changed the beneficiary. He'd previously left everything to a nephew by default. I specifically remember him pointing out that, in his words, the 'no good son-of-a-bitch' never paid him any visits. He knew that you were completely unaware of his wealth. Because he was sure you were helping him out of the goodness of your heart, he wanted to do this for you."

"What does this mean?"

"It means that twenty million dollars will be put into your name very soon. We'll set up another meeting at my office to make sure that all of the funds from the various accounts are transferred over properly."

I just stood there speechless.

Carter looked at me then over at the attorney. "I don't know what to say. I don't feel like I deserve this."

"Well, whether you deserve it or not is irrelevant, Mr. Clynes. The money is yours."

IT TOOK A FEW MONTHS before it really sunk in.

Carter ended up donating some of the money to charity and setting up a scholarship in Bruce Reitman's name. There was certainly a lot left over, enough to keep us set for life. We didn't feel guilty about keeping the rest of the money, since it was what Gordon intended.

The irony wasn't lost on us, that once we'd stopped thinking about money and stopped letting it impact our lives, we ended up running into more than we knew what to do with.

Carter continued to work as a pilot for now while I moved into his Florida condo permanently. He said he'd know when the time was right to quit. It was a good feeling for him to not *have* to work, though, but to only fly because he enjoyed it. It wasn't until he was given the choice to quit that Carter realized he did truly love being a pilot. There would come a time when kids entered the picture, when he would likely cut down or quit. We would deal with that when it came.

As for me, I was giving the old ladies here at Silver Shores a run for their money. I'd notified Carter's Angels (as I'd dubbed them) that they could scale back on the meals for my man. It actually gave me immense pleasure to learn to cook the things he loved.

Florida was my home now. Even Matilda the cat had given up her determination to scare me away once she realized I was there to stay.

Feeling eternally grateful for the comfortable life Carter had afforded me, I'd also discovered a way to give back. My grandmother used to always say if you want to change the world or make a difference, you don't have to travel very far. Just look in your own backyard for the people who need you.

Carter was the best example of that. One day, I'd been thinking back to what he used to do for Gordon, and it hit me that there were many basic things that elderly people could no longer do for themselves. Things we take for granted, like the ability to bend over and cut one's toenails, were impossible tasks for them.

After taking a short cosmetology course, I began offering my services around the Silver Shores community for free. Travelling a few hours a day from condo to condo, I would schedule appointments to give some of the women pedicures and manicures. I would give them my time, and in return, they told me stories and dished out great advice. Some of the women became like mother figures to me. Estranged from my own mother, I appreciated that more than they knew.

The best days, of course, were those that brought Carter home to me. It wasn't uncommon for me to greet him stark naked in our kitchen, holding a freshly made Caipirinha when he'd return from a long trip.

One particular day, though, he'd asked me to meet him at the airport instead. He instructed me to pack a suitcase along with my passport. We'd be meeting at the very lounge where we first met.

When I arrived, Carter was sitting at the same table where we'd sat that first day. He was also wearing the very same brown leather jacket with his wings pinned on it. It gave me a serious feeling of déjà vu. Laid out on the table were mozzarella cheese sticks, wings and egg rolls—the same appetizers he'd ordered back then.

He gestured for me to sit. "Do you know what today is, Perky?"

I wracked my brain. "I don't."

"You don't?"

"No."

"Two years ago today, Kendall."

"It's the two year anniversary of the day we met? How did I not know that?"

"Well, I'll never forget it. July twenty-eighth."

"So much can happen in two years, huh?"

"Yes. But some things stay the same. I'm still a man hopelessly smitten with a beautiful, braless blonde."

"So, tell me, where are we going?"

"In keeping with tradition, that's up to *you* to decide." Pulling up the flight schedules on his phone, he said, "The world is at your fingertips, baby."

"Are you serious? You're gonna let me choose?"

"Yes. We'll go wherever you want. But choose wisely. This is gonna be an important trip you'll remember for the rest of your life."

My body filled with adrenaline.

Oh my God.

He was going to propose to me there?

"Is that so?"

"Yes. Trust me."

"I don't know, Captain. The last time I did that, I ended up getting pissed on by a monkey, got arrested in Dubai, and turned myself into an Amsterdam whore."

He closed his eyes. "That night in the Red Light District was so fucking hot. That was the first time you really shocked me." Shaking it off, he said, "Okay, where to?"

Scrolling down the lineup of flight options, I said, "How about Australia?"

He smirked. "That reminds me of a girl I met once. Her name was Sydney. Sydney Opera House. She had amazing, supple tits."

I smacked him playfully. "So, Sydney then?"

He took the phone. "Yes. Qantas Flight 853, leaving in two hours. Let's do it."

I SHOULD'VE KNOWN that nothing with Captain Carter Clynes was predictable.

We'd settled into our first-class seats as the aircraft

cruised. It was nighttime, and the plane was dark. I'd dozed off and had woken up to the sight of Carter watching me.

"Were you watching me sleep?"

"I was."

"And what were you thinking?"

"I was thinking about how easy it was to slip that ring on your finger while you were out."

My heart seemed to jump. I straightened up in my seat and when I looked down, a massive cushion-cut rock sat wrapped around my ring finger.

Covering my mouth with my other hand, I said, "Oh my God."

"Kendall Sparks, will you do me the honor of becoming my wife during our trip to Australia?" He'd whispered it, wanting to keep this a private moment between the two of us.

"Yes. Yes!" I shook my head over and over. "This wasn't what I expected."

"I know." He lifted my hand to his mouth and kissed it. "Do you like the ring?"

"It's phenomenal."

"It's Carter with an 'I' in the middle." He winked.

It took me a few.

Oh!

Cartier.

We embraced each other for several minutes.

"I love you so much, Carter."

"I love you, too, Mrs. Clynes." He grinned. "Hey, can I ask you something?"

"Yes. Anything."

"Will you still love me when I'm sixty-four?"

"That's an odd age. Why did you pick that?"

He winked. "Beatles song, babe. *When I'm Sixty-Four.*"

"I should have known. Don't ever change, you crazy man." Puling him into a kiss, I spoke over his lips, "I love you so much! I can't wait to marry you Down Under."

We kissed for several minutes. The people around us seemed to be oblivious to our life-changing moment.

Carter broke the kiss. "You know...speaking of down under...I'd love to go there right now. I suddenly have to use the bathroom. Wanna come with?"

"After all this time, how are we only just *now* about to join the mile-high club together? You're a pilot, and I was a stewardess for Christ's sake!"

Carter beamed. "Never too late to start."

EPILOGUE

FIVE YEARS LATER

carter

"COME ON, PICK IT UP! You don't want me to win the race, do you?" I looked back at my son, who trailed behind me. We were both wearing matching helmets as we scooted along the empty road. I was on my Segway, while he rode a traditional child's scooter.

Days like these, I never regretted retiring from the airline. I couldn't imagine missing out on these precious moments with Brucey.

Today, I took him to visit the old neighborhood at Silver Shores. We'd moved to a bigger house about two miles away when he was a year old but still came back to visit the residents all the time.

I pointed to my old condo. "We took you home to that house right there when you were a baby."

"That was where I was made?"

Unsure as to how to answer that, I said, "Technically, you were made in Australia, but you were born here."

"Australia?"

"Yes."

"I'm like a Koala bear?"

"I guess so." I chuckled.

Kendall had found out she was pregnant with Brucey shortly after we returned from our private Australian wedding. We'd gotten married under a sunset just outside the Sydney Opera House.

We lived modestly in a typical one-level, three-bedroom house in Boca. Kendall was adamant that she didn't want our son to grow up like she did. She didn't want him placing so much value on material things.

Kendall was loving being a stay-at-home mom. Meanwhile, I took a contract pilot position for a private jet company that allowed me to choose when I wanted to work. It was the best of both worlds; I still got to fly but on my own terms.

As we continued down the road, I was careful to look out for any oncoming cars.

I pointed to Gordon's old condo. "See this house here?"

"Yeah?"

"That was where your Grandpa Gordon lived."

"Gordon? Like Trash Gordon from Sesame Street?"

"Same name, yes. Your grandfather was a great man, way cooler than Trash Gordon. Someday, when you're a little older, I'll tell you a really neat story about him and how you got your name."

"Okay."

Slowing down, I asked, "You tired? Want to take a snack break?"

He nodded.

We ended up stopping under a shady tree. I took out the juice boxes and various snacks that Kendall had packed.

Brucey looked up at me. He had my dark hair and Kendall's blue eyes. "Daddy, tell me one of your stories."

"Which one?"

"Lucy."

I smiled and mussed up his hair. Starting when he was about two years old, I'd make up stories to tell him at bedtime. Sometimes, he'd randomly ask me to recite one during the day. Lucy in the Sky with Diamonds was his favorite one, partly because—as he always pointed out—Lucy rhymed with Brucey.

"Okay. Lucy in the Sky with Diamonds, it is."

Letting out a deep breath, I put my arm around him and started.

"Once upon a time, there was a girl named Lucy who lived in the sky..."

THE END

Dear Readers,

Want to know when we release a new book? You'll never be spammed, and each month we surprise one member of our mailing list with a free ebook or signed paperback!

To sign up for our mailing list, please visit:
http://eepurl.com/brAP09

ACKNOWLEDGEMENTS

First and foremost, thank you to all of the bloggers who have spread the word about our joint books. You are our lifeline, connecting us to readers every day. We are eternally grateful for all of your hard work.

To Julie – This year, you brought new meaning to what it means to be one tough bitch. You are not only an amazing writer but an amazing person and friend.

To Elaine – Thank you for your attention to detail in proofing and formatting and also for your sound advice in making this story the best that it could be.

To Luna – What would we do without your magic? Thank you for devoting so much time to bringing our books to life.

To Cleida – Our Portuguese would have been totally wrong were it not for you. Obrigada!

To Lisa – Thank you for organizing our release blitz and tour and for always being there for us.

To Letitia – Yet another awesome cover to add to the list. Thank you for keeping our Cocky Bastards looking similar but different.

To our agents, Kimberly Brower and Mark Gottlieb – Thank you for working to bring the Cocky Bastard series to many eyes and ears all throughout the world.

Last but not least, to our readers – Your excitement keeps us going. As long as you want us to keep writing, we will. Thank you for the abundance of support you've given us. You are a treasure.

Much love
Vi & Penelope

OTHER BOOKS BY PENELOPE WARD & VI KEELAND

Stuck-Up Suit

Cocky Bastard

OTHER BOOKS BY PENELOPE WARD

Neighbor Dearest

RoomHate

Sins of Sevin

Stepbrother Dearest

Jake Undone (Jake #1)

My Skylar

Jake Understood (Jake #2)

Gemini

OTHER BOOKS BY VI KEELAND

Standalone novels
Bossman
The Baller
Left Behind (A Young Adult Novel)
First Thing I See

Life on Stage series (2 standalone books)
Beat
Throb

MMA Fighter series (3 standalone books)
Worth the Fight
Worth the Chance
Worth Forgiving

The Cole Series (2 book serial)
Belong to You
Made for You

www.ingramcontent.com/pod-product-compliance
Lightning Source LLC
LaVergne TN
LVHW092005090526
838202LV00001B/3